SPIRIT OF THE NORTH

To Liz,

Fear not the Ghost.

All is Well!

Tyler R. Tichelaar

"This book is a page turner. I could not put it down. It is a great add on to the Marquette Series, but the nice thing is that it stands alone! I hope there are more to come like this."

— Melissa Strangway, author of *56 Water Street*

❄

"*Spirit of the North* flawlessly weaves together a heartfelt family struggle with just the right touch of supernatural peculiarity. The characters are brilliantly detailed by means of a deep connection to their heritage that is conveyed throughout the story. Tyler R. Tichelaar has succeeded in writing a timeless *tour de force* with accomplished originality!"

— Devin Dugan, author of *The Malocas Mission*

❄

"Barbara and Adele's story reminds us that we are all safe, that the universe is there to guide and protect us if we will only listen. Readers will never forget the characters in *Spirit of the North* and they will learn to find strength in their own spirituality."

— Marjetka Novak, author of *Channeling and Working with Angel Cards*

❄

"The power of love is hopefully something every human being has the opportunity to experience. In *Spirit of the North*, Tyler R. Tichelaar demonstrates yet again the special relationship he has with his readers, bringing universal themes to timeless and vibrant life."

— James Dwight, author of *As Worlds Burn: A Tawdry Tale of Spiritual Healing*

SPIRIT OF THE NORTH

a paranormal romance

Tyler R. Tichelaar

Marquette Fiction
Marquette, Michigan

SPIRIT OF THE NORTH

Copyright 2012 by Tyler R. Tichelaar

Marquette Fiction
1202 Pine Street
Marquette, MI 49855
www.MarquetteFiction.com

ISBN-13: 978-0-9791790-6-8
ISBN-10: 0-9791790-6-8
Library of Congress PCN 2011917000

Print coordination:
Globe Printing, Inc. Ishpeming, MI
www.globeprinting.net
Printed in the United States of America
Publication managed by Storyteller's Friend
www.storytellersfriend.com

To Diana, Garee, Helen, and Sarah
and all my Abrahamland friends who already know
the *Secret* Barbara learns.

Love is very patient and kind, never jealous or envious, never boastful or proud, never haughty or selfish or rude. Love does not demand its own way. It is not irritable or touchy. It does not hold grudges and will hardly even notice when others do it wrong. It is never glad about injustice, but rejoices whenever truth wins out.

If you love someone you will be loyal to him no matter what the cost. You will always believe in him, always expect the best of him, and always stand your ground in defending him.

All the special gifts and powers from God will someday come to an end, but love goes on forever.

There are three things that remain—faith, hope, and love—and the greatest of these is love.

—1 Corinthians 13: 4-8, 13

PRINCIPAL CHARACTERS IN *SPIRIT OF THE NORTH*

The Traugott Family

Sybil Shelley—publisher of the manuscript, granddaughter of Sarah Bramble Adams

Sarah Bramble Adams—recorder of the manuscript for her grandmother Barbara Traugott

Barbara Traugott—author of the manuscript, a young woman from Cincinnati who comes to live in Marquette in 1873

Adele Traugott—younger sister of Barbara

Roderick Shepard—Uncle of Barbara and Adele Traugott

The Whitman and Henning Family

Cordelia Whitman—keeper of a boarding house in Marquette

Nathaniel Whitman—her husband

Edna Whitman—their unmarried daughter

Jacob Whitman—their married son

Agnes Whitman—Jacob's wife and daughter to Gerald Henning by his first marriage

Mary Whitman—Jacob and Agnes' oldest daughter

Sylvia Whitman—Jacob and Agnes' younger daughter

Gerald Henning—Agnes' father, a prosperous local businessman

Sophia Henning—Gerald's wife and sister to Cordelia Whitman

Madeleine Henning—Gerald and Sophia's daughter

Other Principal Characters

Mr. James Smith—lawyer to Roderick Shepard

Mr. Wainscott—a resident at the Whitmans' boarding house

Two Shopgirls—residents at the Whitmans' boarding house

Ben—a logger

Karl Bergmann—Ben's logging partner

Mrs. Montoni—Karl Bergmann's mother

Samuel Stonegate—a landlooker

Annabella Stonegate—Samuel's sister

HISTORICAL PERSONS IN *SPIRIT OF THE NORTH*

Charles Kawbawgam—Last Chief of the Chippewa in the Marquette, Michigan region

Foreword

I, Sybil Shelley, certify that I found this manuscript in the home of my grandmother, Sarah Bramble Adams, soon after her death in 2001. I further certify that it was written completely in my grandmother's handwriting. I ask that you read this work with an open mind, beginning with my grandmother's astonishing explanation of how it came to be written. It is a fascinating story, and as I will explain in my afterword, for me it was a revelation that helped to determine the future path of my own life. I believe you will equally find it of incalculable value.

How This Book Came to Be Written

The other day, my granddaughter came over to help me pack and weed through a half century of accumulated items. I am moving now to Snowberry Heights, the senior citizen high rise in Marquette. I am looking forward to the move, the comradeship it will provide, and the freedom from the care of a house and all its possessions, yet it is hard for an old woman to leave her home; here I first came in 1941 as a young bride, here I raised my daughter, here I lived as a widow when my husband passed away, and then later, here I raised my granddaughter, Sybil, after her parents died in a car crash when she was a young child. Now she is in college, living in the dorms at Northern Michigan University, and I have no need for so much space as my house gives me. In my life, I have acquired so many items, both my own, as well as those I packed away after my husband, my parents, and grandparents died. Since I inherited my house from my grandmother, and raised my own daughter and granddaughter here, the house contains the collected possessions of five generations. I felt too overwhelmed to sort through and toss out everything on my own, so I asked Sybil to help me. I came to write this explanation as a result of what happened that day as we were cleaning and packing.

Sybil was standing on a chair in front of the back bedroom closet. She was pulling down boxes from a high shelf while I sat on the bed, sorting through old wedding invitations and funeral cards for people half of whom I could no longer remember.

"Grandma, what's this?" Sybil asked.

I looked up to see an old notebook in her hand; she had it open to a page filled with handwriting. I knew at once what it was, but to put off giving her an immediate answer, I said, "There should be another one just like it up there."

She dug for a minute before she pulled another notebook out from under a box.

"What are they, Grandma? Did you write them?"

"I guess you could say that." I didn't know what else to say. I had never told anyone about those notebooks. I had always wanted to tell someone, but I had feared no one would understand, except maybe Sybil. Many times I had thought about explaining them to her, but I kept telling myself she was still too young. Finally, I had decided I would just leave them for her to find after I'm gone. I was not prepared to explain them to her that day, perhaps because she would think me crazy, but also because she was always such an odd girl—probably from living with an old lady all these years, and from the blow of her parents' tragic deaths in that car crash—a crash she survived. I cannot imagine what affect that must have had on her. She's always been a moody child, given to odd outbursts of enthusiasm followed by moments of severe melancholy. I'm afraid I was not the best companion for her to grow up with. I worry about what will become of her when I am gone—I hope I live to see her finish college, start a career, and find a husband. I hope college will allow her to find the friends she failed to find in high school because she was always so different from everyone, such a loner as her generation says. I've always felt for some unexplainable reason that it was important she learn what the notebooks contain, but I have just never been sure she was ready for that knowledge—maybe she is more mature than I believe, but the notebooks are strange, and I have not always been sure she would be emotionally stable enough to handle the information.

Yet the story is meant to be known by her—meant to be known by everyone who cares to hear it really. My own fears are what have kept it from the world, fears I have held onto since I wrote the notebooks back during the Second World War. My grandmother insisted the story be told, but I was always afraid to tell it, and somehow I've sensed it is Sybil who is to make the story known; I have just had to wait until the right time to make it known to her. I'm not really sure it was meant for me because while it is quite a curious tale, my life has been basically happy, and the knowledge of that story has made little difference to me. But I trust my grandmother, Barbara Traugott, knew better than me when she had me write it down. My role in the story is probably intended to be minimal, only to act as a link between generations to pass the tale from my grandmother to my granddaughter. Sybil will be the one to decide how and when to bring the tale before the world.

As Sybil held the notebooks in her hand that afternoon, she said, "Grandma, I didn't know you were a writer."

"I'm not," I replied. "That's about the only thing I ever wrote."

"But it looks like a whole book," she said, flipping through the pages of the first notebook.

"Yes, but it's the only book I ever wrote," I replied. "Let me have it."

She was resistant to hand it to me.

"Didn't you think it was any good?" she asked. "The few sentences

I've read sounded interesting."

"Don't read any more of it, please. Bring it here."

She looked disappointed, but she obeyed. I took the notebooks and set them behind me on the bed. She frowned.

"You can read them when I'm gone," I told her. "In fact, I'll make sure you get them, but not until then. Now, pull down that stack of records. There's no sense in my keeping them. I haven't had a record player for years."

When she turned her back, I slid the notebooks under a box—to leave them visible might only entice her to further questions.

Later, after Sybil had gone home, I pulled out the notebooks and reread them. I had not thought about them for many years, and often when I did think about them, it was dismissively, as if they were the result of some delirious fantasy of my mind, but as I read them again that night, I was struck by just how remarkable they were, and how utterly impossible it seemed that, even at my most imaginative, I could have written them. They contained information about life in early Marquette: names of pioneer families—the Ridges, Whitmans, Hennings; families whom I had no knowledge of—and terms from the nineteenth century I had never heard. I know it would have been impossible for me to have written this book, even though it was in my own handwriting.

I'm probably confusing the reader now, the first of whom I imagine is Sybil. Be patient, dear, and you'll understand it all shortly. The story of how those notebooks came to be written goes back to a day similar to the one when you found them. On that day, I had gone over to my grandmother's house, the very same house I inherited and the one you grew up in.

I was a young woman then, and I had just finished my courses at the Northern State Teachers College and was still looking for a position. My grandmother knew I had little money, so she asked me to come over and help her clean in exchange for a few dollars.

My grandmother was an ornery old woman, but God rest her soul, she tried always to rise above her nature. She would go the extra mile for those she loved, but in return, she demanded strict obedience to whatever she asked. Even in her eighties, her eyesight remained impeccable enough to notice every speck I missed when I dusted her hutch cabinet.

On this particular day, I was cleaning in her bedroom. As I lifted the edge of her dresser scarf to dust beneath it, a young man in an old tintype photograph stared up at me. He was very handsome, and not more than eighteen, I would say. Although the picture was quite old, his face was still clear. He looked as if he would have been blond, and tall, and strong, what the young girls today would call "a hunk" I suppose. I had never seen a photograph of my grandfather, so I naturally assumed it was him, but when I looked at the back of the photograph, it was signed, "To Adele. Love, Ben." And below that was written some sort of poem, although the paper had rubbed away in so many places that I could not fully make out the lines.

I knew Adele had been my grandmother's sister—dead long before I was born. But I had no idea who Ben was—perhaps some secret lover—but certainly not Aunt Adele's husband, for she had never married.

While I pondered the handsome man's face, my grandmother came into the room. Despite her age, she could still manage to sneak up on people; she was not yet feeble enough to warn others of her approach by clumping down the hall with a cane.

"Haven't you finished in here yet?" she snapped.

"I'm almost done," I replied.

"What's that you've got there?"

"I don't know," I lied. "It just fell out from under the dresser scarf when I was dusting."

She came up to me and put out her hand. When I gave it to her, her face started to go pale. Lifting the edge of the dresser scarf, she stuffed the photograph back where I had found it.

"Well, come on. I've made us dinner."

I followed her to the dining room where she had set sandwiches for us on the table. I waited until we were both seated, then boldly asked, "Grandma, who was in that photo? The back said it was to Aunt Adele from Ben, but Aunt Adele never—"

"Best to leave the past alone," she said. "They've both been dead so long now it doesn't matter."

"Was Ben her boyfriend?"

"You are too nosey," she replied. She took a sip of her coffee and then looked me straight in the eye. "You must get that nosiness from your father's side of the family; you sure didn't get it from mine. In my day, a person only had to be told once that something was none of her business."

"But Grandma," I said, "if they're both dead, what would it hurt to tell me about them?" If there were nothing to tell, she would have said so, but her resistance to talk revealed that there had to be a story behind that picture, and my curiosity made me persistent.

"There really isn't much to tell," she grumbled. She sat down, then picked up her sandwich and inspected the meat in it. "I can't believe I let that butcher sell me this ham. I don't know how I'll ever chew it. I could barely slice it. Seems as if there's chopped up little bits of bone in it."

"Grandma," I scolded. "You're changing the subject."

"There isn't much to tell," she repeated. "He was just a boy my sister knew when we first moved here to Marquette—just a friend. We didn't know him long. That wasn't long before my sister went to—"

Before she finished the sentence, my mother knocked on the door and entered. My mother was always such a talker that others could scarcely get a word in. She and grandmother could gossip with the best of them, but if the conversation turned personal, Grandma would instantly clam up; she feared if people knew her business as she made a point of knowing theirs, she would never have any rest from others' tongues. Apparently, the mysterious Ben was too personal for her to talk about because when I tried to mention the photograph to my mother, Grandma purposely changed the subject by asking me about my future plans now that I had finished my schooling. I forgot about the photograph for the time being.

That fall, I got my first teaching position in another town too far away for me to live in Marquette. While I was gone, Grandma passed away. That same week, a teaching position in Marquette opened for me. And although Grandma had three sons and a daughter (my mother) for her children and plenty of other grandchildren, she had left the house to me. As her only granddaughter, I had always suspected I was secretly her favorite. At that time, my fiancé, Earl, lived in Marquette, but we had put off getting married until we could afford it, and my living in another town had only complicated the situation. Now everything seemed to have come together for us. We married that summer and moved into grandmother's house. Everything would have been perfect except that the United States had entered World War II, so Earl soon found himself enlisted. A month after he entered the service, I learned I was expecting a child.

Earl and I had no time to clean out Grandma's belongings before we moved into the house, but now I decided to turn Grandma's bedroom into the nursery. While cleaning her room, I again found the photograph of Ben. I don't know why, other than that I fancied Ben's looks, but I hung onto the picture, hiding it in my own dresser. I was even a little afraid Earl would find it when he returned. I admit I peeked at it fairly often. I knew there had to be something terribly romantic behind that picture—Ben looked like such a naturally heroic young man with that great blond curl waving over his forehead. No harm existed in looking at his handsome face; Grandma had told me Ben was dead anyway, and even if he were alive, he would have been about ninety by then, and I was a married woman. But I never did show the picture to my husband. I placed Earl's picture on my dresser where I could see it each morning as I woke, but I confess I looked at Ben's picture almost as much. Perhaps it was only a misdirected longing for my husband, but I started to feel a serious infatuation with Ben; I started imagining some remarkable stories about whom he had been and what his relationship may have been with Great-Aunt Adele. I convinced myself that she had been in love with him.

It is silly now, even embarrassing, to admit how infatuated I was with that photograph. I rather fancied Ben looked as if he wanted to talk to me, as if he were trapped in that flat black and white world and yearning to escape. He looked so alive, so vibrant, though seventy years had passed since the photo had been taken. It seemed a shame that a young man with all that energy should not be alive now. I bet he could have taken a dozen Japs with his bare hands. What an asset he would have been to the war effort. How did Aunt Adele ever let him slip through her fingers? Grandma had said Ben and Aunt Adele were just friends, but I found it difficult to believe any woman could settle for just being friends with such a good-looking man.

Sometimes I daydreamed so much about Ben that I felt guilty, and then I would try to make it up to Earl by writing him an extra sweet letter, and saying my rosary to pray for his safety. And now comes the hardest part to explain—far harder than to explain my infatuation with Ben.

I was sitting at the kitchen table one evening, trying to write to Earl, but I had nothing to say to him other than the usual about how much I missed him. When he had first gone away, I had written to him everyday, but after the first couple of months, it felt like a chore to write more than once or twice a week. I wished I'd had the baby before he had gone—then I could have written to him about its first tooth, its first word, its first attempt to walk. But until the baby was born, what was there to say? My life was dull compared to the dangers Earl was experiencing in the Pacific. All I could talk about were the school papers I had to grade, and how once or twice a week I went to my parents' house for supper because my mother worried I was lonely. I was lonely, but I didn't want to express that to Earl—he would only worry about me, and that might distract him from paying attention to whatever battle he was facing, and then he might not come home to me. And then I would wonder whether that was how Aunt Adele had felt—that Ben had not come home to her—I didn't know what had happened to Ben, but he hadn't married Aunt Adele; I was certain there had to be some great heartbreak there, yet I could not believe any man so outwardly attractive could be anything less than inherently good, so I remained curious why they had not married.

One evening, I decided to write to Earl before I made supper, but instead I found myself just sitting at the table, long after dark came, without turning on the light, letting my mind wander until I dozed off.

I dreamt I was writing something, not a letter to Earl but some sort of beautiful story, even though in my sleepy state the words did not quite make sense. Finally, I woke to find myself sitting in the dark. When I turned on the light, I found I still had the pen in my hand. I had scribbled all over a sheet of paper, scribbled, not written any words. I crumpled up the sheet, threw it in the wastebasket, and then made myself supper. By the time I finished the dishes, I realized I did not feel well. Fearing that if I became sick, the baby would be in danger, I decided to go to bed early.

I was asleep by eight o'clock, and slept until after midnight; then I woke up sweating and lay awake in a miserable state for hours, too tired to get up, yet unable to fall back asleep until the early morning. Then I slept fitfully, dreams flitting through my head. I know I had many dreams that night, yet when I woke, the only one I remembered was of lying on my stomach, trying to write a story on my pillowcase with an imaginary pen.

I got up with the first glimmering of daybreak and made myself some tea since I doubted my stomach could take anything more substantial. I thought I should finish writing my letter to Earl before the mailman came—if I became more ill, I did not know when I would be able to write again. But I got no farther than, "Dear Earl" when I felt so tired and groggy that I thought I should go back to bed. My mother had feared that having Earl away during my pregnancy would be too much of a strain for me. I began to think she was right—I suddenly felt overwhelmed by my entire life—the responsibility of teaching so many students, being alone and pregnant, worrying about my husband overseas—it all seemed so unreal, so nonsensical, so absurd to believe it was my life.

I stared out the window until the sun rose—its rays breaking pink over the lightly snow-covered ground. The snow looked so smooth in the early morning light—smooth like Ben's boyish cheeks. Earl, by comparison, had a very rough face, even after he shaved. I wondered what it would be like to touch a smooth face on a man. For a second, I sort of reached out my arm, as if Ben were before me so I could stroke his cheek.

A sudden jolt shot through my arm, from my shoulder to my wrist, and then my left hand began to tingle. My hand picked up the pen, gripping it tightly, and in a fury, it began to pour out words onto the blank paper. I was terrified—I had lost control of my arm, but I was too astonished to try stopping it. It felt numb, as if separated from my body, yet it was functioning perfectly. I stared as I scribbled words onto the paper. I felt as if I were leaning over someone else's shoulder, watching her write. I wondered whether I was possessed by a demon; should I grab the phone? But who would I call? St. Luke's Hospital? A priest to come do an exorcism? I could not move from the chair; my arm would not stop writing, and my body could not move without my arm.

Then I started to read the words my hand was writing. My fear turned to amazement and curiosity. I had no way of knowing what power or intelligence was forming the words, but I saw names on the paper, sentences written about people whose names I did not know except those of my grandmother and Great-Aunt Adele. Then after a few paragraphs, I recognized the tone as my grandmother's voice. Curiosity overcame my fear as I read further. My grandmother's spirit—I don't know how else to describe it—was somehow flowing through me, forcing me to write for her a tale from her own life. And while my hand continued to jot down words, in my head, I heard my grandmother speaking. "Every morning before you go to school, you must wake up early to write until the story is finished." I still could not believe this possession was my grandmother, but as the writing continued, I realized it could not be otherwise. Later, although I never told my mother about the experience, I asked her questions about my grandmother's life; my mother confirmed knowing some of the people mentioned in this manuscript in her early childhood, and she confirmed those people's positions in the community so that I cannot doubt my grandmother herself wrote this story through me, although I find it unexplainable. There is nothing in the writing that makes me believe I was possessed by an evil spirit, even if some of the story's message does not perfectly coincide with the Church's teachings. The way the sentences are turned, the words put together, all sound so much like my grandmother's way of speaking that the only explanation is that her spirit was using me to perform some type of automatic writing, so she could tell me her story now because she had been afraid to speak it during her lifetime.

I don't want to say much more. Every morning after that for several weeks, I woke up in time to spend a quiet hour or two allowing my grandmother to use me to perform her writing. I think it best I say no more about the manuscript's contents but that I leave it to speak for itself. Perhaps because I am old now, people might dismiss this story as the ravings of a madwoman trying to put one over on the public. I do not know what people will say about it—that is why I have always been afraid to show it to anyone, so I leave it for Sybil to decide how to use it. I only know it was an experience I can never explain. I know, during those hours of writing, my arm moved at an alarming pace I never could have maintained by sheer human stamina. I don't know what made me susceptible to the spirit world's influence—although I have an idea it had something to do with my family background, and perhaps because I felt such an attachment to Ben's photograph, an attachment that in itself felt almost otherworldly.

I verify that this story is written in my grandmother's own words— she never spoke a word to me about anything it contains during her actual life. Neither did I change a word of it from how it was channeled through me. I don't believe there is any way I could have known this information, or provided the historical details the work contains. Never could I have imagined with such clarity what my grandmother's life would have been like when she first came to Upper Michigan, seventy years before I wrote this manuscript.

I leave it to the reader to decide what to believe of this strange story. Perhaps the people of the twenty-first century will be less skeptical than those of my own largely atheistic twentieth century.

Sarah Bramble Adams
Marquette, Michigan
August 27, 1997

PART I

1

My first sight of Marquette was not promising. I have heard others speak of their first glimpse of Marquette as they sailed into Iron Bay—on a sunny summer day when Lake Superior sparkled, when the trees were lushly green and the beaches golden—and how they instinctively knew they would find the life they sought in this charming little town surrounded by breathtaking scenery. My sister, Adele, and I had no such experience.

We came by railroad from Cincinnati, where we had been born and raised, and which was larger, more productive, and far warmer than Marquette. We had had a long, tiresome journey by train, interrupted by several delays, including an early blizzard that meant we had a two-day layover in Milwaukee while the railroad tracks were shoveled out in Northern Wisconsin and Upper Michigan. Nothing about the journey had been pleasant, and the arrival was depressing. We were greeted at the depot by nothing but a cloudy, gray sky, a dusting of snow, and frigid temperatures that promised more snow to come. After looking about for a moment at such an unwelcoming land—for even the streets were largely deserted on this cold last day of October, 1873—a feeling of despair rose in us—our uncle had not come to meet us, and we had no idea where to find him.

"What should we do?" asked Adele. "Do you think Uncle is just late, or did he forget?"

"I don't know," I replied, although I feared he had not received the letter I had sent him, or worse, did not want us to come, for we had come without waiting for his reply, feeling we had no other choice now that we had no other family. "Maybe he had to work so he couldn't come to meet us, and with the delays we've had, he can't be expected to wait at the depot for every train that comes into town."

"Barbara, are you sure you don't see anyone who could be Uncle?" Adele asked. "We don't even know what he looks like since we've never met him."

But the platform was deserted. Everyone from the train had been met by loved ones and departed. No one appeared to be waiting for us. I did not know what to tell her. I stood, staring up at the gray overcast sky, as light snowflakes began to fall. Then I looked over at Adele, shivering, appearing cold and forlorn. I wished I could have done anything but bring her to this terrible, frigid land. She was really no more than a child. I was twenty-one, and used to taking charge, having run the household for Father after Mother had died, but Adele was only seventeen—she had never known what it was to be unprotected, to have to fend for herself. I would do my best to take care of her, but with Father now gone, I was afraid myself.

"Well," I said, not knowing what else to do, and wishing Father were alive to advise me, "there's nothing for it but to find out where Uncle lives. I have the address in my bag."

"But how can we go find him? We can't carry the trunk with us."

We were standing outside the depot building beside our trunk; the conductor and another man had been kind enough to carry it off the train.

"Silly, we'll leave the trunk here. Someone will watch it for us."

"Who?" she asked.

"I don't know," I said. "Wait here. I'll see what I can do."

I went back inside the depot, only to find it empty. After the train had pulled away and our fellow travelers left with their family and friends, the station workers must have also gone. No one was even around to ask for directions. What would we do? I felt sick, almost ready to panic. I stood still, clutched my stomach and tried to breathe. "Barbara Traugott," I told myself, "you are not going to let worry get the best of you, and you aren't going to frighten your little sister. Hasn't she been through enough since Father died?"

I could not scare Adele with our situation. I knew what it was to worry over money, to wonder how we would put a meal on the table—I had taken over that responsibility while still a little girl after Mother's death, but I did not want Adele to know that fear. She was now nearly twice as old as I had been when Mother died, yet she still acted like an innocent child, and I was proud of that, for it meant Father and I had done well in protecting her from life's hardships—but without Father to help me, I feared I would no longer be able to protect her.

"Barbara Traugott," I scolded myself again. "For Pete's sake, all you have to do is find Uncle's address. It's not that much to do. Surely you can manage that. And no one will steal the trunk. Why it weighs a ton! Once we find Uncle's place, he can come back with a wagon to fetch it. If we hurry, I bet it won't take more than twenty minutes."

I went back outside, determined to appear confident and in control of the situation.

"Adele," I said, "I'll go look for Uncle's place, and you can—"

"Oh, I couldn't possibly stay here with the trunk," she said. "I'm afraid to be alone in this strange town. What if some rough railroad men come along?"

"Silly girl," I feigned laughter, although I had intended to have her stay with the trunk, "I meant we could go find Uncle together. We can just leave the trunk here with a note attached. I don't think anyone will bother it. This is a small town, not like Cincinnati, so it should be safe."

I opened my little handbag to dig for a piece of paper but quickly realized I had nothing to write with. "I guess we'll just have to leave it and hope it's okay here. I'm sure once we find Uncle, he'll come right down and collect it for us. Everything will be just fine; you'll see."

I smiled to exhibit my confidence in this solution, the only solution available, although I did not feel confident about anything at the moment. Adele did not look convinced, and I could not blame her. It was a foolhardy thing to leave the trunk here—it contained all we had in the world other than the money in my handbag, but what other choice was there when she would not stay with the trunk? I knew she would never walk around town alone to find Uncle.

"Barbara, my hands are getting chapped," she said as I turned toward the street.

"Well, put on your gloves," I replied.

"They're in the trunk."

"Why don't you have them with you?" I asked.

"I didn't know it would be so cold here."

I could not blame her for that. It was only the last day of October, yet it was already snowing. Cincinnati did not get snow this early.

"Well, if we walk to Uncle's house, I'm sure we'll warm up. The town isn't very big so we'll probably find him within ten minutes."

"Do you know where he lives?"

"No, but I have the address right here," I said, digging again in my handbag until I pulled it out.

"There," I said, unfolding a piece of paper to read the address. "Now we just have to find someone to ask for directions."

Fortunately, the train depot was near Marquette's business district, so in a few minutes, we came to a dry goods store.

"That's the Whitmans' boarding house," said the clerk at the counter when I showed him Uncle's address. "Keep walking up this hill here; then take a left. It's a big yellow place. You can't miss it."

"Are you certain?" I asked. "I thought my uncle had his own place?"

"What's his name?" asked the clerk.

"Shepard. Roderick Shepard."

"Never heard of him. But if that's the address he gave you, then if he doesn't live at the boarding house, Mrs. Whitman will probably know where he's gone off to."

"Thank you," I said. I led my sister back out to the street.

"A boarding house!" said Adele.

"Now, don't fret yet," I told her. "Maybe he doesn't live there anymore. The last letter Father got from him was a few years ago. I'm sure when Uncle was married to Aunt Marie, he must have had his own place."

I was not convincing myself, much less Adele. I did not feel very positive about our prospects in this town. I feared we had wasted the last of our money coming to Marquette, where our only relative in the world was a man we had never met who was not even of our blood, but had been married to our father's sister, and she had been dead many years. But we had no one else to turn to. I wished now I had waited longer for a reply to our letter; even if Uncle were willing to help us, we could not all crowd together into one or two rooms of a boarding house.

Following the store clerk's directions, we climbed the hill past the town's main shops until we came to a residential area.

"Is it much farther, Barbara?" Adele asked.

"How should I know?" I said, instantly feeling ashamed of the impatience in my voice. But she was such a slow walker, and I was shivering from the cold. I had no gloves either, and my hair and hat did little to cover my ears and neck.

"I sure hope Uncle's house is warm," Adele puffed. "I'd like to sit in front of a nice fire."

I sure hoped Uncle had a house. That was the most I could hope at the moment. We turned onto the next side street and walked another block. Then I saw the large yellow house the store clerk had described. It looked like a respectable enough establishment. An older, bearded gentleman was shoveling the front steps. As we turned up the walk, I strained my eyes to get a good look at him, wondering whether he were Uncle.

"Hello, ladies," he said, setting down his shovel and lifting his hat. "May I help you?"

"Thank you. We've just arrived in Marquette," I said. "We're looking for our uncle, Mr. Roderick Shepard. Do you know him?"

He stared at me for a moment. I thought maybe he was trying to catch his breath since the air was so cold; when I spoke, I could see my own breath before my eyes.

"He used to stay here," the man mumbled. He hesitated, then added, "Best go inside and talk to my wife. She may be able to help you."

"Thank you, sir," I said. "Please, what is your wife's name?"

"Mrs. Whitman. I'm Mr. Whitman," he said.

"I'm Barbara Traugott, and this is my sister, Adele."

"Pleased to meet you," he said, again tipping his hat. Then he led us up the front steps. After opening the door, he shouted inside, "Cordelia, come here! There are two young ladies needing to speak with you."

Mr. Whitman stepped aside so we could enter the front hall. Then he shut the door and went back down the steps to his shoveling.

We stood in the front hall several seconds, wondering whether anyone had heard his bellowing. As we waited, I was relieved to note it was a clean looking establishment.

In half a minute, a young lady came down the front hall stairs.

"Hello, I'm Edna Whitman," she said. "My mother will be down in a moment. Are you needing a room?"

"Certainly not," said Adele, repulsed by the thought of staying in a boarding house. I did not like the idea either—we had always lived in our own home, no matter how hard it had often been for Father to keep a roof over our heads.

"Oh, I'm sorry," said the young lady.

"No, I'm sorry," I said. "I'm afraid we're a little irritable from our long journey. You see, we just arrived in Marquette. We've been traveling by train for several days, all the way from Cincinnati."

"Oh, no wonder you're tired," she smiled. "Please, come, sit down in the parlor."

She led us into the next room and graciously gestured us toward a little sofa. The room did look favorable, the furniture in fact better than anything we'd had at home, even if the room were obviously a common one for use by all the boarders.

"Now," she said, sitting down across from us, "how can I help you?"

"We've come to Marquette to live with our uncle, but the only address we have for him is this boarding house."

"Oh, perhaps he's one of our boarders now, only—no, I don't think Mr. Wainscott could be your uncle, is he?"

"No," I replied.

"Well," she said, "he's our only male boarder right now, and he's only twenty so I didn't think so. Then we have a couple of girls who work at the shops in town. I was hoping you might need a room since we do have an empty one right now."

"Do you know our uncle?" I asked. "His name is Roderick Shepard."

"Oh!" Her response was almost a shriek, as if I had just mentioned a criminal's name. "Oh, dear," she said, jumping up from the sofa, "you had better speak to Mother. Just a minute." Clearly flustered, she returned to the front hall, and like her father, bellowed up the stairs.

"Mother! Mother!"

"Edna, quit hollering," snapped an older woman's voice. "You're lucky Mr. Wainscott isn't in his room right now; he'd be repulsed by your rude manners."

I could hear Mrs. Whitman coming down the stairs, although the angle of the parlor door blocked her from my view. I was tempted to glance at Adele, to see whether she were as alarmed as I was by Edna's reaction to Uncle's name. But I did not really want to know how my sister was adjusting to the situation; I felt on the verge of failing as a big sister; my own fears for our future were beginning to overwhelm me.

"Mother, come quick!" Edna shouted. "There are two young ladies here who need to speak to you."

"Are they looking for a room?" Mrs. Whitman asked, stepping into the parlor. She was a tall, strong woman, a lady in her movements, yet obviously capable of cooking for—maybe even leading—an army if necessary. "Hello, ladies. You've come to the right place. I have the most respectable boarding house in Marquette."

"No, Mama, they don't need a room," Edna said. "They are looking for their uncle."

Mrs. Whitman's smile left her face. She waited a second for further explanation, before she replied, "I don't understand."

"Mama," Edna said, taking her mother by the hand and leading her to a chair opposite Adele and me, "these young ladies are Mr. Shepard's nieces. They've come to Marquette to visit him."

"Oh," said Mrs. Whitman, hesitantly perching on the chair's edge.

"To stay with him, actually," I said. "We plan to live with him."

"Oh," Mrs. Whitman repeated, her face growing pale as her eyes widened.

"Is something wrong?" Adele asked.

"Oh," Mrs. Whitman said again.

"Mama, tell them," Edna said.

"I'm sorry," said Mrs. Whitman, gingerly choosing her words such that I feared them all the more. "I didn't know Mr. Shepard had any relatives. He never mentioned any, but then we rarely saw him. We barely knew him really—he would come stay with us for a short while each winter, but he always kept to himself. And now—well, I'm afraid that poor Mr. Shepard has gone to the Lord."

No one spoke for a minute. From Edna's reaction, I had feared I would be told Uncle was a criminal, but this news was worse. My heart sunk as numbness spread through my limbs. I was paralyzed by the question of what to do now, and simultaneously, I felt horribly wicked, for I did not feel sorry for Uncle, only for Adele and me, especially when Adele began to sob.

"I'm so sorry," said Mrs. Whitman, getting up to hand Adele her handkerchief. "It just happened a few days ago. I think he must have picked up some sickness out in the woods. In fact, I was afraid we might have to go into quarantine, but the doctor has assured me we'll be fine. I did boil all the sheets and curtains, and I burnt his clothes just to be safe."

I did not know what to say. I did not know what to do.

"Mama," said Edna, "they came here from Cincinnati. That must be—did you ladies send your uncle a letter?"

"Yes," I said, "I wrote to him a couple of weeks ago to say we were coming."

"Oh dear, yes, we did get that letter," said Mrs. Whitman. "We were surprised to get a letter for him because he usually only stays with us in the winter for a few months, and I don't remember him ever getting any letters before. We thought all his relatives were dead, so when that letter came, I didn't know what to do with it. I didn't like to open it, but since he was dead, I was going to write back to whoever sent it, only now that you're here, I—"

"Mama, we should show them the letter to make sure it's the one they sent," Edna said.

"Oh, yes, of course," said Mrs. Whitman. "Let me go see whether I can find it."

She practically rushed from the room, eager to use the letter as a crutch to deal with the awkward situation. I could see the poor woman felt as uncomfortable as we did.

"So our uncle didn't live here then?" asked Adele, folding up Mrs. Whitman's handkerchief now that she had finished wiping her tears.

"No, he only stayed with us once in a while when he came into town," said Edna. "He had his own place out in the country."

"A farm?" I asked.

"I don't really know," Edna said. "I think it might have been a cabin of some sort, but you see, none of us really knew much about your uncle. He usually only stayed with us for a month or two during the coldest part of winter. We never expected him before Christmas, so we were surprised when he came to stay with us in October this year. I think he must have only come into town because he knew he was sick, although he didn't say a word about it when he arrived. Mother and I were out the day he came, so my father showed him up to his room, not noticing anything was wrong, and not asking him why he had come into town so early that year—I beg your pardon, but your uncle did not like many questions—he, well, he would sort of bark at you, but Mother always said not to mind so long as he paid us regular. When my father showed him up to his room that day, he never came down again, so finally, the next morning—it was almost noon—Mother sent Father upstairs to check on him, and that's when we discovered he had died in his bed."

"Oh, it was awful," said Mrs. Whitman, returning with the letter in her hand. "I've never had anyone die in my boarding house before. Here, did one of you young ladies write this letter?"

"Ye-es," I said, recognizing my handwriting on the envelope as she handed it to me. I knew well enough what it said, but I opened it anyway.

"It came just yesterday," said Mrs. Whitman. "I didn't know who it was from. Like I said, I was going to write back to the sender, but I just didn't have the heart to do it yet."

"It's all right," I said. "We left Cincinnati a few days after I mailed it, so we wouldn't have gotten the letter if you had written us back."

I unfolded the sheets of paper. Reading the letter again gave me a moment to take in our situation and wonder what it was best to do now. I had so carefully weighed every word I had put on the sheet of paper before me. I had so wanted to convince this unknown uncle that it would be an advantage to him—in no way an imposition—to have his deceased wife's nieces stay with him. Now all my effort had been for naught.

October 20, 1873

Dear Uncle Shepard,

I am writing to inform you that yesterday my father, your late wife's brother, passed away. He had been sick with influenza for the past few weeks, and because we could ill afford it, he would not let me send for a doctor. You have my deepest sympathies upon his loss. He often spoke of you fondly, and of how glad he was that his sister had found a good husband to care for her. I know he regretted that he lost contact with you after the death of my aunt.

Uncle, now that Father is gone, Adele and I have nothing. Father was only renting our house, and because of his illness, he could not even pay the last couple of months' worth of rent. The landlord has agreed to let us stay for a couple of more weeks, but we have no money to live on. Father told us if anything ever happened to him before we were married, that we should go to you as our only living relative. I hate to think we might be a burden on you, but we have no other options. We will work hard and do whatever we can to make your life easier, so I hope you will not be perturbed by our arrival. I know it is awkward since we have never even met. I apologize if you feel we will give you any trouble, but I hope you will honor our father's wish by welcoming us. We will do our best not to inconvenience you any more than necessary.

We will be taking the train to Marquette. I will go tomorrow to purchase our tickets. I do not know exactly when or how long it will take for us to arrive there, but I write now to give you due warning as it will probably be within a week of your receipt of this letter.

Sincerely,
Barbara Traugott

I had not known how else to end the letter other than "Sincerely." I had thought about fondly, but that sounded awkward when I had never met him. Now, as I folded the letter back up, I realized how fruitless had been all my worrying about Uncle's response to our arrival.

"It's too bad he never got your letter," said Mrs. Whitman. "Had he known you girls were coming, maybe it would have given him strength to hold onto life. I don't know though—my husband said your uncle looked fine when he arrived, but you know how unobservant men are. I remember when I went upstairs to put coins on his eyes, he looked so deathly pale. I can tell you it was quite a shock to me, and we did not even know which church he belonged to, so we had the funeral at the Methodist church that we go to. We sent the bill to his lawyer here in town—I hope that was the proper thing to do since we didn't think he had any other relatives."

"We're very sorry for your loss," said Edna, looking embarrassed by the way her mother rambled on.

I was more embarrassed by their expressions of sympathy. I looked down at the rug. I did not mourn Uncle's death—how could I mourn for a man I had never known? Instead, I grieved that Adele and I now had nowhere to turn. We did not have time to mourn for uncle. I could not help but ask aloud, "Where will we go now?"

No one answered. After a minute, I raised my eyes to find the other three women all likewise staring at the rug. I could see I was the only one capable enough to figure out what was to be done. Mrs. Whitman and her daughter were not responsible for us, so as the older sister, I had to take charge.

"Mrs. Whitman, my sister and I have very little money, but might we stay here tonight until we figure out what to do?"

"But where will you go then?" asked Edna. "Back to Cincinnati?"

"No, we haven't the money for the train fare," I replied. "I imagine we will have to find work."

"But Barbara, you know Papa wanted me to finish school!" Adele said.

"Yes," I agreed. I doubted school would be possible for her now, but I also felt it unwise for us to argue before strangers. "Perhaps I can work while you finish school."

"You can stay with us until you find work," Edna said.

"And then when you do, you can pay room and board from your salary," Mrs. Whitman added. Her mouth had pursed up at her daughter's offer, apparently from fear of taking in unemployed boarders.

My spirit recoiled at the thought of taking charity until I had work.

"You're very kind," I replied. "But didn't you say our uncle had some property outside of town?"

"He had a cabin out in the woods, out near the plains," answered Mr. Whitman, stepping into the parlor. I don't know how long he had been standing in the front hall and listening to our conversation.

"Did he legally own it?" I asked.

"Yes, I imagine so," said Mr. Whitman.

"Then," I said, slowly, unsure of myself but seeing no other solution, "since Adele and I are his only living relatives, I presume we are his heirs. In that case, the cabin is ours, so we can live there."

"Oh, you can't live there!" said Edna. "It's out in the middle of nowhere, miles and miles from town. How ever would you manage, especially with winter coming on?"

"We will manage," I said. "The Traugotts always manage."

I secretly had my own doubts, but I would not accept anyone's charity.

"Mr. Whitman," I asked, "do you know how to reach our uncle's property?"

"No, I'm afraid I've never been there. You would have to ask Mr. Smith—he was your uncle's lawyer. He can do the legal paperwork for you to inherit the place, and I imagine he'll know the cabin's whereabouts."

"Thank you. Where is Mr. Smith's office, please? I'll go see him straight away."

"Oh, Barbara, I'm so tired," said Adele. "Can't we stay and rest for a while first?"

"Of course, dear. Why don't you go upstairs? I'll see about the property. You'll need your rest if we are to move out to the cabin tomorrow morning, especially if it's a few miles ride from town."

Adele was uninterested in the property or the state of our future home. She simply whispered to me, so Mr. Whitman would not overhear, "Don't forget to fetch the trunk, Barbara. I can't sleep without my nightclothes."

"Come; I'll show you both up to the room," Edna said. "Then, Miss Traugott, you can freshen up before you head downtown."

"No, thank you," I replied. "It's already mid-afternoon, and I know lawyers are busy men. I want to get there as soon as I can in case I have to wait. And I don't know how long it will take to get our trunk brought from the train depot. But I will be back for dinner, and I will pay you now in advance, Mrs. Whitman, for the room."

"Oh, that's not necessary," Mr. Whitman said. "You can pay us after you work out your legal issues and get your inheritance—perhaps your uncle left you some money."

"No, I insist," I replied. As I expected, Mrs. Whitman did not object but quoted me her prices without hesitation as I dug into my handbag for money. Thankfully, her prices were quite reasonable, even a bargain compared to what it would have cost us to stay in Cincinnati. And I was grateful when Mr. Whitman offered to take me down to the depot in his wagon to fetch our trunk and then to accompany me to Mr. Smith's law office. In five minutes, Adele had gone upstairs, and Mr. Whitman and I had headed back toward Marquette's business district.

2

"Yes, I was your uncle's lawyer," said Mr. Smith once Mr. Whitman and I were seated in his office. "In fact, he came to see me last summer to make up his will. I guess it was timely considering the present circumstances, although I'm afraid the property can't be worth much—it's not good farmland, though he had a little crop planted on it, and the cabin he built is rather dilapidated from what I remember the one time I went out there. He didn't build in the best location either—a good mile from the creek. He left everything to your father—his brother-in-law, his only living relative he said in his will—and since you say your father is dead, I guess you and your sister are his legal heirs. Strange how these things happen, that you should just happen to show up right after he dies, as if it were fate or something—if you believe in such things."

"More like plain old bad luck," I frowned.

"Well, you would be best off to sell the property," said Mr. Smith. "It's not worth much, and two women couldn't possibly live out there by themselves. I'd be willing to take it off your hands for you—I deal quite a bit in real estate, so I could probably sell it more easily than you. Like I said, it's not really worth much, but I could probably get something for the timber on the land—how about I pay you five hundred dollars for it?"

Mr. Smith rather surprised me. He did not even bother once to express sympathy to me for my uncle's loss—not that I was upset over Uncle's death, but it only would have been polite. I had felt myself somewhat coarse to worry about money when many would expect my first concern to be acquiring my mourning weeds—which I had no money to purchase anyway—but Mr. Smith was not concerned with such social proprieties. He was clearly a man of business, and a prosperous one at that. He wore the finest linen suit I had ever seen, finer than what most well-to-do men could afford to wear even to church; his office shelves were filled with gilded volumes; he sat behind an expensive finished veneer desk. He had a leather chair, and on the edge of his desk sat a decanter with spare glasses so he could freely offer whiskey to his clients. He was scarcely a year or two older than me, so I could not imagine he had acquired such wealth by concerning himself with others' welfare. Even should I be certain five hundred dollars was a fair amount to pay for my uncle's property, I knew it would not support Adele and me for long if we did not have a steady income. I suddenly envisioned us working that land, farming it, finding a hired man if necessary—that property might bring in a recurring income— whereas five hundred dollars in the bank would dwindle quickly if we had to pay rent at the boarding house and depend upon an employer to pay us wages.

"Of course, before I can purchase the property from you," said Mr. Smith, perhaps sensing my hesitation over his offer, "I will need proof that you and your sister are the children of Hans Traugott, since neither of you are named in your uncle's will."

"I can have our baptismal records sent from our parish church in Cincinnati," I replied. "Our father's name will be on them."

"That should be fine then," said Mr. Smith. He leaned back in his chair, putting his hands behind his head. "Funny, your uncle never mentioned that he had two pretty nieces."

"Funny," I thought, "that you haven't even seen my sister yet you assume she's pretty. I know you're only flattering me." Adele had golden curls, but my mousy brown hair proclaimed me undeniably plain.

"My uncle never actually met us," I replied. "I'm sure he knew he had nieces—our aunt, his wife, used to send us little birthday cards when we were children before she died—my father always said she loved children." And then I had a strange memory—something I had forgotten, and could barely recall whether it were true now, and though I feared it would ruin everything, I could not be dishonest without remarking, "I thought at one point, though, that my father had told me my aunt and uncle had had a child."

"Really?" Mr. Smith raised his eyebrows and leaned forward. "Your uncle never mentioned one."

"If they did though," I added, "the child would be grown now—probably be about Adele's age, seventeen or eighteen since my aunt died when I was about six."

"Must have died then—so many children do," said Mr. Smith. "Your uncle clearly told me he had no family except his brother-in-law."

"Well, perhaps I'm remembering wrong too," I replied. "Father and Uncle did not write to one another often, and Father rarely mentioned my aunt after her death."

"Well, I wouldn't worry about it," said Mr. Smith, sitting back up at his desk to light a cigar. He offered one to Mr. Whitman, who simply motioned it away. "You and your sister are your uncle's heirs. I'm sure there won't be any trouble about the inheritance. As soon as I get those baptismal certificates, I'll do the necessary paperwork, and then prepare the purchase agreement to buy the property from you. That'll give you plenty of money to travel back to Cincinnati."

But I would not have decisions made for me so easily. "My sister and I have nowhere to stay in Cincinnati or Marquette," I said. "May we stay at the property until our baptismal records arrive?"

"You don't want to do that," said Mr. Smith. "There's nothing there—it's no place at all for women, especially when winter's coming on."

"I can't decide that until I've seen the property," I replied. "And I need to know what I own before I can determine a fair price for selling it."

"Oh, well, now," he said, "I just don't want you to be disappointed is all." He stood up from his desk and crossed the room to the window overlooking Marquette's harbor. "That cabin's no real place for young ladies, but I suppose if you want to see it—well, I could drive you out there—it's a good twenty miles I imagine—I'd have to take you on Sunday—I have business to do every other day. I could stop by the boarding house just about noon perhaps for you and your sister."

"It's twenty miles?" I gasped. "If we did live there, how would we get back into town?"

"That's why I said two women couldn't possibly live there. You can't walk into town, at least not at this time of year—the roads are all mud, and you never know when you might get caught in a rainstorm or a blizzard in this country—you could get lost in a snowstorm halfway between here and the cabin—it's only a logging road after all. No, you can't walk to town and back from there. You'll see what I mean when we go out on Sunday, provided the weather is good. Trust me—one look at the place and you'll be happy to have me take it off your hands."

"I would greatly appreciate your taking us there," I replied, unwilling to argue with him, although I had already made up my mind we would find some way to stay there and work the farm and make a living from it. "My sister and I will have to go to Mass Sunday morning, but we would be available for you to drive us out there in the afternoon."

"Oh, you're Catholics," he said. "I thought most Germans were Protestants. I'm an Irish Catholic myself."

I nodded in acknowledgment, too annoyed to speak—why did people assume Martin Luther had decided the religious question for all Germans?

"I don't imagine you even know where the cathedral is," he said. "I'd be happy to take you and your sister to Mass before we drive out to the cabin."

"Miss Traugott, that could make a long day for you," Mr. Whitman told me. "Mr. Smith, why don't you come have Sunday dinner with us after church and before you and the young ladies head out there?"

"Thank you," Mr. Smith replied. "I would enjoy that. It isn't often a bachelor like me gets a home cooked meal."

"Well, you need to find yourself a wife," smiled Mr. Whitman.

"Yes, in good time," said Mr. Smith.

"Thank you, Mr. Smith," I said, rising to my feet. "I'll make sure Adele and I are ready when you come to pick us up Sunday morning. In the meantime, I'll buy some provisions to take with us to the cabin. I don't know what supplies Uncle had, but I wouldn't want to make an extra trip into town once we're settled there. I imagine if Uncle did plant a crop, there'll be plenty there for us to eat through the winter."

"You won't find much growing at this time of year," said Mr. Whitman. "He probably harvested everything weeks ago."

"Miss Traugott," Mr. Smith said, "you surely can't intend to live out there."

"I don't know that we have much choice," I replied. "My sister and I have very little money. We can't afford to stay with the Whitmans for long, kind as they are. Before I make any decisions, I'll have to find out whether my uncle sold his crop, and whether there's any money to be made from the farm. And until the legal paperwork is done for our inheritance, I can't sell the place; we need to live somewhere in the meantime."

"I doubt," Mr. Smith said, "that your uncle grew enough on that land to feed himself. What little money he had I believe he got from trapping and selling animal furs. I wouldn't be surprised if his sickness weren't the result of being malnourished."

"I don't see any other choice for now," I repeated. "I'll buy supplies in town tomorrow so I'll be prepared to move out there Sunday."

"I trust, Miss Traugott, that you will reconsider when you see the property—it is not a place for young ladies."

"Thank you for your kindness, Mr. Smith," I replied, turning toward the door. "I will see you Sunday morning."

❄   ❄   ❄

Mr. Whitman and I returned to the boarding house in time for supper. The other boarders, after expressing sympathy for the unexpected loss of Uncle Shepard, inquired what I intended to do. I explained that I was going out to see the cabin for myself and that Adele and I would probably live there. The two shopgirls protested it would be a dreadful place, out in the woods, so far from town. Mr. Wainscott agreed with the shopgirls, although I gathered it was less from concern for my welfare than to ingratiate himself with the young ladies. I was not forthcoming with answers to their many other questions, largely because I did not have answers. Mr. Whitman kept saying, "Just give the young ladies time to decide." Finally, the conversation turned to other topics; meanwhile, I ate without saying another word, all the while wondering whether it were foolish of me to go live in the cabin. I just could not see another workable solution.

After supper, I was ready for bed, but Mrs. Whitman insisted everyone have dessert in the parlor. She had made a special pumpkin pie "just because we have guests." Mr. Whitman led the other boarders into the parlor while Adele and I hesitated until Mrs. Whitman told Edna, "Go take the young ladies into the parlor and entertain them. I can manage getting dessert by myself, and it won't take me but ten minutes to cut up the pie and make coffee."

Seeing escape was impossible, Adele and I followed Edna into the parlor.

We all sat around for a couple of minutes, dreadfully bored, Mr. Wainscott commenting that it would probably rain. "At least it will melt the snow," said one of the shopgirls, and the other said, "Miserable drizzling weather would be appropriate for Halloween."

"Why, Pa!" Edna then perked up. "I had forgotten it was Halloween. You should tell us one of your ghost stories."

"Oh no, your mother wouldn't like that," he replied.

"I bet you could tell us one before she even finishes cleaning up."

Mr. Whitman raised his eyebrows to suggest Edna should be helping her mother, but she said, "Mother told me to come in here and entertain the Miss Traugotts, but your stories are far more entertaining than my conversation, and it is Halloween, Pa."

"Very well," he said. He had filled his pipe with tobacco as his daughter spoke. Now he lit it, took a good puff, and exhaled enough smoke to raise a sinister fog along the New England coast where his tale took place.

"Now this story," he began, "was told to me by my Grandfather Whitman when I was young. It dates back to the beginning of this century, and every word of it is true. It concerns a young man named Enoch, and Sabrina, the pretty young girl who had the misfortune to love him. They had grown up in the same little seaside town—known each other since birth in fact, and gone to school together—and when they came of age, they fell in love, and there was talk of their marrying.

"Now Enoch was by no means a handsome boy, and he was not strong or athletic like most of the other young men, but he had a tall figure that stood out in a crowd, and his hard features suggested a determination not really there. Some say he had a little scar over his lip where his older brother had once struck him with a rock when he was a boy—I don't know whether that's true or not, since I was not there, but what is true—and you can verify this in the town's records—is that his older brother went missing for several days, and when his body was found, it was lying on some rocks along a cliff above the sea. The townsfolk whispered that Enoch had murdered his brother to get revenge for that scar, but it's just as likely his brother's death was an accident and no fault of Enoch's.

"Sabrina paid no heed to any ill rumors about the young man. She had her heart set on Enoch, and he had his heart set on her, and none of their parents was opposed to the match. But that spring, Enoch's mother and father both died of the diphtheria, and then that summer, a terrible drought struck. Now Enoch had been raised a farmer, but his father had done all the hard work on the farm, and with his parents no longer there to keep a steady eye on him, he did not care for the crops as he should. The long and the short of it is that his crops failed, and ultimately, he knew he could not make a go of the farm. Plenty of other farmers had a hard time that year, but they struggled and got by, while the determination that appeared on Enoch's brow did not compensate for the weakness of his character and his lack of backbone. Finally, he confessed to Sabrina that he wanted nothing to do with hard dirty work like farming, so he was going to sell the farm and seek his fortune elsewhere.

"Sabrina's parents were beside themselves with dread when they heard this, for they did not know how Enoch would support their daughter. They had two sons of their own who were to split the farm between them, so Sabrina was expected to find a husband to care for her. When her parents considered breaking off the engagement, Sabrina flew into a fury, declaring if she could not marry Enoch, she would marry no man but throw herself off the same cliff that had caused the death of Enoch's brother so the ocean would swallow her body for all time.

"As you can imagine, Sabrina's parents were frightened by her outburst, for they truly believed their daughter meant to destroy herself if they did not let her wed Enoch. They told themselves the boy was young and foolish, but he came from a good family, and in time, he would settle down; they would do what they could for the young couple in the meantime.

"And so one day in early spring, Sabrina and Enoch were married, and a few weeks later, he went off to sea. He promised Sabrina he would make his fortune and come home with enough money to buy ten farms, or better yet, they might start up a tavern in the town, or even their own shipping business. Sabrina, because of the great love she bore for Enoch, allowed her soul to be fed on such dreams, while her parents worried their daughter and her unsteady husband would starve after they had gone to their reward.

"Well, Enoch's ship sailed off—out to the South Seas it was. The summer and the autumn passed and then the winter came. An entire year went by, and in that time, not one letter came home from Enoch. You can imagine Sabrina's anxiety and excitement when the ship finally sailed back into the harbor, but I don't think any of us can imagine her disappointment when all the other sailors disembarked from the ship, yet no Enoch appeared.

"One young man on the ship was a couple of years older than Enoch and had known him since their schooldays. When Enoch's brother had died, this young man had taken it upon himself to look after Enoch; it was said when one of the other boys at school had called Enoch a murderer because of his dead brother, this older boy had thrashed the accuser so hard no one else ever dared whisper such a rumor again. This young man was the last to come off the ship that day, and when he saw Sabrina standing on the dock, her eyes welling up with tears, he hated to be the one to tell her, but he felt it was his duty.

"'Enoch decided to leave us,' he told Sabrina, 'in a foreign port'—I forget the name of it now—'he...' and then the man paused, trying to find words to soften the blow, but Sabrina could not bear the silence, and suddenly, everyone on the dock heard her shout out, 'Why? Why? Where's my Enoch?'

"So the young man quickly put his arm around her and led her from the crowd, and then to calm her, he said, 'Enoch has great prospects. He believes he can make his fortune in that place, and—'

"'How?' she demanded, for in her heart, Sabrina had begun to doubt Enoch's fidelity.

"'He has a plan,' said the young man. 'He thought he'd start up a plantation there—pineapples and bananas—and he'll make a great deal of money. He's just starting out now, so he told me to give you all his love, and to ask you to be patient. He's going to send for you to come to him just as soon as he can. He kept asking me to tell you that he loves you very much.'

"Sabrina tried to find comfort in these words. She let the young man walk her home to her parents' house, and there he told the same story again, and her family politely thanked him and then let him go home to his own folks.

"But Sabrina's family was not pleased. 'Who does Enoch think he is to expect our sister to live in the wild with him?' and 'I don't believe any of it—it's all lies,' said her brothers, and her mother confessed, 'I always did fear that boy would come to no good.' But her father only put his arm around Sabrina and consoled her by saying, 'We can't say whether his plans are right or wrong until we know more. We'll just have to wait for word from him.'

"They waited all that next spring, and that summer, and into the autumn, and when winter came again, and they knew no word could reach them in those months because of the storms at sea, all their spirits fell, and in her heart, Sabrina began to doubt Enoch would return—she feared he might have died—that's what she told herself— that's what she almost hoped had happened, for the other possibility would have been just too much for her to bear.

"Now the other sailors who had been on Enoch's ship had gone out again that spring, but when the next winter came and ice froze along the shores so it was not safe for ships to sail, the sailors had nothing better to do but drink in the tavern, drink and talk, and the drink loosened their tongues so that they said things perhaps they should not have. That's when it came out—rumors that Enoch had gone native. When Sabrina's brothers heard these stories, they feared they must be true because Enoch's friend would have spoken out against such rumors if they were not, and soon Enoch's friend quit coming to the tavern, ashamed perhaps to have been friends with such a one as Enoch."

"What do you mean by 'gone native'?" Adele interrupted Mr. Whitman.

"Well," giggled Mr. Whitman. "I don't know whether I should say in front of young ladies—but I guess I mean he went to live with the natives and follow their ways."

"You mean with the savages?" asked one of the shopgirls.

"I don't know whether they were savages or not," said Mr. Whitman, "but the rumors were that he had gone to live among them, and some even said that he had taken a woman from among them."

"Oh my!" said Adele.

My sense of propriety at that moment made me want to get up and leave the room; I would have expected Mr. Whitman to have a better sense of decorum, but I also perversely found myself wanting to know what had happened to the poor Sabrina.

"The brothers kept all these rumors from their sister," Mr. Whitman said, "but I imagine some of the sailors told their own wives and fiancées, and you know how women talk, and so I'm sure if these rumors never actually reached Sabrina's ears, she sensed the rest of the town knew Enoch had done something disgraceful, and her heart broke over it.

"The years passed, and Sabrina's parents died. Her brothers married and started families of their own, and they prospered enough to build their own homes while Sabrina continued to live alone in her parents' house. Her brothers begged her to come live with them, but she refused. She could no longer find joy in human companionship. Her house was near the ocean, and so she had a widow's walk built upon the roof, and they say in the evenings at dusk, she could be seen pacing about there; sometimes she would walk the entire night while the rest of the town slept, for she craved no human company save that of her Enoch, and he was absent. Those children who dared creep near the house at night to catch a glimpse of the mysterious solitary woman said they heard her weeping and begging God to bring back her lover. That is when the story began to grow truly strange.

"The young man who had been Enoch's friend had grown to love Sabrina, perhaps out of compassion for her pain, perhaps because he had always loved her, but he had been too loyal a friend to Enoch to speak earlier. Finally, he went to Sabrina and explained to her how unlikely it was that Enoch would ever return, that enough time had passed to presume Enoch was dead, and that if Sabrina would have him, he would be honored to marry her and care for her the rest of their days.

"Sabrina thanked him, but she refused his offer. She continued to live in that house alone, and after a few years, the young man gave up waiting for her and married another. He became a good husband and father, but the townsfolk whispered it was always Sabrina whom he truly loved.

"And then one night, many years after the day Enoch had sailed away, when Sabrina's beauty had begun to fade, and she had shut herself up so that scarcely anyone ever saw her, the townsfolk heard a piercing scream coming from her house. When they ran and knocked on her door, there was no answer, but the screaming continued until finally,

Sabrina's brothers broke in through a window and went upstairs. They found their sister sitting up in bed, her hair turned gray overnight, her face pale with horror, blood soaking through all her bed sheets. She stood staring out the window, shrieking so that her brothers could barely stand it, and it took them several minutes before they could shake her enough to bring her to her senses.

"Some said she had tried to kill herself—to slit her wrists—though her brothers refused to let a doctor see her. I don't know why they didn't send for the doctor, but people say it was because they were afraid to know the truth about what had happened to her; others say she had not hurt herself, for there was a woman who came to clean for her, and she told everyone she had seen no scars on Sabrina's wrists the next day.

"I hesitate to mention this part, but Sabrina was clearly mad after that night, such that her brothers ordered her tied to her bed so she would not hurt herself, and often she would thrash about in the bed, screaming out Enoch's name. Most frightening of all, some say she went mad because her prayers had been answered—that Enoch had returned to her—only it was not the flesh and blood Enoch, but his ghost—come back to claim his wife in their bed.

"Really, Father!" said Edna, but I could see a smirk of pleasure on her face.

"Now, I'm only repeating the story the way my grandfather told it to me, and whether it is true, who is to say," Mr. Whitman replied. "Anyway, after that, Sabrina grew weaker and weaker, and though she thrashed about in the bed for several more nights, soon she wasted away until she died before the year was out.

"Her brothers boarded up the house after she died, for they could not bear to go near it, their pain was so great, and they were too sentimental to sell or tear down their childhood home.

"And it is still said that to this day, Sabrina's steps can be heard at night, pacing up and down the widow's walk, and sometimes, a scream is heard in the night, and while some say it is just the wind during a storm at sea, no one can prove that it is not Sabrina, crying for her demon lover."

Everyone was silent after Mr. Whitman finished his tale. I thought it completely distasteful and wanted to go upstairs to bed all the more now except that Mrs. Whitman had still not come in with the pie and coffee.

After a couple of minutes, Edna said, "It's such a sad story."

"Rather freakish," laughed Mr. Wainscott. "I mean, especially that a dead man would come back to torture his wife like that."

"I don't believe it would have happened that way," Adele said. "I can believe part of it—that Enoch might have come back to her, or that her ghost haunts the house because she still longs for him—I believe people can love like that, but I don't believe he would return as her demon lover. If anything, I think he would have come back, repentant for deserting her, and if she saw his ghost, it would only show how great love is, that whatever our sins, we can make peace with one another after death."

"What a romantic idea," Edna said. "It's like something out of a Brontë novel."

It was on the tip of my tongue to say the whole story was ridiculous when Mrs. Whitman appeared with the coffee. She handed me my cup first, then gave a cup to one of the shopgirls, who rather than thanking her, said, "Mr. Whitman has been frightening us with ghost stories, so it won't be the coffee that keeps me awake tonight."

"Nathaniel, you and your ghosts," Mrs. Whitman frowned.

"What? It's Halloween after all," he said.

"That any Christian man would find pleasure on the devil's day," his wife scolded. "And these poor young ladies mourning their uncle— you'll have them so frightened they won't dare go live in the woods, though perhaps that would be a good thing."

"It really wasn't that frightening," Adele said. "It was more of a love story."

"Well, I don't know whether that makes it any better or any more true," Mrs. Whitman replied. "Those love stories are all make-believe and can do a great deal of harm."

The coffee was too hot to drink. I would have to wait for it to cool, and that would be many more minutes—I was so longing for bed, so tired. At least Mrs. Whitman's presence would keep her husband from telling more terrible tales, so I could excuse myself when I had finished dessert. I needed a good night's rest so I could think more clearly and make the right decision about living at the cabin. I had not met anyone this day I could truly depend upon for sound advice. Everything would be solely up to me. As soon as Adele and I drank our coffee and ate our pie, I excused us both, and we went upstairs.

❄   ❄   ❄

On Saturday, Mr. Whitman was kind enough to take me in his wagon to get supplies for the cabin. I think he was surprised when I bought enough flour and sugar and coffee to carry us through many months, but I had heard about the long winters in Upper Michigan, so I knew we might well be snowed in for weeks at a time if the winter were hard. I was growing more frustrated with Adele, who refused to stir out of doors until Sunday, wanting only to rest. She even suggested to me that I should just sell the property to Mr. Smith so we could return to Cincinnati. But I had always hated the busyness of that bustling city. Marquette seemed more quiet and restful to me, and I had worked hard all my life, so I hoped to find some peace in the woods even if I still had to work hard. Our prospects might not be greatly promising, but each time someone tried to persuade me otherwise, be it Mr. Smith or Mrs. Whitman or my own sister, I grew all the more determined to prove we could survive in Uncle's cabin through the long winter. I would be self-sufficient, not relying on someone else's kindness for my daily bread.

On Sunday morning, I awoke with a determination that not even Adele's worries could dissuade. I had personally repacked all our belongings into the trunk the night before so Adele could not claim she had forgotten anything and needed to return to Marquette as an excuse. We were going to live in that cabin all winter, and fix it up if need be, and live off whatever we could find of the crops, and plant anew in the spring. It was going to happen, and it was all going to be fine, and we would not have to depend on anyone but ourselves.

Mr. Smith was not too cooperative. For starters, he was late picking us up. Not once in my life had I been late for Mass, yet Mr. Smith did not arrive until five minutes before the service began. Adele and I were literally waiting on the sidewalk when his wagon came around the corner.

"Good morning, Miss Traugott," he said, tipping his hat as he pulled up before the boarding house.

"I was starting to think we would have to walk," I replied. I walked around the wagon to climb up, and in the meantime, he jumped down from his side to give my sister his hand.

"I'm afraid we haven't met, Miss. I'm Mr. Smith. I was your late uncle's lawyer."

"I'm pleased to meet you," said Adele.

"The pleasure is all mine. Miss Traugott did not tell me how lovely her sister is."

"Mr. Smith, we better hurry or we'll be late," I said.

"You won't be able to go to Mass once you're living out in the woods," Mr. Smith replied as he climbed up beside me. I had purposely taken the middle of the seat to separate him from my sister.

"Can't we come into town on Sundays?" asked Adele.

"Not unless you have a wagon, and I wouldn't advise it even then in winter unless you want to get caught in a blizzard."

"Father and Mother wouldn't like our missing Mass," Adele said.

"We can say our rosaries at home as we did a couple of years ago when we were too sick to go to Mass," I replied. "God will understand."

"I suppose," said Adele, doubtfully. Again I wondered whether I were making the right decision, but all we had in the world was that cabin in the woods, and whatever its state, we had to make the best of it. Then Adele added, "I trust God will provide a way for us to get to Church."

"You'll need a miracle," Mr. Smith grunted. I already felt some distaste for the man, but after such a blasphemous remark, I did not like him. And his making us late for Mass did not help matters.

Yet I did notice how gently he handed Adele down from the wagon, then gave her his arm to walk her into the cathedral. I could not completely dislike anyone who admired Adele, for I loved her almost like my own child, yet I feared the day a man might take her from me.

I was not impressed when I saw the church. In those days, St. Peter's Cathedral was not the magnificent edifice it would be in my old age, after it had twice burnt and been rebuilt in the 1880s and 1930s. No, in

1873, it was a simple little church, only designated as a cathedral, to my understanding, after the diocese's founding bishop, Frederic Baraga, had decided to move his see from Sault Sainte Marie to Marquette. Even had it been a magnificent cathedral, it would not have struck me with admiration that day when I was so anxious about the future. I paid little attention to the Mass, distracted by the attention Mr. Smith gave to Adele as he helped her remove her coat, found the correct page for her in her missal, and kept sneaking glances at her, even winking once when she returned his look. I would have to endure him the rest of the day, but once he left us at the cabin, Adele would be safe from his groping eyes. I worried that she liked his attention—for Father and I had kept her sheltered at home from men's eyes, and although Mr. Smith was not particularly good looking, he was well dressed. Someday, his wife would be well dressed as well, but I did not want Adele to be that wife. She was too young to marry—hardly more than a child, and she could not leave me yet, not so soon after Father's death, not for at least a couple of more years. And then—well, I would try to find her a wealthy husband, and one who would take me in as well— after all, I would be her husband's sister-in-law.

I would not write Mr. Smith off as that future husband, if I found none better, but he had decided drawbacks, which were obvious just from sitting beside him at Mass. During the recitation of the Nicene Creed, he faltered three times in his words, and during the Eucharistic prayers, he was not prompt at kneeling or standing; he was obviously out of practice, and that spoke volumes to me about what kind of man he was. No matter how much money he had, my sister would not wed a godless man. She would have to wait until I found one worthy of her.

After Mass, Mr. Smith took Adele's arm as if it were expected of him. I followed behind them to the wagon. He helped her up into the wagon, and then politely did the same for me, which awkwardly put me on the end of the seat. Unlike the pew in church, the seat was so small that his leg brushed up against Adele's. I told myself the ride back to the boarding house was only a few minutes in length, but I would not permit him to give her such attention on the ride to the cabin. I would sit between them. That was absolute.

On the way back, Mr. Smith tried to engage my attention with gossip about the people at the church, making such remarks as, "That Mrs. Montoni—some nerve she has going to Mass when her husband owns a saloon," and "Carolina O'Neill wouldn't even look at me when I smiled at her—snooty little thing." But worst of all was when he told me his own ambitions. "They say this financial panic, as they're starting to term it, if it gets much worse, will result in many people having to leave Marquette, but that doesn't bother me any. I'll buy up their properties lickety-split, and resell them at higher values once this little depression is over. A man can make a tidy profit in times like these if he knows what he's doing. It's what needs to be done if a man wants to support his family—or if he is planning soon to have a family."

I caught his insinuation—that he would be able to provide for Adele—but I chose to ignore it. How could he think of profiting from his neighbors' misfortunes! He might as well be a usurer—or at least a confidence man. I was disgusted by him. I wished we had not agreed to have Sunday dinner with the Whitmans. The sooner we reached the cabin, the sooner I could end my acquaintance with Mr. Smith. I would definitely have to write him off as a prospective suitor for Adele.

The other boarders had gone elsewhere for Sunday dinner, Mrs. Whitman reserving that day for family only—so it had truly been a special invitation she had made to us. There were family guests at the table, whom she introduced as her sister and brother-in-law, Mr. and

Mrs. Henning, and their daughter, Madeleine. "My son, Jacob, and his family," Mrs. Whitman added, "decided not to come because his wife Agnes isn't feeling well. He's a very devoted husband, although I would think Agnes could rest better if he brought the two little girls over here."

I did not mind the absence of two little girls; they would have only screamed and whined through Sunday dinner, and I soon found Mrs. Henning intolerable enough. She was a busybody of a woman— one who might have fit Mr. Smith perfectly had she been thirty years younger. She certainly was an odd choice of a wife for Mr. Henning, of whom I never heard an ill word spoken during the years the family remained in Marquette.

I disliked Mrs. Henning thoroughly. All she did was chat with her sister about her house and the new carpet she wanted to order for one of the parlors, and what color it should be, and how frustrating it was that she had to rely on a catalogue when she used to own a mercantile store and could have gotten it at a better price, "not that money is an object, mind you, but I don't want to spend all Gerald's hard-earned money on a rug when I could use it to buy other things for the house." From her elaborate laced and bustled and colorful costume, I doubted seriously she had any concern for how she spent her husband's money, and considering I did not even have a home at present, it was nothing but obnoxious to me to hear about her palatial residence.

Her husband was far more personable. He made several attempts to include us in the conversation by saying, "You must find our change of climate a surprise" or "I'm sure the train ride was not that comfortable, but it was far worse when I came here twenty-four years ago on a schooner across Lake Superior." I could barely reply to him before Mrs. Henning would again interrupt with trivial decorating comments. After nearly an hour, and its being discussed whenever she stopped speaking for a moment, she managed to realize Adele and I really did mean to go live out in the cabin in the woods. Then she declared, "Why, how can you? It's not civilized. It's not as if you're Indians or something."

"They look like capable young ladies to me," said her husband.

"But it's nonsense," Mrs. Henning replied. "If you were Irish even it might be understandable—the Irish all live in dirt floor cottages—but you were raised in an American city."

"There is no dirt floor in that cabin," Mr. Smith said, "and there are many Irish who have never had a dirt floor in their home."

That Mr. Smith was of Irish blood was lost upon Mrs. Henning.

The meal finally concluded. Throughout, my stomach had been twisting in knots over my decision to go to the cabin. Now that it was time to leave, I feared someday we would come back into town, admitting defeat before all these people because I had made the wrong decision. If things did not work out, what would I do? Sell the cabin to Mr. Smith? Manipulate him into marrying Adele? But I doubted he would be charitable enough to take me in as well. Perhaps Mrs. Henning would let me be one of her maids? From her descriptions of her house, I would bet the maids had Persian carpets in their rooms. But I did not have to give up yet; I would try to persevere, to achieve my goal of independence. I could not determine whether I was making a mistake until I had seen the cabin.

When the dessert plates were cleared, Mrs. Henning suggested Madeleine entertain us with a song, but I protested we could not stay.

"We wish you a safe journey," Mr. Henning graciously said, so I did not have to argue with his wife over our departure.

"I wish you could have stayed longer," said Edna.

"I'll fix you up some leftovers to take with you—you can make yourselves cold chicken sandwiches for supper tonight," Mrs. Whitman insisted. She had begun our acquaintance with concern we would not pay for our room, but now that she was getting us off her hands without financial loss to herself, she was becoming more generous.

We said our goodbyes to everyone and went out on the porch. I insisted we need not be walked to the street. Mrs. Henning began to complain about her lazy maid, thus making everyone feel obligated to remain at the table and listen to her, so we departed alone.

"Mr. Smith, we have some supplies on the back porch if you'll be good enough to put them in the wagon," I said once we were outside. For a moment, I thought of returning inside to ask Mr. Whitman or Mr. Henning to help him, but Mr. Smith simply smiled at my sister, gave me a look as if to say, "I'm not your servant," and then made three trips between the back porch and his wagon to load our supplies. I did not care whether it annoyed him to help us—I needed the supplies brought with us, and I could not lift them myself—I think he was most annoyed to see I was serious about living at the cabin. Keeping him occupied allowed me to climb into the wagon and plant myself in the middle of the seat to separate him from Adele. However much he might help us, my sister's beauty would not be his compensation.

"You are a determined woman, Miss Traugott," he said as he took his seat beside me. I stared ahead without replying. Truthfully, I was afraid if I spoke, I might change my mind about going to the cabin.

"Giddup," he said, shaking the reins. We started down the street. Until then, I had no idea in which direction Uncle Shepard's property lay, but Mr. Smith led us south through town; we passed the cathedral, then journeyed parallel to the lakeshore a little way until we had passed through the valley just south of Marquette. Once we entered the forest, the town became invisible.

It was a long, dull ride. The road was very rough. I doubt it had been there more than a couple of seasons. It was a dirt road—had it been raining or snowing, we never could have made our way along it. Mr. Smith said it was a logging road, but he explained that since most logging was done in winter because it was easier to get the logs out by sleigh than wagon, the road itself was not very accessible. The sky was cloudy, and the afternoon became bitterly cold—hardly more than forty degrees; the leaves had all fallen from the trees, making the forest bleak and frightening, like something from the worst of Grimm's Fairy Tales. For the first half hour, we saw nothing but dead vegetation in all directions. The forest was thick with bushes, ferns, and berry bushes, but all were in a brown and yellow state of decay. Gradually, we passed beyond the birch, maple, and oak trees to a great spread of pines—pines were almost the only trees for miles and miles, and while these were green, they felt more unfriendly than the leafless maples and oaks.

"Doesn't anyone live out here?" Adele nearly whispered through the scarf she had wrapped over her mouth to keep from breathing in the cold air. She had insisted she would not need the scarf when we left the boarding house, but I had known better and made her wrap it around her face when we first started out of town. I was grateful to notice it also hid her pretty face.

"No, there's not much out here," Mr. Smith replied. "People haven't started farming this area too much yet. There's a railroad track—goes to Escanaba, but that's about it."

"Where's Exsanobwa?" I asked.

"Escanaba," he repeated. "It's on Lake Michigan, a good sixty or seventy miles from here I would say. It's just a little village—I've only been there once myself—not much more than a stop for the railroad really."

"If we ever needed anything out here, would the trains stop for us?" I asked.

"You're probably a few miles from the railroad tracks, but if you stood by the track and flagged one down, it might stop—not that you would know when a train was coming—and in winter, with the snow drifting and all, few trains run and even if they do, it might be days before a train could get through."

Our life in these woods did not sound pleasant. But I knew of nothing else we could do—perhaps I was being stubborn and we should have stayed in Marquette—but we had no money to accomplish that, and we could not go back to Cincinnati. At least Uncle's cabin would give us a roof over our heads.

I don't know how long we traveled down that road, but I would guess it was well over an hour and perhaps closer to two. Finally, the road grew quite narrow as it wound through the thick pine trees. We climbed up small hills, then went down little dips into valleys, then up again, with Mr. Smith continually having to put on the brake; twice he got out of the wagon to lead the horses around a sharp bend or a rock that cropped out into the road that might break the wagon wheel if he were not careful. Finally, at the bottom of a thickly wooded hill, we turned off the main road onto an overgrown path, so narrow I did not at first think the wagon would pass between the little saplings growing up on both sides. Then we moved into a large copse, full of moss and dead berry bushes, followed by another dip into a small valley. But once we were up again out of that valley, through the leafless trees, the cabin came into view.

"There it is," Mr. Smith said, as he turned the horses into another curve in the road. At first glimpse, it looked so small that I began to quake inside. But we were still half-a-mile away, and as we drew closer, I could see it was two stories. Adele had not yet said anything; I was afraid she was depressed by the sight of it, so I put on a good face, saying as pleasantly as possible, "It looks respectable enough."

"Frankly, I'm surprised it's still standing," said Mr. Smith. I did not reply, convinced he was only trying to rile me. "I remember noticing some of the wood was starting to rot on it when I came out here last summer to write up your uncle's will."

Dismissing his remark, I said, "Adele, look at all the land we have for our yard. It makes me feel quite rich."

She said nothing, only waited for the wagon to stop, and then let Mr. Smith hand her down.

"There you are, Miss," he said, setting her on her feet. I noticed his hand linger in hers, but again I told myself not to be rude since he had driven us out here—he would be gone soon enough.

He offered me his hand, but I pulled mine from his the second my foot touched earth.

"Shall we go in?" I said.

"Please," Adele replied. "I'm so cold."

Mr. Smith led us to the cabin, on the way pointing out the field where Uncle had a garden—it was not large enough to be called a crop—being at most a quarter acre and surrounded by pine trees. Uncle had obviously not been ambitious about maintaining his property, although Mr. Smith said he had lived here about twenty years.

"You can see this place isn't much," said Mr. Smith as we stepped inside the front door. "I'd be surprised if the roof holds up through the winter. You better be prepared for a good soaking first time it rains. Anyway, I'll go fetch your supplies in."

I did not see any signs of structural weakness—not that I would have known where to look. It had rained the night before, yet the cabin floor was dry, and there was no musty smell, so I doubted I needed to worry about leaks. Considering there would be only Adele and me, there was plenty of space. The downstairs was all one large room, nearly forty feet long and half as wide. A set of stairs along the back wall led up to a loft, just slightly over half the size of the downstairs. A large fireplace near the stairs would heat the entire cabin. Two good-sized windows were downstairs, and I was thankful to see the windows had glass on them with wooden shutters outside to protect the glass.

But glass windows soon proved to be the only luxury Uncle had included. There was no pump for water—Mr. Smith said we would have to fetch it from the creek nearly a mile away. There was a stove, thankfully, for I hated cooking over an open fire and had not done so in years, but the stove looked so dirty and a bit rusted that I was skeptical it would work. Some cupboards with cracks and chipped wood made me believe I would find little inside them. Everything looked forlorn, without any effort having been made to provide comfort. A lone rocking chair near the fireplace with a cushion tied to its seat was the grandest piece of furniture. The dining room table actually had four wooden chairs, only one being lopsided. A large bin along the wall held firewood. Some tools and other paraphernalia hung on the downstairs wall—snowshoes, a rifle, a couple of kerosene lanterns, a hammer, a saw, and a few other tools I did not recognize. A shelf by the stove contained a few scratched and dented pans, four plates, one with a crack in it, another with a chipped edge, and a handful of utensils. Any woman would have found it a nightmare. More than anything, the dilapidated kitchenware nearly made me agree to return to Marquette. But I forced a smile, and said, "Adele, we have some curtains and a tablecloth in our trunk which should make things look better. With a little effort, I'm sure we can make ourselves quite comfortable here."

Before Adele could reply, Mr. Smith came in with the last of our supplies, set them on the floor, and repeated, "It's not much of a place for young ladies."

He needn't have told us that. Adele went to the rocking chair and started rocking as a way to keep warm. Too unsure of myself to know what more to say, I went upstairs to investigate. I expected Mr. Smith would follow me to ensure we had everything we needed before he left, or to try further to dissuade me from staying, but he remained downstairs to build a fire, under the guise of kindness, but more likely to talk with Adele.

Upstairs I found one double bed, torn at the bottom so that the feathers were falling out. On top of it were three blankets with little rips in them. A disgusting bear skin hung on the far wall—that, I decided, would be the first thing to go, although upon reconsideration, it might make a good rug to keep the floor warm—I would decide that later.

After a few minutes, knowing it was time to go downstairs now to tell Mr. Smith he could leave, I sat down on the bed to calm myself. When I stared out the one tiny window, all I could see were pine trees for half a mile until they obscured my view of what could only be more pine trees beyond. I did not want to live here. How would we survive? We had brought a few months' worth of supplies, but even if we found some food in the garden, we could not possibly make it through the entire winter, which I had heard might last into May. Of course, there was the rifle downstairs, and hopefully, there were bullets. I would learn to shoot if needed—my heart withered at the thought—but if I grew hungry enough, I could do it.

"Barbara Traugott, you are a stubborn woman," I told myself, "but there's nothing else for it. You can't live on the mercy of others, expecting their charity. You have to make due for yourself and Adele. You have to, and so you will."

When I went downstairs, Mr. Smith was sitting on the floor beside Adele's rocking chair. A log was crackling in the fireplace.

"Barbara," said Adele, "Mr. Smith has started us a fire. Isn't he clever?"

"Thank you, Mr. Smith," I said, but I was rather annoyed—it did not seem quite cold enough to warrant a fire—we could not waste wood, unless I were to learn to cut down trees as well. I had seen Uncle's ax hanging beside the tools.

"Now, Miss Traugott," said Mr. Smith, getting to his feet, "you can see this place is far too rough for young ladies like yourselves who are used to city ways."

"On the contrary, Mr. Smith," I replied, "it is the first home Adele and I have ever had. Even in Cincinnati, Father only rented our house—this is our first real home, and we'll take to it just fine once we add a few feminine touches."

"My offer to buy it still stands," he said. "Of course, what with this financial panic that's starting, I might not be able to give you full price, but we could come to some sort of mutually beneficial agreement—say three hundred dollars."

The day at his office, he had offered me five hundred, and I had thought that a rather large sum, though I knew we could not live on it for long. Now I felt insulted that, apparently not remembering his previous offer, or hoping I did not remember it, which was more likely, he would offer me less. Three hundred dollars would mean definite poverty to Adele and me once the money was gone. I was still too proud to work in a shop or hotel, or as Mrs. Henning's maid, and I could certainly not see Adele performing menial labor. No, we would stay here. The cabin, despite its appearance, was security nonetheless. It was a roof over our heads and forty acres. Even if those forty acres contained only pine trees, they would provide firewood, and once the trees were chopped down, we could plant the land to make prosperous fields. It was our property, and I was proud of it, no matter what anyone thought.

"Thank you, Mr. Smith. If we decide to sell, I will let you know, but for now, Adele and I will live here."

"Winter could come any day. You don't know the kinds of winters we have here—often three feet of snow within a day or two—the temperature can drop below zero and stay there for days. One night last winter, why it was forty degrees below zero. You just can't stay here. Even a man would have a hard time of it in a solitary place like this—that's why your Uncle would always come into town for the coldest months."

"Adele and I are well used to solitude," I replied. "We will be fine."

Mr. Smith and I both looked at Adele, but she continued silently to rock and stare into the fire.

"It's a damn shame; that's what it is!" he exclaimed.

"Mr. Smith, please!" I said.

"Pardon my language, but it is a shame to have a pretty girl like your sister have to stay out here in the wilderness."

"We appreciate your concern," I replied, although I did not appreciate that it seemed to be solely for Adele. "But you had better head back to town now before it gets dark."

He grunted, said, "Good day, Miss Adele," and opened the door. She only nodded at him; I was glad to see he held no interest for her.

I followed him outside, closing the cabin door behind me. I was not yet ready to be alone with Adele's disappointment over our remaining.

"Provided the road is still accessible and the snow doesn't fall," Mr. Smith said, putting on his hat, "I'll come by with the paperwork once I get those birth certificates."

"I sent a letter requesting them on Friday," I replied. For a second, I was half-tempted to say he could take us back to town next time he came if by then we had found life unbearable here, but I bit my tongue and only said, "I appreciate everything you've done for us, Mr. Smith."

"I'll try to come out," he repeated, "but you never know. Winter could blow in any day now, and then there'd be no reaching you until spring. Miss Traugott, your sister is a lovely young girl. You look strong and capable, but she seems rather dainty to me. She should be gracing some man's dinner table, not living in this cabin. Please reconsider. She would find a husband soon enough in town, and—"

"We appreciate your concern," I repeated. "I hope you have a safe trip back."

This time I sounded annoyed. He was clearly smitten with Adele, but who was he to think he deserved her? We did not even know him— he might have money, but the way he tried to barter with me over the cabin, I was doubtful he had always gained his wealth honestly, and I knew nothing of his family. I did not care how much security he might provide for Adele. Being separated from her own flesh and blood so soon after our father's death could not be in her best interest.

"I'll see then if I can't come back in a week or two," he said and climbed up into his wagon.

I watched him start down the road. I bet myself he would be back within a few days; I doubted he would get Adele out of his head quickly. And I knew, whatever trials faced us, I would send him off again when he came. But between now and then, I would have to figure out how we could live in this wilderness. I tried to gather my courage, rather than concentrate on the harsh stories of winter I had heard—surely most of them had been exaggerated. I was not sure how strong Adele was, but I would make up for it. We were not absolutely forlorn in this land—I could strap on Uncle's snowshoes at anytime and make my way back into Marquette—I could probably walk there faster than Mr. Smith had driven us, considering he had to be careful with the wagon, and the poor horses had pulled three of us and our supplies. There was no reason to despair. We would adjust in a few days and then everything would be fine.

I stood outside in the cold until my hands grew numb. I kept telling myself that whatever was needed to survive, I could handle it. I kept telling myself that because I was not yet ready to go inside and face Adele. But eventually, I was so cold that I had no choice.

3

And so my sister and I had been abandoned to a little cabin in a remote foreign land—it might as well have been a foreign land since we did not speak the language of Nature, its trees or wildlife, and we knew nothing about long, frigid winters. But abandoned was probably not the most accurate term to describe our situation. Mr. Smith had not abandoned us; I had stubbornly insisted he leave us here. Uncle Shepard had not abandoned us; he had not known we were coming to live with him, nor had he chosen to die. And Father had not abandoned us; he had not chosen to die either.

Yet I felt abandoned. Adele seemed in shock at our situation—she had always been fastidious; I could tell she was overwhelmed by the dirt in the cabin, not to mention the permeating cold, so overwhelmed that she had not budged from the rocking chair since we arrived, not even to say goodbye to Mr. Smith. I could not completely blame her, especially when she had always been weaker and more sensitive than me—I told myself to give her a few days to adapt, although I was skeptical she would—I did not know how I would adapt myself. Truthfully, I think I found the situation more difficult than she did;

she at least had me to rely on; I had no one. In the frightened recesses of my heart, anger and resentment welled up, and not knowing whom else to blame, I secretly blamed God. How could He be so cruel to take what little we had possessed in Father and our Cincinnati home and exchange it for this deteriorating cabin in the middle of nowhere? I knew I had my faults, but I could not believe I had committed any sin grave enough to deserve such punishment.

Once Mr. Smith's wagon disappeared, I returned inside, wishing I had a shoulder to cry on, but when I saw Adele, barely rocking in her chair, looking dazed and depressed, I knew I must be strong for her sake. Yet the most confident words I could muster were, "It'll be dark soon—too dark to look around the place. I wish I had asked Mr. Smith to show me where the stream was. Why don't we go to bed? Then we'll be well-rested in the morning so we can make plans."

When Adele did not answer, I went over to the trunk and started to unpack. I thought perhaps she wanted supper, but I was too tired to attempt using that frightening stove, and we had eaten a large meal at the boarding house so it was senseless to waste our supplies. The cold chicken leftovers Mrs. Whitman had given us would last until tomorrow.

As I unpacked, I made a few comments about how lucky we were to have such warm clothes for this winter, or how mother's old tablecloth would cheer up the room. Still, Adele just sat. I don't know whether the cold made her unwilling to move, or whether her silence came from despair, or worse, anger at me for bringing her here. She had no reason to be angry—she had not found any better answer for our situation. She was my sister and I loved her, but at times, I grew tired of always being in charge.

Finally, I walked over to her and said, "You can take off your coat now. It's not that cold in here anymore."

The fire had made the room warmer, although not much warmer—sixty degrees at best, but I was trying to see the best in everything.

Slowly, she stood up and removed her coat.

"There. We'll be warm enough tonight," I said, returning to the trunk. "I think there are enough blankets upstairs, and I should be able to finish sewing my quilt before the snow gets very deep. Now, let me just find our night clothes."

"Barbara," she barely whispered.

"Yes, dear," I said. Her tiny voice made me fear she was becoming ill; sickness would make things near unbearable for us.

"I don't want to go to bed yet. Let's read a little from the Bible first. You know Father would want us to."

"All right," I said, smiling. I found the request a relief; it would provide a small degree of normality to our strange evening. I dug down to the bottom of the trunk until I found our father's English Lutheran Bible. Adele, meanwhile, returned to her rocking chair. I pulled one of the kitchen chairs up to her and perched on it to read.

Adele and I had been raised Catholic because our mother was Catholic, and Catholics in those days did not read the Bible, but we were not a very typical Catholic family since Father had been a Lutheran. According to him, he and Mother had left the old country due to their families' intolerance for their union. Aunt Marie had accompanied them, being the only family member who understood their love and could rise above the religion question. Religion mattered less to Father than Mother I think, although he was always a God-fearing man. He let Mother take us to Mass while he stayed home to read the Bible, and eventually, our curiosity over why Father did not accompany us resulted in his giving us little Bible lessons after Mass. I don't think

Mother quite approved of our Bible studies, but she knew Father was too good a man to teach us any severe heresies. After Mother died, we read the Bible with Father every night, and after his death, during the few days we remained in Cincinnati, Adele had insisted we continue the ritual. I had little trust in God at the moment, but observing our normal routine provided a little comfort.

I was always the reader. Adele complained she could not concentrate on the meaning of the words when she read aloud. We always read straight through the Bible, from cover to cover, and tonight we were to start the Book of Job, which I had scarcely paid attention to in the past, but now I found it intolerable. Job had possessed everything, only to have it all taken from him by no fault of his own, but by a frivolous wager between God and Satan. I grieved for Job, feeling how his unjust fate seemed to parallel my own. Again I wondered whether I should have accepted Mr. Smith's offer to buy the cabin. Again I tried to convince myself we had no other choice but to live here. I felt such despair that if Adele had not been there, I believe like Job I would have rent my clothes, sat on the floor, and poured ashes in my hair. Such despair sounds ludicrous to me now, but at the time, I could understand the man's grief. When I reached the part where Job's friends come to give him advice, I could not bear to read any further.

"Adele, my throat is so dry, and since we have no water, I think it best I stop reading for tonight."

"All right," she said. "We'll be okay tonight without water. In the morning, we can go find the stream together."

That was the first sign of interest she had expressed toward our new life here. I felt heartened that she was willing to help me, even though I felt thirsty right then.

"We should probably go to bed," I said. "We don't want to waste our firewood, and with the blankets over us and the cabin already warmed up, it shouldn't be too cold."

I set down the Bible and lit one of the kerosene lanterns. Then I walked over to the fireplace. With the poker, I toppled the logs over until the flames were smothered.

"Barbara, are you sure it won't be too cold without the fire?"

"We can restart the fire if it is, and we have plenty of blankets," I repeated. I remembered she had not yet been upstairs; I thought that all the more reason to put out the fire—so she could not see the state of the blankets we would sleep under. However cold it became during the night, I was determined we would not make another fire until morning—I had seen a woodpile outside, and several small logs were in the wood bin, but I was deeply concerned we would quickly run short of firewood if we were not careful, and I did not relish trying to swing Uncle's great ax. Tomorrow, I would count all the logs, then divide them by the estimated number of days of winter to determine just how many we might burn each day so we would not run out—yet, I already doubted there would be a hundred and eighty, which would be the minimum needed even if we only used one each day—it could be six months before it was warm enough to go without any fire at all.

Adele said nothing more, just got out of her chair, picked up her nightclothes from where I had laid them on a kitchen chair, and headed upstairs.

By the time she reached the loft, the fire was out. After fetching the kerosene lantern I had bought in town, I followed her upstairs, tucking my own nightclothes under my arms. I could tell from how slowly she moved that she was very tired and would quickly fall asleep. I doubted I would get much rest—my mind was racing with trying to imagine how we would survive all winter. I was also afraid to fall asleep. The door had no lock, although there was a board to place against it, which should keep any wanderers out. A bear might easily break one of the glass windows, but I doubted the windows were large enough for him to crawl through—although a wolf might. And I had left the rifle downstairs. But if I went to fetch it, Adele might realize how precarious was our safety; then she might not sleep at all, and I did not want to listen to her worries all night. I needed time to be quiet, so even if I did not sleep, I could lie there and strategize what we could do to survive. At least now we had a roof over our heads, and despite Mr. Smith's remarks, I did not think it would collapse on us. But how was I to keep food on our table, and wood in the fireplace, and fresh water in the house once the snow came with the creek so far away?

After Adele and I had changed our clothes, and she crawled into bed, I extinguished the flame in the lamp; then I felt my way into the bed beside her. I had barely pulled the cover over me when she snuggled up against me, and putting her hand on my shoulder, said, "Good night, Barbara. Don't worry. Everything will be all right."

I was surprised by the remark. Had I appeared worried to her, or was she only comforting me to reassure herself? "Of course it will, dear," I replied. "Go to sleep." Then I rolled over so she would not be touching me. I did not want any tenderness now—not from someone I would have to protect. I did not have her liberty to drift into an easy sleep because no one was there to protect or care for me.

❄   ❄   ❄

Adele and I went the next morning to find the stream—we were afraid if only one of us went, she might get lost in the woods. I had not thought to ask Mr. Smith in which direction it lay, although he said it was less than a mile away and marked the border of the property. I did not even know exactly what was our property, save for what was between the cabin and the undiscovered stream. After finding a water bucket in a corner of the cabin, we set out to explore our new surroundings. We began by heading straight from the cabin door, and then diverged after a few yards from where the driveway went back to the main logging road, which was not even visible from the cabin, being a good mile away. Our distance from the main road made me both fearful and relieved, for in an emergency, we would not see anyone who passed by, but neither would any vagrants or rough lumberjacks come to our door for handouts or out of curiosity, and the path from the road was overgrown enough that it suggested it was no longer used. Clearly Uncle had rarely gone into town from the look of the overgrown path. We had started toward the main road because Adele had said if the stream lay in a different direction from the cabin, there would be a worn path since Uncle must have gone to the stream every day. At first, this idea seemed reasonable to me, but in the two weeks since Uncle had gone into town, most of the trees had lost their foliage, so it was possible the path was now buried under dead leaves. I had thought the bare trees might make the stream easier to spot, but that was not the case. We walked down the path a mile without seeing any stream until I was inclined to think the leaves had fallen and covered the stream itself. Only when the cabin was scarcely visible anymore did we turn to the right and go off the trail. I suggested we slowly make a circle around the cabin, certain we would find it that way. We walked and walked, stopping every hundred feet or so to peer in all directions, yet no stream came into view.

"Maybe it's more than a mile," Adele said. "Do we even know how far a mile is?"

"Yes," I said. "The church back home was exactly a mile from our house and I used to count my steps to it, and now I've counted just beyond that number, so if we went farther than need be, we'll eventually come to it because it will have to cross in front of us."

"But Barbara," said Adele, "the woods are harder walking than city streets, so maybe your steps weren't as long as in Cincinnati. Still, I think we've—oh, Barbara!"

Suddenly, a great rustling shook the bushes. At first, I feared it was a tremendous beast about to break through and attack us. But the trees were all spindly little things, filled with dead leaves between their stems so we could see right over them but not through them. No bear could fit in there. Still, Adele clutched my arm and slowly we backed up—it might be a weasel or a rabid raccoon or even a skunk. And then the creature burst out, jumping right in front of us! For a second I did think it a bear, until I saw it was not even a foot tall. Then it ran into another bush before I could get a good look at it.

"Some kind of bird," Adele gasped.

"Probably a partridge," I replied. I was not quite sure what partridges looked like, but Mr. Smith had told me they would be good eating if I could shoot one. I wished now I had thought to bring Uncle's rifle with me. I had no idea how to shoot it, but such chances for meat might be rare.

"Once we find the stream," I said, "we'll come back and look for that bird. He would probably feed us for a couple of days."

"Oh, Barbara, I couldn't eat it."

"Why not?"

"Not a live creature like that."

"We eat chickens all the time," I said.

"But we don't kill them."

"We buy them from the butcher," I said, shaking my head in frustration over her delicate feelings. "The butcher kills them, and we eat them, so I don't see what difference it makes if we kill them. There isn't any butcher around here to do it for us."

She had no answer to that. I felt irritated by her, so I started to walk faster, leaving her to dawdle behind. I had so much to do, and I was frustrated we had not yet found the stream; I did not want to add to our troubles having to deal with her qualms about something so natural as killing and eating a bird. You would think she had been raised in some fancy place like Paris. She would eat partridge when she was hungry enough—I knew that—but I was annoyed that I would be forced to do the killing—she would never offer to hunt herself. I had always had to do the dirty work, and it was my own fault for babying her so much after Mother died. I had always tried to protect her, but she was seventeen now; she would have to learn to care for herself since we had no man around.

"Are you coming?" I hollered over my shoulder. "We don't have all day to find the stream. We have to clean the cabin—it's full of dirt, and we'll want to take inventory of the woodpile—we'll probably have to start chopping wood before the snow covers the ground—Uncle sure didn't leave us enough wood to get us through the winter. And if we want to eat tonight, I'll need to figure out how to use that stove."

"Chop wood? Barbara, you can't chop down a tree."

"Why not?"

"However would you?"

"With Uncle's ax."

"But you're not strong enough."

"Do you see any men around here to do it?" I demanded.

I had been shouting over my shoulder, but now I turned around.

She stood staring at me.

"Well, do you?" I repeated.

"No," she said.

"Then I guess we'll have to learn to chop down trees."

I purposely said "we." If I had to learn to chop wood, she would too. Yet while I figured I could swing the ax and get by through trial and error, I doubted she could even lift the ax.

And then came what I had been expecting. Her face burst into a torrent of tears. For a second, I almost laughed as I envisioned hanging the bucket around her neck to catch her tears since we had no drinking water. But when she sat down on an overturned tree, I saw things were only going to get worse if I didn't motivate her.

"Don't do that," I said. "You'll dirty your dress. We can't wash it until we find some water."

"Barbara, how can you be so cruel to me, telling me I'll have to chop down trees and shoot birds?"

I wanted to scream, "Because you're weak! Why couldn't you have been a boy? Why do I have to be the strong one? Why did Father have to die and leave me to care for you? I'm not being cruel to you. I just want you to accept reality."

But I held my tongue until I could control my temper. I counted five-and-twenty, then stepped over to the stump, reminding myself she was frightened, just like me. And if I showed fear—which I had just done by listing all the work to be done—it would only further overwhelm her so she would be no help to me. I could not break down, not even show my fear—then no one would be there to cheer up either of us.

"Adele, I'm sorry," I said, trying to sound kind, although I did not feel kind. "I'm sure the stream can't be too far. We've already circled more than halfway around the cabin, so we must be close to it now."

She said nothing, just stared at the dirt and decaying leaves between her sniffles. I was not going to beg or plead for her do anything. I did not have the energy even if I were so inclined. I just stood there, shivering in the cold, looking out into the forest, wishing desperately to spot the stream. After a few minutes in her ridiculous posture, Adele placed her hands firmly on the cold dirty earth, then pushed herself to her feet; I had not seen her in such an unladylike posture since she had been a little girl, but at least she was standing up—that was the most I could expect. I turned my back to her and continued to walk forward, looking for the stream, assuming she would follow me. I refused to look back. I hurt just as much as she did, and if I saw her sitting down again, I knew I would crumple down beside her. Then we would both have a good long cry together, a cry so long that no one might find us until spring, after the snow had melted and our bodies thawed.

Yet a couple of minutes later, I spotted the stream. It wasn't much of one—barely two feet wide, and so shallow I could barely scoop the water out of it without getting mud in the bucket, but perhaps later, if I walked farther along it, I would find where it grew wider and the water was clearer. For now, I would settle for it being a little cloudy. At least I had water, and now I was so cold I just wanted to be back inside the cabin. Adele did not show any relief or enthusiasm for my discovery. She stood idly while I filled the bucket; then she walked slowly beside me as I tried not to spill any water. I had to keep switching arms because the bucket was so large and heavy, probably holding two gallons at least. It was a long walk home, but I did not dare ask Adele to carry the water from fear she would topple the whole bucket, or worse, I would have to listen to her complain about its weight.

And so we had water. Once we were home, I thought I would pour the water into some sort of basin, and then go back for more—so we would have water for drinking and water for washing and cooking. But I soon found there was no extra basin—only this one bucket. Had Uncle washed? Then he had done it from this bucket, or gone to the stream to bathe. Had Uncle needed a drink? He had gotten it from this bucket. Had Uncle needed water to cook with—he had gotten it from this bucket. It was unbelievable—this was our only source of water. I had a coffee pot I could pour a little in, and a few cups, but nothing else to contain it. I was disgusted. How had Uncle managed to live in such a situation? I had not known him, but obviously, he had lived a far rougher life than two young ladies from Cincinnati had ever expected to know. Surely, he could have afforded to buy or at least he could have made another bucket. Men are just unbelievable at times.

I had not brought any of my mother's old china or utensils to Marquette; I had sold them for train fare, knowing they would have been too much trouble to carry, and I had naturally assumed Uncle would have such items. Now I would have to learn to go without. Lack of water basins and buckets were only the beginning of the scarcities I would endure.

Not being able to fetch more water, I went to the woodpile to do log inventory—one hundred twenty-nine logs. We would never get by on that number. Even if we only burnt one log a day, the pile would only last until the first week of March. I knew better than to depend on an early spring thaw. Realistically, I figured we would be out of wood before Christmas. So I took down Uncle's ax from the wall. I could barely lift it, but I would have to. I noted with disapproval that Adele had retreated to her rocking chair with the Bible, as if reading it would miraculously convince God to provide us with everything we needed. Then I went out to the woodpile, set a large log on the ground, and practiced swinging the ax, trying to lift it and swing it sideways, then above my head. I nearly fell backward when I lifted it over my head; to keep my balance, I had to drop it. It fell, catching the edge of my dress and tearing it; I was grateful it had not hit my toes. I wanted to give up then, but I could not. I would learn to swing it, and before the snow fell, I would have enough wood for the rest of winter. I lifted that ax and brought it down on that log, and after something like a hundred swings, at least fifty of which missed the log, I managed to crack it enough to pull it apart. I had not added to our wood supply, but I felt I had accomplished something nevertheless—tomorrow, I would try to chop down a tree.

The next day, I went out by myself to the stream, leaving Adele embroidering a lovely set of pillowcases. We had more important things to do, but I begrudgingly told myself if I allowed her a quiet day with her needlework, as she had often known back home, perhaps her spirits would rise to the challenge before us. If her spirits did not rise, mine were sure to fall from exhaustion. I began to doubt anything could keep our spirits up through the long winter, and I further doubted it when as I reached the stream, snowflakes appeared in the air. As I dipped the bucket in the water, I got my mittens wet. My hands nearly cramped with cold as I walked home. Soon the stream would probably freeze over. Then how would we get water?

When I returned to the cabin, Adele said, "Aren't the snowflakes beautiful?" I saw nothing beautiful about them. They were impending doom for us, the harbinger of a long, lonely winter, perhaps starvation and imprisonment in the cabin; whatever crisis might occur, we would not be able to get into town for help. Without answering her, I set down the water bucket, removed my wet mittens, and put Adele's gloves on to keep my hands warm, a better way to warm them than by starting a fire, which would only cost us wood. It was still morning, and bound to get warmer by midday, so I told myself we did not need a fire yet. When the day got warmer, the snow would stop; then I would go out to find a dry, dead old tree to chop down. In the evening, we could start a fire, and then I could dry both my and Adele's gloves beside it.

"Barbara," Adele said, "when we get more snow, you won't have to fetch water."

"What do you mean?" I asked, annoyed by her assumption that it was my job to fetch water. "When the stream freezes over, we won't have any water."

"No, Barbara. The snow is a blessing. We can melt it for drinking water whenever we want so we never need worry about running out. We'll even be able to waste water. Aren't we lucky?"

Yesterday she had sobbed in despair; now she thought winter's approach made us lucky. Oh, she irritated me. It was easy for her to be cheery when she didn't have to face the reality of hard work. If I could find nothing better to do than embroider and watch the snowflakes fall, I would be cheerful too.

I was so cold from my walk. Even wearing Adele's gloves, I had to sit on my hands to warm them. I was almost convinced the blood in my fingers would literally freeze. Adele continued to embroider. She had on her heaviest petticoat and a shawl around her shoulders, yet I still did not know how she could not complain about the cold. Perhaps moving her needle kept her hands warm. Even if I were willing to start a fire, I felt too cold now to get up. I tried to imagine the room being warm, but my imagination failed.

By noon, the snow was coming down hard. The light through the windows grew so faint Adele could not see her work. I did not want to chop wood in the snow, so I suggested we eat. Adele said she was not hungry, but I insisted she eat an apple and a piece of cheese. I did the same. After our meager meal, we stared out the window; it was too dark to do much else. We had a few candles among our supplies, as well as the kerosene lanterns, but I was not going to waste fuel during daylight hours. So there was nothing to do. I had envisioned we would have never-ending work while living here. I certainly could have swept the floors or dusted, but I was too cold right then to move about. Even if I swept the cabin, fetched water, chopped firewood, and prepared all the meals, I could see that after a few hours of work, I would have accomplished all necessary for our day-to-day survival; the rest of our time would be left to boredom and silence.

I went upstairs and dragged a blanket from the bed. Then I returned downstairs, wrapped in the blanket, and sat on a kitchen chair to watch the snow. Adele remained in her rocking chair with the cushion, the only comfortable chair in the house, which she did not think to share with me. She started to hum some hymns. Her humming was annoying, but I didn't have the energy to snap at her, and nowhere could I go to escape it. I felt so frustrated and irritable that, despite my polite upbringing, I laid my head down on the table. After a short while, I fell asleep.

I don't know what time it was when I woke. The storm had caused darkness to fall early, but I felt it must be well into the night. I must have slept for hours, one of those slumbers so sound that upon waking, a person feels disoriented as to time and place. A large cracking sound had jolted me awake; I awoke in alarm, hoping it was merely the sound of a branch breaking against the wind. I tried to focus my eyes, but in the dark, I could not even see the table before me. Then I was struck by the cold. The cabin had not had a fire in it now for twenty-four hours. I did not know whether Adele was still in her rocking chair, but I doubted she would have gone to bed without waking me first.

I stood, barely able to push myself up from the table, my hands stiff from the cold. Reaching out so I did not stumble against something in the dark, I shuffled across the room to the stove where I kept the matches. After fumbling about, and knocking a wooden spoon to the floor, which did not wake Adele, I found the matches, then groped back to the table and carefully ran my hand along it until I found the kerosene lantern. I could scarcely bend my frozen fingers to hold and strike the match, but after several determined attempts, I got the flame lit. As my eyes adjusted, I saw Adele still in her chair. I considered waking her to send her up to bed, but the room was too cold to disturb her yet. For the first time, I felt fear that if we did not leave the fire lit at night, we might literally freeze to death in our sleep.

There was no kindling in the wood box. How could I have forgotten to bring any in? I had intended to fetch some when I went out to try my hand again at chopping wood, but I had been so cold, my hands so white and numb, that I had forgotten all about returning outside. I should have filled the wood box that very first day we had arrived; Mr. Whitman and Mr. Smith had both warned me about the cold, long winters, and the treacherous snow drifts, one of which might easily form between the cabin door and woodpile. And now, with the snow coming down, even if I brought in the wood, it would be wet, so I might never get it dry enough to light. Why couldn't Adele have thought to remind me? No matter how cold my hands had been, had I fetched the wood when I came back from the stream, we would be warm now, and I could have fetched it when there had still been a gentle snowfall, not a blizzard, as there obviously was now from the way the wind was roaring. I did not want to go out in the storm, but as I sat shivering, I also knew I could not go back to sleep in this cold. What if Adele became sick from the cold because I delayed making a fire? Then what would I do, all alone? It was as much her fault as mine I had forgotten the wood. She had done absolutely nothing since Father had died—I had figured out how to get us to Marquette, I had talked Mr. Smith into bringing us to the cabin, I had gone with Mr. Whitman to buy our supplies, and since we had come here, I had fetched the water, I had made the meals, and I had even started the fire last night. Why had God put me in this situation where I was so alone, without anyone but a useless sister who only added to my work?

I wanted to cry. I had not yet cried, not even when Father died, because I did not want to upset Adele, but I was bitterly close to it now.

"Barbara Traugott, stop your sniveling," I reprimanded myself. "Where on earth is your gumption? Get up and go fetch the firewood and then everything will be fine."

I picked up the kerosene lantern and went to the door. I still had on my coat and Adele's gloves. I slipped on my boots and then removed the board that barred the door shut. I had barely touched the latch before the wind blew in so strongly I had to set the lantern down in the snow outside the door, and then use my body to block the lantern from the wind, while reaching in with one arm for the door handle, my other hand holding the doorframe so I would not lose my balance. I am still amazed I managed to get that door shut. Then I picked up the lantern and started toward the woodpile, the wind all the while whipping about me, turning my hair white with snow. At least six inches of snow had already fallen, so I hiked up my skirt with one hand to step over where the snow had swiftly drifted into little hills. I only remember once, in my girlhood, such a storm in Cincinnati, and the snow had all melted the next day. Even now, I could not imagine what it would mean when this was common weather every week.

I struggled as the wind blew miniature ice bullets into my face. I bowed my head against my chest, my hand covering the kerosene lantern to shelter it from the wind. The lantern did me little good since I could not look up to see where I was going, and the deluge of snow made the night almost black. When I reached the woodpile, I realized I would be unable to return with both the lantern and the logs. And I would have to make a few trips to the cabin and back if I were to bring in enough firewood to keep us warm, especially if the storm continued through tomorrow—who knew how deep the snow would be by then? Why had I even brought the lantern with me? I should have left it outside the cabin door to light my way back. And then, as I carefully set the lantern down in the snow, the wind blew out the flame. Biting my lip to keep my frustration from welling up, I ran my hand over the logs, scarcely able to see them, trying to find small ones I could easily carry back. I felt like just resting against the woodpile, already feeling exhausted from walking against the wind, but if I rested, I feared the storm would only get worse and I would not find my way back. If I were not so desperately cold, I might have cried, but then my eyelids would have frozen together. As angry as I was at Adele, I told myself I had to get back to the cabin before she awoke and was frightened to find herself alone. I took off my scarf and covered the lantern's opening with it so the wick would not get wet from the snow and become unusable. Then I lifted two light logs and trudged back toward the cabin, trying to step in my own tracks to make my journey easier. I dropped one log halfway, but kept walking with the other until I could set it by the cabin door. Then I rested a second before going to retrieve the second log.

Once I had both logs beside the door, I thought of going inside to start the fire before I fetched more wood. But I did not want to leave the lantern by the woodpile in case a falling branch should break it, or even the bitter cold should shatter the glass. The snow might even bury the lantern so I could not find it.

So I trudged back to the woodpile, hoping to find another small log I could carry under one arm while I returned with the lamp. Three logs should be enough to start the fire and warm the house for tonight. Perhaps by morning, the storm would be over, or if not, at least it would be daylight so I could see what I was doing. At the very worst, I could then strap on Uncle's snowshoes so I wouldn't sink in the snow as I went to the woodpile.

"Barbara, you're going to be fine," I consoled myself. "You're made of sturdy stock. One more trip to the woodpile and your work will be done. That's all you need to do at this moment; anything else is in the future, so you don't need to worry about it right now."

I don't know where I found the courage to follow that advice when my fingers felt brittle enough to break off like icicles. Recalling tales of people who had suffered from frostbite, fear more than courage propelled me back to the woodpile.

At first I could not find where I had left the lantern, but peering closely I saw my footprints in the snow; in another ten minutes they would be drifted over. Beside them was the lantern. Stepping to my right, I spotted several small logs, almost sticks, which would be good kindling. I clutched several under my arm, then reached down for the lantern. That's when I lost my balance and found myself lying backward in the snowbank.

I thought I had landed in the snow, but when I tried to get up, I felt something quite firm beneath me. I pushed against it to lift myself, but it was not the ground or even a piece of wood. It felt like fur. In terror, I rolled off it. My first horrible thought was that I had touched a hibernating bear, but as I tried to stand, my foot rubbed against something that looked like a log, and then I realized, it was a leg. A human leg!

Astonished, I got to my feet and bent over to brush the snow off the figure at my feet. First I cleared off what became a pair of trousered human buttocks, with a fur coat curled up above the man's waist—the coat is what I had initially touched. The cold now forgotten, I dug with my hands at the snow, uncovering the man's back, his legs, his head. I lifted the head to make sure his face was not against the ground so he could breath. Hardly any snow was about his face, so he could not have been lying there long—an hour at most—probably less since the drifting had piled up more snow against him than had actually steadily fallen. Had the lantern not blown out, I probably would have spotted him earlier. I took off my glove to feel his face—it was still somewhat warm, despite the cold. I tapped his cheek to wake him, but he only moaned. At least that meant he was still alive. I was rather frightened to wake him—it was too dark to see what he looked like, so I was unsure whether he were someone I should fear. In truth, I feared any man I might meet in the woods, but he was obviously too weak and sick to hurt anyone. I had to get him inside, but how? I was not strong enough to carry him to the cabin.

I stood up, selfishly remembering to gather up the sticks and lantern. I headed back to the cabin, moving effortlessly this time, too determined to let myself stumble in the snow.

"Adele, wake up. Help me!" I shouted as I opened the door. I dropped the sticks on the floor to make further noise.

"What's wrong?" she cried out in alarm as I stumbled about the room, looking for the matchbox again.

"There's a man by the woodpile. He's half-buried in the snow. You have to help me get him inside."

"A man!"

I heard fear in her voice, but I also heard her get out of the rocking chair. I don't think I ever moved so fast in my life. Within a minute, I had relit the lantern and left it on the table so we could see when we returned. Reading the urgency on my face, Adele said, "Oh Barbara, what should we do?"

"You have to help me get him inside. I can't do it alone."

"But a man, Barbara! We can't have a man stay here with us."

"We can't leave him out there to freeze. Come on!" I ordered. I was irritated that her concern for another was subservient to her reputation. I didn't want a man living with us either, but we would figure that out later. Running back into the storm, I left the cabin door open as a sign she had better follow me.

I reached the young man in a matter of seconds since I had now made a fairly good path to the woodpile. I immediately grabbed him under his arms and tried to pull him backwards, but I could only move him an inch or two at a time.

"Adele!" I shouted in frustration, but before I had to call again, she was beside me.

"Grab him under his left arm," I said. "I'll take his right. We'll have to drag him."

"He looks so heavy," she groaned.

"We have to do it," I said. "He's still alive because he moaned when I first found him. We have to get him inside and start a fire right away."

Any other time, I would have doubted my sister had the strength, but somehow she was able to compensate for what I lacked. We stopped several times to rest a few seconds, but when the man started to moan again, we were encouraged to continue, even if we were hurting him. When we got to the cabin door, we had to push him up into a sitting position so we wouldn't hurt his back as we yanked him up the two steps.

"The rug," Adele said once we had him in the doorway. Before I understood, she let go of him and ran upstairs. In a few seconds, she was stumbling downstairs with the bearskin. "Help me move him onto it—then we can slide him on it to the fireplace."

She had some cleverness. I was glad for it. It was not an easy task to get the bear rug under him, but once we did, we pulled him quite easily across the floor toward the fire.

Then I went back to shut the door. After putting the board over it so the wind would not blow it open, I grabbed the logs and sticks I had left against the wall. While I carried the logs to the fireplace, Adele went upstairs again and returned with our blankets. Before I could protest, she told me to help her lift the man up so we could take off his snow-covered coat before the snow thawed and made him wet. Then she wrapped him inside our blankets.

"I'm as cold as he is," she said, but she covered him anyway.

I felt my sudden energy start to fail, but I struck matches, trying to light the fire. Adele came to help me, bringing the kerosene lantern and the Bible. I did not think reading the Bible would help our guest, but I was astonished when she ripped out the blank pages in the back and inserted them into the lantern. As soon as they caught fire, she tossed them into the fireplace, and in a minute, the log caught the flame and began to crackle. I had a wicked thought then—she had only burnt the blank pages at the back, but if we had another such emergency, the Book of Job could serve a similar purpose.

We watched, breathing heavily, as the fire spread across the sticks and logs. Our goal accomplished, we did not know what to do now. I rested a moment while Adele got up to return the Bible and lantern to the table. Then she sat down on the floor beside me, leaning over our guest and tucking the blanket up against his neck.

"I wonder what his name is," she said.

"I wonder whether he'll live," I replied.

I placed my hand against his face. It was so smooth. He was hardly more than a boy, perhaps no more than Adele's age, but he was quite large—at least a hundred and eighty pounds I estimated. He had beautiful blond hair and a gallant curl that I pushed back to feel his forehead. He definitely had a fever. I hoped he would be all right. He was so handsome I could not help but wish him well. I felt a sudden maternal instinct for him, although he could be no more than a few years younger than me.

"What should we do?" Adele asked.

"I don't know," I said. "We'll just have to keep him warm and hope his fever breaks." I did not add that whatever sickness he had, I hoped we did not catch it.

We sat watching him sleep—he seemed to breathe easier now. He did not moan anymore.

I felt my head begin to nod.

"Barbara, you're exhausted," said Adele. "Go sit in my chair and rest. I'll watch over him. I can't have you sick too."

I felt like telling her the rocking chair was not hers, but I knew she meant to be kind. If she were going to watch over him, she would be more comfortable in her chair, so I told her I would go up to bed. She had left one of our blankets up there. That would have to be sufficient for tonight, and with the fire going, the cold would not be unbearable.

I went upstairs, too tired to fear leaving my sister alone with a strange man. He could not possibly hurt her in his condition, and he was so handsome I felt almost certain he was kind. Perhaps when he became well, he could teach us how to live here—at least show me how to chop down a tree or shoot Uncle's rifle. I told myself his presence was a good thing.

Little could I foresee how much he would hurt us both.

PART II

1

I had intended to sleep an hour or two, then insist Adele go to bed while I watched over our visitor. But I only woke when sunlight was streaming into my eyes through the upstairs window. I rolled over and buried my face under the same blanket I had shivered beneath all night. When I noticed how quiet it was, I realized the storm must be over. Then I remembered our guest; I listened carefully, but the silence suggested all was well downstairs. I carefully climbed out of bed, hoping not to step on a creaking board and wake anyone. I walked to the window to look outside. An unbelievable blanket of snow covered everything; the woodpile looked like a little lump in a bowl of porridge; tree branches were caked with three inches of snow standing upright on them, with a few little breaks where the warm morning sun was slowly causing the snow to fall from the branches so it almost looked as if it were still snowing.

Then I heard Adele's rocking chair squeak and decided I had better go downstairs before our guest woke. Last night I had acted out of fatigue, desperation, and a Christian sense of duty, but this morning, I feared to leave this strange man alone with my sister.

Before starting downstairs, I peered over the railing; Adele was still asleep in her rocking chair; the stranger did not look as if he had moved from before the fire, which had died out. I hesitated to wake them, but if he were ill, he would need to stay warm. I quietly went downstairs and then fetched the matchbox and the Bible. I was tempted to rip out the Book of Job, but I took the Table of Contents instead and scattered the pages in the fireplace. On top of them I placed a couple of the small logs I had withheld from the fire last night; then I lit one of the pages sticking beneath them. Father would be horrified that we were burning his Bible, but we were doing it respectfully, the least significant parts first, and if God did not understand, well, what did it matter since He had abandoned us? But perhaps this young man had come as God's answer to my prayers.

Once the fire was sparking, I sat down at the kitchen table and watched the stranger sleep. I tried to imagine what I might say to him when he woke. I had no idea what his disposition, opinions, or background might be. He was such a powerfully built young man, and my sister and I were merely weak, naive women. Yet he was so very handsome, and despite being ill, he looked peaceful—which I thought must be the source of his beauty. And he had such a smooth face, with barely the hint of a beard, which made him look like only an oversized boy. He was mildly snoring, breathing steadily; I thought of touching his forehead to see whether he still had a fever, but he slept so easily I assumed the worst was over. He had probably just been warm from struggling against the storm, and his exertions had exhausted him. He must have walked several miles before he came to our woodpile, and then perhaps had tried to seek shelter beside it, probably not seeing the cabin since we had not had the fire or a lantern lit. If he were a decent man, he would be grateful we had saved his life. Rather than wish to hurt us, if anything, he would stay long enough to teach us how to live in this rugged land. Mr. Smith had offered me help, but I had been unwilling to take it from him, unwilling to be in debt to anyone, but this young man did not strike me as the type who would keep score, expecting anything in return, while I suspected Mr. Smith's generosity sprung from calculating what would benefit him. Now I felt willing to accept help, even from this stranger, if it were necessary to survive what I now understood would be a long, horrid winter.

When the strange man moaned and rolled over, I worried he might wake to see me staring at him. I thought about waking Adele, but I was afraid her chattering would disturb our guest. Yet I hoped Adele would wake first so I would not be alone to talk with him. When my stomach growled, I decided to start breakfast, but I would need more wood if I were to light the stove. The man was bound to have a huge appetite, especially after his long walk and heavy sleep. I had bought several dozen eggs in town, probably more than Adele and I could eat before they spoiled, so I figured I might as well cook him some.

I dreaded leaving Adele alone with him, but as I put on my boots and coat, I told myself it would only take me a couple of minutes to go to the woodpile for kindling to light the stove; however, when I opened the door, so much snow was piled against it that had it opened outward, I never would have budged it. I grabbed the shovel and began clearing off the couple of steps I could not even see; I would have to dig a path to the woodpile; the snow was a good foot deep at its lowest points so that I could not simply lift my dress to step over it. The woodpile was only thirty feet from the door, but with the snow so heavy, it took me a good half hour to shovel a path barely wide enough to walk in. The sun shone brilliantly, making the snow crystals nearly blinding as they reflected its rays; by midday, I imagined the cabin roof would be melted off.

Alone in the quiet white world, I felt a sense of security—perhaps just from the warmth of exerting myself—I had not been so warm in two days—but I also felt safe in the possibility that God had sent this man to us—not that the man had done anything yet to verify such a belief, but once he were better, I could foresee him shoveling, chopping wood, shooting game, or at least teaching us how to do so. If he had been lost in the woods, he might not know how to find his way to where he was headed, so instead he would stay to protect us; but I trembled at the thought of a strange man living with us; still, I wasn't sure it could be helped—two women could not survive in this country without a man—at least not two women from the city like Adele and me.

Once I finished making a path, I carried the shovel back to the cabin and laid it by the door. Then I returned to the woodpile, filled my arms with a few small logs, and despite my shoveling, stumbled back along the narrow path to the cabin. As I tried to balance the logs with one arm and reach for the latch with the other, the door unexpectedly opened. The stranger stood before me.

"Let me take those for you, Ma'am. They're too heavy for you to be carrying."

A moment passed before I spoke. He had the logs half out of my arms before I muttered, "Thank you." I had not dreamt our meeting would occur so awkwardly.

"Don't mention it," he said. "It's the least I can do after you rescued me from the storm. Your sister explained it all to me."

As he turned around, I was both awed and frightened by how broad his shoulders were, how massive his back, which for a moment completely blocked my view of Adele calmly rocking in her chair as if having this man build us a fire were the most ordinary occurrence.

I tried to catch Adele's eye to obtain some hint of what had happened while I was outside, but she was intent on watching the stranger. Perhaps I, being the eldest, should speak first.

"I hope you weren't too cold last night. I wanted to get the fire going before you woke up."

"No, Ma'am. I wasn't cold at all," he said. "It's warmer in here than it was out in the storm last night."

He stood up, brushed bits of bark from his hands, and turned around.

"I'm Ben," he said and gave me his massive hand to shake, although he did not close on my hand, but was quite gentle.

"I'm Miss Traugott, and this is my sister, Adele."

"Pleased to meet you. I'm sorry I didn't come out to help you shovel. I'm afraid I was a little disoriented when I woke. For a moment, when I saw your sister sleeping there, I thought I must be dreaming—she looks so much like how I remember my mother when I was a boy."

Adele smiled. It was a pleasant compliment, but it alarmed me that he had awakened before her; what might he have done to her had he been a ruffian? But he seemed safe, even pleasant, so I couldn't think ill of him—I was rather afraid to.

"You're not sick then?" I asked.

"No, I think I was just exhausted. I knew the cabin was here, but I couldn't quite see my way. I just paused there at the woodpile to catch my breath; I don't know what happened then—must have passed out like a girl," he laughed. "Sure am glad you found me though or I might have frozen to death. I don't know how the two of you managed to pull me inside—I know I'm not light, but I do appreciate it."

"It's what any good Christian would do," I said. He had such a pleasant voice that it embarrassed me to hear my own. I could not get over his luscious messed up head of blond curls sticking out all over; I had the urge to comb them as if I were his mother, and his gentle boyish face made his size less threatening so that I could almost imagine he would let me comb his hair for him.

"Barbara," Adele finally said, "Ben works at a logging camp not far from here. He was on his way there when he got lost in the storm."

"It wasn't even snowing when I left Marquette yesterday afternoon," he said, "but a few miles from town, the snow started blowing so hard I didn't even know whether I were on the right trail. I apologize for the inconvenience I've caused you."

"It's no trouble at all," I said, then added "Um," as I tried to think what more to say, but no words came to me, or to him, or to Adele. After a moment, I noticed his coat on the floor. He followed my glance, instantly assuming I meant for him to be on his way because he sprinted across the room to pick it up and looked as if he were about to put it on when I thought to ask, "Are you hungry? Let me get you some breakfast."

His face broke into a glorious beam, as if one of the angels were shining its radiance on me. I would do whatever necessary to keep him here, and if he were a decent sort, as he now seemed to be, he would realize he owed us a debt for saving his life. I would at least make certain he helped us before he left—I did not know how I would do it, but I was determined to keep him here for a short time at least. It would be a relief to have a man's assistance since Adele was completely useless, and I, one single woman, could not do everything alone in this rugged land.

"Let me give you a hand," he offered, following me to the stove.

"Oh no, I can do it," I replied, not having intended for cooking to be among his tasks.

"I don't mind. I've helped the cook in the logging camp many times. When I first joined the camps, I wasn't much more than a boy so they often stuck me with helping the cook until they realized I was a lot stronger than my twelve years would suggest."

"You've been logging since you were twelve?" gasped Adele.

"Yes," he said. "Didn't have much choice. Didn't have any parents to look out for me."

"What happened to your mother?" Adele asked.

"She died when I wasn't much more than five or six."

"And your father?" I asked.

"We weren't very close so I left home. Here, I can crack the eggs for you at least," he said, taking them from my hand.

It broke my heart. A young man, about my and Adele's age, yet an orphan sooner than us, with no one to care for him, having to make his own way in the world. Having known hardship already, he must know how we felt; he would have to be willing to help us.

"Do you have any brothers or sisters?" asked Adele.

"No. I think I have relatives somewhere that were my mother's, but after she died, my father didn't stay in touch with them, and now he's passed on, so I doubt I'll ever meet them."

"So you're all alone," Adele sighed.

It was sad, perhaps too sad for him to discuss since he said no more about it. Once he cracked the eggs, he insisted on making the coffee. We hardly spoke as we made breakfast. Adele left her rocking chair to sit at the table. I cooked the eggs and made toast while Ben stared at the brewing coffee as if that would help it along. I wanted to ask him when he would leave for his logging camp, but I was afraid he would say right after breakfast. He had apparently come on foot so he couldn't take us into town, and he wasn't heading in that direction anyway. I thought, however, he might take a letter with him, and then if someone from the camp went into town, they could deliver it for us. I could write to Mr. Smith and ask him to come back to fetch us—now that the snow had fallen, I did not think he would come out on his own, at least not before spring, and by then, he probably would have forgotten about us. But I did not want to go back into town—of course, I desired the comfort there, but I was not yet ready to concede failure. Perhaps I could convince Ben not to go back to his camp—perhaps he would stay here all winter to protect and provide for us. It was probably an unrealizable dream, but I could not help selfishly wishing it.

I was more interested in what he could do for us than who he was, but Adele's priorities were the opposite. He had poured coffee into our cups and carried them to the table. Now, as I turned from the stove to carry the plates of eggs to everyone, I noticed how Adele stared at him, her eyes adoring. I could not blame her—he was beautiful, like some mix between Adonis and Jesus caught in reverent prayer, joyful serenity radiating from his face—only Ben did not have a beard like Jesus and he was blond, but still, I did think of Jesus—almost as much as Adonis.

Once I set the eggs on the table, we all sat down to eat. When Ben asked Adele to pass him the toast, he flashed at her such a brilliant smile that she blushed. Then I knew everything was ruined; he would have to go, even if it meant us freezing and starving this winter. He was no better than Mr. Smith—worse actually because of his charm and looks—I would not let him take Adele from me.

"So, Ben," said Adele, "tell us about yourself. Are you from Marquette?"

"No, Ma'am, not really. I grew up in the woods like how you're living. My father and I lived in a cabin until I left him."

"Were you born in Upper Michigan?" she asked.

"Yes, Ma'am."

"And what about your parents? When did they come here?"

Why was she asking so many questions? Why did she need to know his family history?

"I honestly don't know much about my folks. My father and I never spoke much, and like I said, my mother died when I was little. She was good to me though. She taught me how to read, and I remember her singing to me."

"Our mother also died when we were little," said Adele. "And now, both our father and uncle have died, so we're all alone in the world."

How could she tell him that? We did not need a stranger knowing we were alone and unprotected. Granted, I had considered he might become our protector, but I wasn't going to look vulnerable until I knew he could be trusted. How could she admit such a thing to a total stranger, even if it were fairly obvious we were alone in the woods?

"How did you two ladies come to live here?" he asked.

"When our father died," Adele continued to blab, "we came to live with our uncle, but he died before we got here. This was his cabin. We've only been here a few days now. We have nowhere else to go."

Ben raised his eyes in surprise. Men are always surprised when women live on their own, as if they can't survive without a man. And Adele made us sound so pathetic with her, "We have nowhere else to go," as if she hoped he were some knight in shining armor come to rescue us.

"You said your uncle died?" he asked.

"Yes, just a few days before we arrived in Marquette."

"I'm sorry to hear it," he said respectfully.

"Thank you. We felt bad for Uncle Roderick, but we never really knew him," Adele said. "He was a Shepard, an in-law. He married Aunt Marie, our father's sister. We never even met Uncle Roderick, or Aunt Marie either that I can remember, but after Father died, Uncle was the only relation we had left."

Ben frowned, apparently searching for additional words of comfort.

"I guess that puts us in the same boat," he finally said. "I don't have any family either."

"Adele and I have each other," I said. I did not want his pity. I was not even sure I wanted his help, and I was not going to make it too obvious we might need it.

My tone must have been sharp, for he did not reply. We finished our eggs in an awkward silence. I sneaked a few glances at him as he ate—he was just too handsome, like Lucifer must have been before the Fall—somehow I did not quite trust him. Still, he was our guest, so I could not be rude to him. As he nervously sipped his coffee, I thought I should politely ask whether he would like anything else to eat, but such politeness was inconvenient when I feared we would be short on food this winter. I searched for some pleasant remark to make, but he ended up breaking the silence by clearing his throat.

"I believe I knew your Uncle Roderick."

I looked up in dismay.

"Really?" Adele asked.

"Yes," he said, wiping his mouth with the cloth napkin—life would be harsh here, but I had decided using our cloth napkins from home would help us retain a sense that we were well-bred young ladies.

"What was Uncle like?" asked Adele. "Father never told us anything about him—he courted our aunt in Cincinnati before I was born, and then they moved here right after they were married."

"I'm not sure how to describe him," Ben said. "I mean—well, other than that he was tall and had a beard—I guess I didn't know him that well."

"How did you know him?" I asked.

"Just from seeing him around town I guess—and I knew he had this cabin because—I came here once to do some work for him." Then he hurriedly added, "But just for a day and we hardly said two words to each other. That's all. He pretty much kept to himself."

"Yes, that's what Mr. Whitman said," Adele replied. "He was staying in town at the Whitmans' boarding house when he died. He was apparently really sick but didn't tell anyone, and the day after he got into town, he died."

"Yes, that's what I heard in town yesterday," said Ben.

Something in his answer did not seem right. He knew Uncle had died, and he had said before that he knew the cabin was here, but that the storm had kept him from seeing it. It made me doubt he had been lost at all. Had he purposely come here, hoping to steal from the dead man's property?

"Why did you come this way then if the cabin were empty?"

Adele had asked the question. I was surprised—did she suspect something wrong as well? Yet, I was also annoyed. If he suspected we thought something was odd about his behavior, he might become angry—even violent—a thief does not like his intentions revealed.

"I had no idea I would end up here—like I said, I got lost in the storm. I knew your uncle's cabin wasn't too far from the main road, but I didn't realize I had missed the main road—the storm was so bad I had no idea in which direction I was headed."

That sounded honest, but liars train themselves to sound truthful. I hated to think ill of him, but my and Adele's safety had to be my first concern. Better to overreact now than to have him catch me off guard later. I might still ask him to show me how to use a rifle, but—suddenly, a horrid image in my mind—his turning the rifle on me, demanding all my money—but he would not resort to that—he was a powerful enough man that he could physically take whatever he wanted by force, and that scared me all the more. No, I could not let him stay here, and once he did leave, I would make sure the door was always barred in case he decided to come back to rob us—or worse—while we slept.

"What kind of work did you do for Uncle?" I asked, trying to concentrate on the conversation so my fears were not noticeable.

He stared about the cabin a few seconds and then looked up at the ceiling. "Um, well, I helped him repair the roof that day."

He had taken longer than he should to answer, yet I wanted to believe he had helped fix the roof. "How long ago?" I asked. "Maybe seven years ago," he replied. That was a disappointment, but still, seven years ago should not be so long that the roof would leak now. Mr. Smith had only been trying to scare me when he suggested it would leak—scare me so he could purchase the property at the lowest price possible.

"Do you do much carpentry work?" I asked. Maybe I could have him look the place over, just to make sure everything was sound.

"No, Ma'am. I mostly just cut down trees."

"Do you know how to shoot with a rifle?"

"Of course; any man in Upper Michigan can do that."

"Could you show us?" Adele asked. "We don't have any idea. If a bear came, I don't know what we'd do."

She had no qualms about playing the helpless female. Here I was trying to feel him out, but she had to reveal all our private matters before his trustworthiness was certain.

"Sure," he said. "That'd be the least I could do after you both rescued me last night."

"Can women shoot rifles?" Adele asked.

"My ma could—at least that's what my father told me, so I don't see why you couldn't. You'll have to if you plan to eat this winter."

I laughed as if he were joking about the obvious before I replied, "You must understand that since we come from Cincinnati, being in the woods is a bit unfamiliar to us, but I think we've adjusted well so far."

I gave Adele a seething look, warning her to say no more about how we were truly faring, but she was not looking my way. Instead, she was caressing—it's a shameful word but I don't know how else to explain her look—her eyes were caressing his enormous forearms, which he had put on display when he sat down at the table by rolling up his shirtsleeves.

"Better I show you how to shoot than you hurt yourselves while trying," he said. "Looks like you have enough food in that corner for a while, but I doubt it'll last you all winter, and you'll be hungry for fresh meat soon enough."

How long had he been eyeing our food supply? We obviously had nothing else worth stealing. If he were so concerned about food, perhaps he didn't belong to a logging camp, or he didn't even know where he was getting his next meal. Perhaps he was just a vagrant, looking for handouts. But he seemed too handsome to be a vagrant, too well-mannered, and he certainly looked well-fed.

"Good. You can teach Barbara to shoot this afternoon," Adele said.

As usual, I had to carry the burden. Why didn't she learn to shoot? Why did she have to be so soft and tenderhearted?

"I wouldn't mind a bit," he replied, "but would you excuse me a moment?"

He pushed back his chair and went to the cabin door. Once outside, I saw him walk past the window and around back, most likely looking for the outhouse. I was grateful to be relieved of his presence for a moment.

"He's nice," said Adele.

"We don't know that for sure," I replied. "We can't trust him just because he appears to be kind. We don't know anything about him."

"We know he's a logger, and that he knew Uncle and was even kind enough to help him fix the roof, and—"

"And nothing else," I said. "And we don't even know whether those things are true—we only have his word for it. You have to realize, Adele, that the less he knows about us, the better off we are until we know more about him—and I think you've already told him more than we want him to know."

I pushed my chair back, then stood up to clear the table.

"Barbara, don't be so rude. What if he overhears you?"

She glanced out the window.

"What if he does?" I said, but she was right. I had to be careful. He might be unwilling to help us if he heard me speak ill of him, and if he were some sort of scoundrel, he might be hiding behind the door now, eavesdropping. I did not want to say anything he might interpret as our fearing him.

"Barbara," Adele asked, "why are you always so afraid of everything?"

She knew how to make my blood boil. If I were afraid, I was not unjustified. And I wasn't really afraid. I was just being cautious. I had to be prepared for whatever life should throw our way, something to which Adele gave no thought. She should be grateful for my caution. But I would not argue with her now in case Ben overheard. I set to washing the dishes, taking out my frustration on the egg yolk remains.

"It's mighty cold out there," said Ben when he returned. He stood in the doorway to shake the snow off his boots, all the while letting the cold air into the house. "When I woke up, I thought the sun was going to melt the snow, but now there's a nip in the air, like it's going to start snowing again. I guess winter is here to stay, though it's hardly November yet. I bet you ladies are surprised by all this snow."

"We rarely had snow in Cincinnati," Adele said, "especially before Christmas."

"We can get blizzards here as early as mid-October," said Ben, "although I've also known a green Christmas. You can never tell in Upper Michigan."

"At least the weather will keep life interesting," Adele smiled.

Two days ago, Adele had been sitting on the ground crying because she was cold and we couldn't find the stream. Now she thought the weather was interesting! She hadn't even stepped outdoors since then—not even to the outhouse—and as indecorous as it sounds, of course, I had been relegated to emptying the chamber pot.

"Adele, would you bring me the rest of the dishes?" I asked, tired of her laziness.

"I got them, Ma'am," said Ben, carrying the cups and silverware over to the little counter beside the basin.

"Thank you," I said. He stood beside me for a moment, as if wanting to help, but I ignored him, busying myself with putting the dishes in the water. After a minute, he returned to the table.

"Ben, did you say you could read?" asked Adele.

"Yes."

"Barbara and I always read the Bible before we go to sleep, but last night, in the excitement of your coming, I guess we forgot. Would you mind if we read it now while Barbara does the dishes?"

"No, that's fine," he said. I had my back to them as I worked, but I imagine he looked as surprised as I did when Adele fetched the Bible and asked him to read.

"All right," he said. "Where should I read from?"

"Anything but Job," I replied.

"Please," said Adele, "read the Twenty-Third Psalm."

He rustled a few of the thin pages. Then his voice deepened, became reverent, as he read:

The Lord is My Shepherd. I have everything I need.
He brings me repose in green pastures.
He guideth me along the cool streams.
He restoreth my soul.

I didn't pay attention to the actual words. A man's voice reading the Bible stirred within me memories of my father. How sad he would have been to see his two girls living like this, alone, so far from everything we had known; if Father were alive, he would have done all necessary to protect and provide for us. It hurt so much not being able to talk to him.

"Ben, you read so beautifully," Adele gushed. "Your mother must have been a fine teacher."

"Thanks," he said. "Should I read some more?"

"Maybe just one more psalm while I finish these dishes," I said. "Then you better show me how to shoot that rifle before you go."

I was unsure whether I should let him go. I hoped he might offer to stay of his own accord, in the realization we needed his help, yet I was afraid to ask directly for his assistance. My thoughts were so fixated on how I might phrase a request for him to remain that I did not hear the next psalm. Only after he finished reading did I become aware of silence in the room. I set the last dish down to dry and wiped my hands. Then I looked to the table where he and Adele were sitting quietly—they seemed to be meditating on the reading, but actually I suspect they did not know what more to say to one another.

"Are you ready?" I asked, stepping toward him.

"We'll need to wear some snowshoes out there," he replied. "I nearly sunk up to my knees in the snow drifts behind your cabin."

"We don't know how to use snowshoes," Adele said.

"You have some though," he replied, nodding toward the pair hanging on the wall.

"Those were our uncle's," I said. "We've never used them."

"There's another pair by the fireplace," he added.

"There is?" asked Adele.

"Oh yes, look," he said, walking around the side of the fireplace to pull them down from where they hung on a nail. Uncle had so many things hanging on the cabin walls that I had not noticed them before, and along the side of the fireplace, they had been out of sight behind some protruding stones.

"These look like they were made for a child," said Ben, "but you ladies have such small feet that they'll probably work fine for one of you while I wear your uncle's pair."

"Will you show me how to use them first?" asked Adele. "I haven't even been outside since it snowed."

He looked askance at me, but before I could respond, Adele said, "I really want to learn, and we'll need to know how to use them, Barbara.

You show me first, Ben, and then we'll come back in so you can show Barbara, and at the same time, teach her how to shoot."

"Fine," I growled. "If Ben has time to do both."

"Oh sure, I'm in no hurry," he said, "long as I get back to the logging camp by nightfall. It shouldn't be more than a couple of hours' walk from here."

Adele shot me a fast smile, asking me not to be difficult. She and Ben both put on their coats. Then he asked her to sit down so he could strap the smaller snowshoes onto her feet. He looked like Prince Charming trying the glass slipper on Cinderella—which must have made me one of the ugly stepsisters. I tried not to feel irritated so I could concentrate on how he strapped on the snowshoes since Adele would forget by tomorrow how to tie the straps.

"We'll just walk around the house, Barbara, so don't worry about us," said Adele.

"I won't."

She looked like a goose shot in the leg when she waddled to the door, trying not to step on one snowshoe with the other.

"Ma'am," Ben said to me as he opened the door, "you might want to look about for some ammunition. It would be rather difficult teaching you to shoot if there aren't any bullets."

"All right," I agreed before fastening the door behind them. Rather than look for the bullets, I stood by the window, just out of their sight, watching them traipse about in the snow. Even with children's snowshoes on her feet, Adele struggled to move. She tried to slide her feet, as if she were on skis rather than snowshoes. Ben stood beside her, trying his best to model how she should move her feet. She was so clumsy that I wondered how she had even learned to walk as a child. Later, when I tried on the snowshoes, I found them very simple to walk in. Adele had barely gone twenty feet before she tripped herself. Ben tried to catch her, but the width of the snowshoes distanced them so he could not grab her before she fell. She was certainly not a coordinated young lady, but I wouldn't put it past her to be faking it—trying to trick him into thinking her needier than she was. Until he had appeared, I never would have expected such coquetry from my own sister. When she fell over in the snow, she only laughed and willingly let Ben help her to her feet, whereas, two days ago, she would have been horrified to have the snow dampen the hem of her dress. As Ben set her on her feet and guided her along, I could literally hear her giggling!

I knew then it was not only the men I needed to watch—I would have to battle my own sister to hang onto her. She was actually flirting with a man. I was shocked to feel my annoyance turning into disgust over her behavior, and I began to doubt whether I did truly want her with me any longer if she could act that way, completely disregarding my feelings. Had I tried to show her how to snowshoe, she would have only whined and told me to quit scolding her, but she was willing to act like a ninny to please this man. I had done my best all these years to look after her, all the while wishing I had an older sister to look after me. I did not think I could ever understand why I had been given such a heavy cross to bear in this life.

Ben and Adele now turned around to practice walking back toward the cabin. Seeing how they smiled, I wished I were outside with them—then Ben raised his head to look toward the cabin, and I ducked back behind the wall so I would not be caught watching them. I had better things to do than spy on them. I needed to find the bullets. I went over to the cupboard, looking around, wondering where Uncle would keep such things. I wanted to find the bullets before they came in—so they would think I had stayed occupied while they were outside.

But no bullets were in the cupboards. Nowhere could I find a box that said "bullets" on it, or any kind of box or container at all. There was hardly anywhere but the cupboard to look. Not even a chest of drawers was in the cabin. Uncle's few clothes had been tossed over the end of the bed or on the floor—he had apparently been unconcerned with whether his clothes were wrinkled or dirty. I looked all over downstairs and then upstairs, yet nothing looked remotely like it might be a storage place for the bullets.

I went back downstairs, annoyed that Ben and Adele had still not come inside. There was nothing to do. I thought about taking the rifle down from the wall, but I did not think it would store more than one bullet, and if I tried to inspect it, I might blow my fingers off.

What were they doing out there? At this rate, it would be dark by the time Ben finished teaching me to shoot—not that it would matter when I had no bullets—but then he might not have time before dark to reach his logging camp, and I did not want him to spend another night here. Maybe he would go into town to fetch us bullets and return in the morning, just to drop them off and show me how to shoot and then go to his camp tomorrow night. He could stay in town tonight— but how convince him to make the extra trip for us? Hadn't I sheltered him from the storm? It was the least he owed us.

I wished they would come inside. They must be half-frozen by now. I peered out again from the window's edge. No one was in sight; I saw only snowshoe tracks going around the side of the cabin. Oddly, Uncle had not put any windows in the back wall of the cabin. How had he expected to know when he had visitors coming when the road curved around the cabin so you could not see people approach? He could not even check to make sure it was safe to visit the outhouse— he might walk around the corner of the cabin and come face-to-face with a grizzly bear. For that matter, Adele and I might do the same thing—well, probably not Miss I-Can't-Empty-My-Own-Chamber-Pot. It would serve her right to have me eaten by a bear while emptying it. What would she do then? Probably rot inside the cabin, too afraid to venture out unless Ben came back to find her.

But she was outside now, and safe with Ben to protect her. No, I was not sure she was safe with Ben—I didn't even know where they were. I decided to go out and look for them.

As I opened the cabin door, they came around the corner. They did not see me when I first poked my head outside. I felt a snowflake fall on my cheek as I heard Ben say, "Well, Adele, it's going to snow again. It looks like it'll snow hard too. You can tell the way the sky changed so quickly."

Then Adele saw me. "Hello, Barbara. We had a wonderful time. I didn't know snowshoeing could be so much fun."

I was too stunned to reply. Ben had addressed her by name rather than calling her "Miss." How had that change come about in half an hour?

"She's better at snowshoeing now than me," Ben laughed. He was kidding her, as if they were old friends. I stepped back to let them inside. Adele's cheeks glowed red from the cold. Ben sat down to unstrap his snowshoes. "I feel a bit winded," he said. "I wonder whether I do have a bit of a fever. I need to sit down for a few minutes."

"You should rest," Adele told him. "Who knows how long you were laying out in the storm before Barbara and I found you."

"It wasn't long," I said. "He didn't have that much snow on him."

"Oh, that's nothing," he laughed. "I've camped in the snow many nights. My logging partner and I sleep in a tent, winter and summer, no problem at all. I haven't had a cold in years. Being outdoors makes a man tough, but I do feel a little winded right now."

"Do you really sleep outdoors all the time?" asked Adele.

"Most logging's done in the winter," he said, continuing to talk as I grew impatient for him to teach me how to shoot before it grew dark or snowed harder. "That's when it's easiest to get the logs out of the forest. My partner, Karl, and I—we've only been partners a short while, but I'd trust him with my life—we sleep through all kinds of weather in that tent—rain, fog, hail, snow. He snores so hard nothing could wake him, and when you work long days like we do, you're just happy to lie down, so you don't notice whether the earth is cold or even whether there's a rock where your pillow should be."

"And here I thought Barbara and I were roughing it in this cabin," smiled Adele. "I guess we don't really know what hard is."

This from one who had collapsed to the earth crying two days ago!

"Yes, it's definitely going to keep snowing," Ben said, looking out the window.

"Oh, you can't leave then," said Adele. "You said your logging camp is something like ten miles—that's too far to walk in the snow."

"I've walked farther than that in a blizzard, or at least snow-shoed. I didn't expect the snow to come so early, or I'd have brought my snowshoes with me into town the other day."

"You'll just have to stay until the snow stops," said Adele, as if the decision were completely hers, as if having a man, who was no relation, staying with us were of no concern in the world.

"I suppose," I said, "the Christian thing to do would be to loan you our snowshoes so you could get back to your camp."

"Oh no, I wouldn't think of taking them. Besides, it's too early in the year for this snow to last. It'll probably all melt in a day or two. Looks like some even melted this morning."

As we peered out the window, the now steady snowflakes transformed into a swirl of white; a sudden gust twirled the snow in circles before our eyes. I resigned myself, not without some relief, to our guest staying with us again tonight. In time, as I came to experience more Upper Michigan winters, I would become almost indifferent to storms—realizing one might spring up, last twenty minutes, then be over and have all the snow melt within the next hour, just as easily as three feet might fall in a couple of days. That first winter, however, every time I saw a snowflake, doom seemed to settle over my soul.

"Why don't you stay tonight?" I said. "We would enjoy the company and you did promise to show me how to shoot the rifle."

"You can't go shooting in this weather," he replied. "I don't mind spending another day here rather than walking through that storm. Really, we only had a few hours relief from the snow this morning, so back at camp they won't worry. They'll just think I stayed in town because of the weather. Thank you, Ma'am, for your hospitality."

"You're welcome," I replied. I was not going to concede that he was doing us the favor.

"Oh good," said Adele. I was surprised she didn't clap her hands with glee the way she looked so excited.

The rest of that day Ben entertained us. If he were still ill from his adventure the previous night, you never would have known it from the way he kept talking, Adele all the while encouraging him. He was a strange man, not one easy to get to know, offering very little personal information, instead exaggerating things to impress Adele. He talked a lot about working in the woods and the people he worked with, and he had many stories to tell, some of them tall tales, I imagine, because I found it difficult to believe he could chop down as many trees in a day as he claimed. I still distrusted him. I would not have been surprised if during the night, he should sneak off with our food, yet the next moment, he would say something in such a pleasant way that I scolded myself for thinking ill of him. I did find the sound of a man's voice comforting, again remembering Father.

I felt friendly enough to cook Ben an extra nice supper, although the more he ate, the less there would be for us later—but if his stomach were full, he might be less inclined to take advantage of us by stealing our food in the night. I considered giving him a little money in exchange for his returning to us with some supplies from his camp—if he did run off with the money, it would make little difference since I could not get into town to buy more food. I did feel better, however, when he repeated, "Miss Traugott, we'll make a point of going out shooting tomorrow before I leave. After you've done so much for me, I'll have to find you a nice rabbit or turkey to make up for what I've eaten."

Just as dark fell, the snow stopped up again. Then Ben acted disappointed not to have made his journey that day. I did think it odd a big strong man like him would let the snow stop him, but I reminded myself how difficult it had been for me in the cold and wind just to get to the woodpile. I was grateful when he went out to the woodpile twice, bearing in his strong arms three times as many logs as I could have carried each time. We would have enough wood inside for several days now if the storm continued. It was possible he might actually feel some concern for us, some male instinct to provide for us, and Adele's flattering attention could not really hurt that much.

I was both relieved to go to bed that night—tired from the strain of entertaining company—and concerned to sleep while a stranger was under the same roof. Our bed was pushed up against the railing of the loft, so I could peer between the bars to watch him during the night while he would not be able to see me when I was lying down. I would sleep lightly, just to be safe.

"He seems really nice, doesn't he, Barbara?" Adele whispered as soon as we were in bed.

"Yes, I suppose."

"I wish he would stay, Barbara. It'll be lonely when he's gone. But I suppose being a logger is more interesting than staying here."

"I'm sure he'll leave tomorrow," I replied.

"He's the only person I've really liked since we came north. Edna was nice enough, but I feel some sort of bond with Ben."

"Don't be silly," I said. "You hardly know him."

"I feel like I've always known him. Don't you think he's handsome?"

"Shh, Adele, he'll hear you. Go to sleep."

"Sometimes you're so grumpy, Barbara. I would think you'd be glad he's here since tomorrow he'll show you how to snowshoe and to shoot."

"He had better show me to shoot after all the food he ate."

"Shh, Barbara, he'll hear you," she mocked. Then she yawned and rolled over. "Goodnight, Barbara."

"Night," I muttered.

In a minute, I heard her gently snoring. I wished I could sleep. I looked over the railing, but the fire's last embers were dying so I could barely see where Ben was stretched out on the floor. I decided I would just rest my eyes long enough that if he stirred to go steal Uncle's snowshoes or the rifle or our food, I could wake up instantly—not that I had any idea how I would stop him—I certainly could not withstand physical violence from him—but somehow I could not imagine him beating me. I felt almost pleased by the fear—it was better than the loneliness and boredom that would come after he left. Adele would probably cry when he went. Somehow I would have to make him promise to come back—to bring us supplies or send us someone to take us into town—but being in the cabin had not been so bad today with Ben there. If he taught me how to shoot so I could provide us food, and if he came to see us once in a while, winter would not seem so long. We could persevere. Maybe he could teach me how to chop wood too so we would not freeze. Winter would be difficult, but it would not be completely impossible to survive.

When I did fall asleep, I had a restless night, the kind filled with odd dreams you can't remember, dreams of waking, only to find you are not awake. I struggled long to open my eyes, feeling paralyzed, unable to move my limbs, and when finally I forced my eyelids open, the sun was pouring across the bed. It had to be well past eight in the morning. I had not slept that late in years—I was aghast to think I had let down my guard that long. Yet I lay there a moment, listening, until I realized I was alone upstairs.

I heard Adele below, talking to Ben, yet still I could not pull myself out of bed; I only rolled over, telling myself one more minute of rest and then I would get up—if Adele screamed because he was attacking her or robbing us, I could jump up and be downstairs in a minute— of course, I was in my nightgown, but that could not be helped if an emergency arose.

I drifted back asleep, half aware of their voices, him talking of logging, Adele's voice a mutter when she replied. Eventually, I heard footsteps coming upstairs. I imagined it must be Adele, so I tried to wake and lift myself out of bed, but my limbs still felt paralyzed, completely immobile. Embarrassed by my laziness, I pretended to be asleep when she called my name. I did not respond. My eyelids felt as if coins had been put upon them so they would not open. I don't know whether I could have spoken had I wanted to. I heard her return downstairs and say to Ben, "She never sleeps late. I hope she's not sick."

"She's probably just tired," he replied. "It's hard adjusting to a new place, and I bet she's been working hard since you got here."

Then I felt guilty. I had not worked that hard—there had been little I could do with such limited resources. But I hoped Adele would feel guilty for how unhelpful she had been. I certainly wasn't sick—I couldn't be sick.

I drifted back asleep, only to bolt from the bed when I heard a loud voice. I threw the blanket over my nightgown and looked over the railing, terrified that my worst fear had come true—he was attacking her!

Then I realized the male voice was not Ben's. I had heard it before, but I could not place it.

"You should be ashamed!"

I started down the stairs, just far enough to see another man facing Ben, who was seated beside Adele at the table. I halted, realizing I was not properly dressed for a visitor, not when this man was dressed in such a fine suit.

"Where is your sister?" the man asked.

"Here I am," I replied, not yet knowing whom I answered.

He turned to stare at me, my hair in a mess, as I shivered in my nightgown beneath a ragged blanket.

"What is the meaning of this, Miss Traugott?"

It took me a second to answer, to understand the situation, even to recognize him.

"Mr. Smith! We did not expect you before Sunday."

"I can see that," he replied. "I did not expect you or your sister would entertain male guests here. Who is this gentleman?"

"Barbara, I've tried to explain to him," Adele appealed for help.

"Sir, it is because I am a gentleman," Ben answered for me, "that I do not take personal offense at your insinuations, but you owe these ladies an apology. They took me in when I got lost in the storm. They have done nothing but show Christian kindness to a stranger."

"Who are you?" Mr. Smith demanded of him.

"If it is any of your business, my name is Ben."

"Does Ben have a last name?"

Ben paused a moment, uncertain of himself, before replying, "To my friends, Ben is my name, and these ladies are my friends."

"These ladies—" said Mr. Smith, turning to see the sternness on my own face, and then softening his tone slightly. "These ladies I have tried to aid in their time of bereavement over their uncle's death. I only wish to make sure all is well with them."

"They are well," Ben smirked, "and I'm sure, they appreciate your concern."

"All is well, Mr. Smith," I said. I felt excited to have two men both acting so protective toward us, yet I was annoyed that they thought we could not care for ourselves. To lessen the tense moment, I asked, "How ever did you get through the snow?"

Mr. Smith's eyes looked me up and down, not the way they admired Adele, but with disapproval over my appearance. No man had ever seen me in my nightgown before, not even my own father since I had become a woman. I tightened the blanket about me.

"It has been melting all day, but it was rough going in a couple of spots," he replied. I looked out the window to see snow melting from the roof. The sky was so bright it must be noon now. I had been asleep all morning. "I came to make sure you had weathered the storm all right."

"That's very kind of you, Mr. Smith," I replied.

"Yes," said Adele, "but Ben has been here to protect us, so we are perfectly safe. He's taught us to snowshoe, and he's going to show us how to shoot and chop firewood."

"I see," said Mr. Smith.

Ben's smile said to him, "I'm in the ladies' good graces, not you."

Mr. Smith frowned; then he turned to address me.

"Miss Traugott, I brought you the final papers to sign for your uncle's property. I wired for confirmation of the baptismal records. I have yet to receive them by post, but since all seems in order, I thought I would come out. I have brought a purchase deed with me. That way you can sell me the property and have money to stay in town before winter becomes worse."

"You're not selling this property, are you?" Ben asked, jumping up from his seat.

"Sir, this is none of your business," Mr. Smith replied.

Ben hesitated, as if to speak, but then he sat down in annoyance. I was annoyed as well—he had no right to interfere in my affairs, and despite Adele's simpering affection for him, we did not need his protection.

"Miss Traugott, will you sell the property to me?" Mr. Smith asked.

"It—well—I." I was unsure what to say.

"Miss Traugott, surely after a few days being here, you realize this is no place for women. You would be much more comfortable in town. Despite what the Panic has done to make property prices drop, I am willing to increase my offer to three hundred and fifty dollars."

"This property is worth twice that!" Ben shouted.

"Sir," Mr. Smith snarled, and he even took a step toward Ben.

I grew frightened as Ben stood up from his chair. But then Mr. Smith hesitated, taking a good look at a man who outweighed him by thirty pounds. Ben easily could have taken Mr. Smith over his knee like a child who deserves a spanking.

"Mr. Smith," I said, "I am not yet ready to sell the property. I'm sorry, but I need more time to make my decision."

"Well, then," he said, stepping back from the table, not even raising his eyes to me as his chin dropped into a pout. "I guess I've wasted a trip."

"I guess you have," said Ben.

"Ben, we do not need your interruptions," I snapped. I had never raised my voice to a man before, but I was head of this household; no one would speak for me.

"I beg your pardon, Ma'am," Ben replied.

He looked humbled. Adele grasped him by the sleeve and pulled him back into his seat. They began whispering but I ignored them.

"Mr. Smith," I said, "I do appreciate your coming out, but I intend to remain here for the winter so I have time to make the right decision."

"You can't survive out here all winter. I won't allow it. It would be irresponsible for me to let you."

"I do appreciate your concern, but we will be fine. If anything should befall us, the blame will lie with my own stubborn self."

"Is there anything I might do for you before I leave?" he asked, but now he was merely being polite. He was probably already bemoaning the lost hours of his time when he could have been in his office making money. He had only risked this trip to make a profit on my property. I wondered whether Ben was correct that the property was worth twice what Mr. Smith had offered. I had no idea, but neither could Ben. I would need to have it surveyed and an appraisal done by another real estate agent.

"Thank you. We will be fine," I told Mr. Smith. "I am sorry for your wasted trip."

He turned to Ben. "Might I give you a ride back into town, sir?"

"No, thank you. I will be walking to my logging camp this afternoon. But you need not worry about these ladies. I can easily walk here from my camp, and I intend to check on them often. It will be easier for me to do so than for you to come here from town."

"I see," he said, putting on his hat. He moved to the door, but as he placed his hand on the latch, he turned back. "Miss Traugott, might I have a private word with you?"

"Of course," I said. I walked to the door, retaining what dignity I could; I stepped outside onto the front step in my slippers, nightgown, and blanket, closing the door behind me. It was actually quite warm outside, and I did not have to fear any passersby seeing me, but a month ago, I never would have imagined myself standing outside in my nightclothes with a strange man.

The moment I closed the door behind me, Mr. Smith turned red with anger. He spoke rapidly.

"You must realize I am quite taken by your sister," he began to my disgust. "She is a beautiful woman, not one a man is likely to forget. In truth, since I met her Sunday, I have not stopped thinking about her. Excuse me for saying so, but it is obvious your financial situation is not comfortable. I could make it a great deal more comfortable—not solely by purchasing your property, but by taking her hand in marriage. But I will not be associated with a woman whose reputation risks being sullied by a strange man living with you. It is unacceptable. I do not doubt your sister's innocence, but I consider it fortunate I came upon the scene before something regrettable happened. You know how people talk."

"They won't talk if you say nothing," I replied. The words came out before I knew what I was saying. I heard my voice crack from the fury I felt inside. He had no right to threaten me with gossiping—that is what he was insinuating. How dare he suggest either my sister or I would ever be less than virtuous, or even that Ben was not a gentleman? He did not know any of us. What right had he to be so presumptuous even to dream my sister might be his wife? We owed him no obligations. As our uncle's lawyer, had he no moral scruples, no sense of responsibility to his client's heirs that would prevent him from trying to cheat or manipulate us? I detested him thoroughly.

"Mr. Smith, you are without reason for your concerns," I repeated. "I am my sister's own guardian. I can personally vouch that nothing improper would be permitted to happen to her."

He paused, seeking words to further his argument, but I was freezing in the cold, and seething with such anger that I could not tolerate a continuance of this scene.

"I hope you have a safe trip back to town, Mr. Smith. Good day."

He deserved no more of my time. He looked shocked by such a rude dismissal. I knew I had just given up my chance to return to Marquette before the long winter. But at that moment, I felt no regret.

He tipped his hat to me, out of habit rather than courtesy, and said, "You understand my position. I will not be able to come again."

He climbed up into his wagon, shook the horse's reins, and started down the road.

As I watched him leave, I noticed all the snow had melted on the ground, save for a few little patches. It was melting off the roof, had even dripped on me as I stood beneath the eaves. I felt the warm sun on my face, yet I shivered. I wondered whether there would be another warm day before we were trapped here all winter. Even if we survived the winter, could we ever go back into town, or would Mr.

Smith have spread ill words about us? What would we do if we went back to the boarding house, only to have Mrs. Whitman tell me, "Your kind are not welcome here." I felt I might collapse under the weight of the situation. I turned to go inside, planning to tell Ben he needed to leave—but first I would have him teach me to use the rifle.

As I stepped inside and shut the door, Adele said, "Barbara, do you think we might—"

I heard no more. Everything went black.

2

I was ill for several days. I had a high fever, and drifted in and out of consciousness; when I was conscious, my eyelids felt too heavy to open, my legs too sore to lift. I was not surprised to find myself in bed, although I had no memory of how I had gotten there. I imagine Ben carried me upstairs. He was still there when I came downstairs, several days later. I have vague memories of Adele mopping my forehead with a cloth, telling me to lie still, putting a glass to my lips, from which I could scarcely drink. And I think I had some strange, confused dreams—hallucinations—of Father there, caring for me, his voice soothing me as if I were a little girl again, with the chicken pox, but I knew it must have been Adele or Ben who was caring for me.

I have only one clear memory from those many days—I woke, realizing it was afternoon because the room was dimly lit—the sun only came through the upstairs window in the morning. My mind was lucid enough for me to realize I had to relieve myself. For a moment, I forgot I was ill. Almost naturally, I got up to go to the chamber pot, but on my way back to bed, my legs weakened and my head grew dizzy, as if I would pass out. I clutched at the little table under the window and tried to call for help, too weak to make it the few feet back to bed. My returned strength had vanished in an instant, and my throat ached so that I could not shout, but my cry of "Adele!" should have been heard downstairs. I felt my forehead breaking into a sweat and my back shiver with chills. I feared I would vomit or collapse onto the floor before Adele reached me. I lowered my head to keep from vomiting, to catch my breath. After a couple of minutes, I felt well enough to lift my head again and cry for help. That was when I looked out the window. Adele and Ben were outside, playing in the snow, chasing each other around the trees.

Deep rage boiled up in me. How could she leave me alone inside when she knew I was desperately ill? Even if I were sleeping, how could she do it, just so she could be outside with Ben? I saw her throw a snowball at him—he must have taught her how to make them—he dodged it, but he let her chase him around a tree with another. Then he came around the tree so fast he was instantly behind her. He grabbed her by the waist, then fell backward, she on top of him, both of them laughing.

How dare they leave me like this? They were so selfish. I was too angry to watch any longer. Despite my pain, I stepped forward and nearly fell as I reached the bed. Moaning, I crawled back under the covers, pulling the blanket about me to keep me from shivering. I rolled onto my stomach to place the blanket over my head. In that position, I could look down from the loft and watch them when they returned. I tried to console myself by thinking they had only gone outside for a few minutes to get fresh air because they thought me asleep. But as minute after minute passed, I felt abandoned, and I silently cursed them for their selfishness. If I were not ill, I did not doubt they would run off together, without any thought for me.

More than anything, I wanted my father. I missed him more at that moment than any other time since his death. My body ached miserably, but my soul ached more—my only relation, my own sister, would rather cavort with a stranger than tend to me. Soon he or some other equally wretched man would take her from me. My future could hold no happiness. Even as I realized I was making myself miserable, I increased my feelings of self-pity, sinking further and further into agony until I heard the cabin door open. Ben and Adele walked about downstairs while I strained my ears to catch bits of their conversation. I did not have the strength to raise my head and watch them. I closed my eyes, hoping it would improve my hearing, but I only fell asleep.

I don't know how many days passed after that hour of clarity before I woke and felt better. I became lucid again on another afternoon, when the cabin was quiet. Again I thought they had abandoned me, but I lay there peacefully, thankful just to be alive, whatever lay ahead. After about ten minutes, I heard footsteps coming upstairs. Adele appeared with a glass of water and a bowl of soup.

"You're awake!" she whispered with such pleasure I could not sustain my previous anger at her. "How do you feel?"

"Weak, but better. How long have I been sick?"

"Two weeks yesterday."

My eyes opened in surprise. I had not thought it more than three or four days.

"I've been so worried about you," she said, setting the soup and water on the bedside table and scooting a chair up to my side. "I've been giving you medicine, but I wasn't sure it was doing you any good. You didn't even seem to know you were taking it. Your eyes would only flicker, then close again when I slid it between your lips. Ben wanted to go fetch the doctor, but I was afraid to be alone with you, and I knew we had no money to pay for one. But you look so much better now, Barbara. I just know you'll be fine." She gave me an encouraging smile.

"I'm hungry," I said, struggling to sit up. Adele grabbed the pillow and placed it against the loft railing so I could lean against it. I wanted to glance down to see whether Ben were still there—had he stayed all this time? What would I do if he had acted inappropriately toward Adele?

"Here," she said, starting to spoon-feed me the soup. She made me feel like a child, but in sitting up, I had used all the strength in my arms.

"How have you managed alone?" I asked after a couple of spoonfuls.

"I haven't been alone. Ben has stayed to help me."

"All this while? But where have the two of you slept?"

"Downstairs on the floor. I didn't want to disturb you by sleeping here, and Ben was afraid I would get sick sleeping beside you. I did get a bit of a cold a few days ago, but I'm almost over it now."

"You slept beside him?"

"Barbara, don't worry so much. He insisted I sleep in front of the fireplace so I would be warm. He slept over by the stove."

I hoped she spoke the truth. Would she tell me if it were otherwise? He had a charm that may have worked a hold over her in the two weeks I was ill—she was easily suggestible, not knowing her own mind like me. I wouldn't be surprised if they had slept beside each other, while he had convinced her to lie to me about their sleeping arrangements. She knew nothing of the ways of men; one of my schoolmates had told me what her married sister had told her it meant to sleep beside a man. The thought had made me sick, but a woman must put up with it if she is to have children, and a woman's husband is her lord. Nevertheless, as Adele's only kin, I would decide which man would be her lord. And if it were too late now to make the decision—if Ben had had his way with her, then by God, I would make sure he made her an honest woman.

"Barbara, you look so pale. Are you sure you feel better?"

"I'm just—my stomach is a little upset—probably because I haven't eaten in so long."

"Probably," she smiled. "You haven't had anything except water and milk and the medicine I managed to make you take. I bet you've lost ten pounds."

I did feel thinner. Frail. That frightened me. How would I do all the work necessary when I was so weak?

"Ben's been wonderful to me, Barbara. His friend, Karl, came by a couple of days after you fell ill—he's a nice young man, though I do like Ben best. Karl's a good friend to Ben. He came looking for him, worried when he didn't return to camp. He had spent the whole day out looking for Ben and finally saw the turnoff from the main road that led to our cabin. Ben explained to him that he couldn't leave me while you were ill, so Karl went into town and brought us all sorts of things—flour and sugar and medicine for you. He came back that same night, in the dark, having snow-shoed all the way to Marquette and back. Then he slept clear all the next day from exhaustion, but I sure was thankful. I haven't had to worry about anything while you were sick. Karl stayed two days before going back to work, and he and Ben chopped down a bunch more trees for us, and they caught us some game, such big partridges. And they found Uncle's fishing pole too; before he left, Karl caught a fish in the stream, but the stream finally froze over yesterday, so we won't have fish again for a while—although Ben says he could try to drill through the ice to fish—he's so smart— who would have thought you could fish in winter? And best of all, Barbara, yesterday he shot such a big rabbit, so for Thanksgiving we'll have a real feast. Now that you're well, we'll definitely have something to be thankful for."

"How did they shoot anything? Did they find Uncle's bullets?"

"Oh yes, Ben found them tucked away in the walls between some of the logs. No one but he would have been clever enough to look there. He found several dozen of them, so we'll have enough for the whole winter, but Ben said not to worry—as long as they're logging nearby, he'll come by a couple of times a week to make sure we're doing all right. He hasn't wanted to leave me while you were ill, Barbara, but he'll have to get back to work now that you're well, though I'm sure he'll stay another day or two until you're strong enough to be up and moving about. Thanksgiving is a couple of weeks away, but we'll celebrate it early while Ben is here."

She was so enamored with all of Ben's heroic feats that I was exhausted just listening to her. When she finally paused long enough for me to get in a word, I asked, "Where is he now?"

"Out chopping wood. We've used up almost all that Uncle left."

"All the wood! How will we survive without it?"

"Like I said, Ben and Karl have chopped a lot more. Ben just brought in a big load of it this morning. Don't worry, Barbara. He's a logger after all, and he's so strong. Why he showed me his muscle one day, and I just about fainted when I touched it. I never—"

"Adele!" I snapped in disapproval, hurting my throat terribly by doing so. Then I heard the cabin door open. Ben was downstairs, setting wood in the bin.

"Oh, I better get Ben his soup," said Adele. "He'll be hungry from all that work, and you should rest more, Barbara. You'll need your strength to come downstairs for dinner tomorrow."

"Thank you," I said as she stood up and collected the soup bowl.

Had I the strength, I would have gone downstairs that moment to reprimand Ben. How dare he let my sister see his naked arms, much less touch them! I was grateful for all he had done—I knew Adele never could have managed on her own while I was sick—but I could not let gratitude overcome what was proper. Had Ben any sense of decorum, he would have gone into town and found another woman to come and stay with us while I was sick. If he were a gentleman, he never would have stayed here.

I could hear Adele downstairs, speaking to him, but I could only make out some of his words because his deep voice carried farther—simple phrases like "That's wonderful" and "She still needs her rest." I did need more rest—I felt weak and miserable. I was too incapacitated to change the situation now. Exhausted, I fell back asleep.

It was after dark when I woke again. I lay there, listening to muffled voices, interrupted now and then by a crackling log. Heavy footsteps on the stairs made me realize Ben was coming up—I had not requested his presence or given him permission to enter my bedroom, although he must have carried me upstairs before. But Adele appeared with him. "We hoped you were awake," she said. "I thought it might do you some good if we read to you awhile. Ben has such a nice reading voice." I saw him, leaning over her shoulder, a chair in his hand that he had carried up.

I nodded, too tired to argue. If Adele were with me, it would not be so indecorous to have him in my room. They both sat down. She handed him the Bible. As he read the Twenty-Third Psalm, I watched from the corner of my eye. She had her chair right up against his, so close I did not doubt she would have put her head on his shoulder if I had not been present. She clearly doted on him; I hoped he did not take advantage of it. Perhaps I should have a word with him before he went back downstairs. I could not blame her for liking him—even in the dim light from the kerosene lantern, I could see how magnificent he was—my sister was beautiful, so it was odd to think he was even more so. He was so strong and masculine. He had his sleeves rolled up on his forearms—they were impressive, his veins popping out like cords—how could she not have wanted to feel how strong he was? They were perfect for one another, and she needed someone strong to care for her, and of course, that someone should be a man; clearly, I was not strong enough to care for her, not after I had made the mistake of bringing us here, only to have my stamina fail so quickly.

I watched his face as he read. Every minute or two, he would sneak a glance up at her from the page. When she caught him and smiled, he turned his eyes away and actually blushed—that look told me they were still innocent. He read with such reverence that I wanted to think him a gentleman, although I had heard of men behaving well until they got what they wanted. But was I judging him without evidence of ill intentions on his part? To my knowledge he had not yet done anything wrong—in private, I would warn him not to, while expressing gratitude for his protecting her during my illness. That would be the best way to handle the situation.

I tried to lie still, to find comfort in the words of the Bible. He was reading the Book of Ruth. Poor Ruth had lost her husband, and now, with her mother-in-law, she had gone to a strange land. I felt her grief, her loneliness, but also her great love and devotion to Naomi. I wondered how she could have endured, working in the fields with strangers, trusting in a God who was not her own. I thrilled inside when Boaz loved her and claimed her as his wife. At the end, I felt a tear form in my eye. I hoped Ben and Adele wouldn't notice—I would say it was just the fever. Secretly, I wondered whether I could ever be so good as Ruth and thereby find my own Boaz to love me.

"It's a beautiful story," said Adele when Ben finished reading. "That's how marriage should be—based on love. I think my mother and father must have loved each other that way."

"I wouldn't know anything about it," Ben replied.

"Don't you remember your parents together?" Adele asked. "You said you remember your mother."

"Yes," he said, his eyes not leaving the page.

"Did your mother and father love each other deeply?" she asked.

"I don't remember much about it. My mother died when I was so young, and my father would never speak of her."

"He must have loved her a great deal then," Adele said, "so much it hurt him to talk about it."

She waited for Ben to agree, but instead, he said to me, "Miss Traugott, you look tired. I think we should go and let you sleep."

"Thank you," I replied. I was actually sorry when they went back downstairs. I had enjoyed his reading. No one had read to me since Father had died. I wanted to tell him his voice had comforted me, but I still did not trust him. I wished I had asked Adele to leave the room so I could talk to him alone, but I was afraid my warning him not to take advantage of my sister would sound like an accusation, and I could not insult him after his kindness to us. I shut my eyes, telling myself everything was all right, or at least if everything had worked out for Ruth, it could work out for me. Yet my trials seemed more insurmountable than hers.

The next morning, I woke to Adele banging pots around on the stove. I pulled myself out of bed and decided to go downstairs before she came up to fuss over me, or Ben tried to carry me down. I considered getting dressed, but I did not have the energy. I needed a clean nightgown, but I had no other. Once Ben left, I would need a bath. We had no bathtub, so it would have to be a sponge bath, which would take more effort than I could manage. Perhaps Adele could help me take one this evening. I stood at the top of the stairs, my hand on the banister, testing my legs to see whether they had the strength. Then I started down the stairs, firmly planting each foot on each step, slowly without a word so Ben and Adele would not discover my purpose. Adele was sitting in her rocking chair while Ben hovered over the stove—apparently he was making breakfast, which made me wonder whether Adele had done any work at all during my illness.

The stairs cracked, making Adele turn around when I was only a few steps from the bottom.

"Oh, Barbara, why didn't you call me? Ben and I were going to come fetch you."

"I'm fine. Stay where you are."

"Here, sit down," she said, moving her rocking chair closer to the stairs so I would not have so far to walk.

"Why don't you come to the table," said Ben. "We'll be ready to eat in a minute. You must be starving. You can have my eggs. I can make up another batch."

"I'm not very hungry," I lied as Adele took my arm and guided me to the kitchen table. I could feel my stomach rumbling, but I felt guilty taking the eggs Ben had cooked for himself. I did not even know whether they were the eggs I had bought—he and Adele must have eaten all those by now—Karl had probably bought these eggs in town. When Ben set the plate before me, I hesitated, staring at it; after a few seconds, I picked up the fork and slowly started to nibble on the eggs, unsure how they would affect my stomach. In a couple of minutes, Ben sat down beside me with his own plate full.

I didn't say much during breakfast. Neither did they. I felt they were uncomfortable; they had become used to one another's company, and now I made an awkward third party. My stomach felt too weak to eat more than half the eggs and a couple of bites of toast. I refused the coffee, knowing it would gurgle in my stomach the rest of the day. When Adele and Ben did speak, it was only to ask repeatedly how I felt, and to make comments about their work around the cabin—which, as I suspected, had been done primarily by Ben, "while Adele nursed you," he said, making me wince as he used my sister's first name again. When the snow melted, he offered to fix a few things up for us so we would be more comfortable. "We'll see," I replied. I did not want to be here in the spring, but for now, I had to concentrate on making it through this day.

When we finished eating, Ben asked whether he might carry me back upstairs so I could rest until supper; he would carry me down later for our early Thanksgiving dinner. I longed to go back to sleep, but I was determined to stay downstairs so they would not be alone together. When I said I would sit up for a while, Adele insisted I take "her chair." She babied me, running to fetch a blanket while Ben took my arm and walked me to the rocking chair. Adele tucked a blanket under me, and Ben stirred up the fire to keep me warm. I felt too warm, but it felt good—I would not object to wasting wood today, though I was anxious to go outside and see how much wood Ben and Karl had cut for us. I had never imagined winter could be this cold, and it was still only November. What would we do if we ran out of wood? Ben had not mentioned yet when he would leave, and I was afraid to ask. I wanted him to stay until I was fully recovered, until he could show me how to chop down trees and shoot the rifle, but I felt it would be several more days before I was strong enough to learn anything.

Once I was settled by the fire, I was surprised to hear Adele say she would wash the dishes. Ben, to my relief, went outside to chop wood. "I'm going to make sure you ladies have enough firewood to keep you warm all winter; I wouldn't be much of a lumberjack if I didn't, now would I? I'll come in around noon to help Adele cook that rabbit."

I wanted to bless him then. How could I have thought ill of him— he was like an angel now, completely altruistic. What a difference compared to Mr. Smith, even if Mr. Smith's money could make us more comfortable than all the trees Ben might cut down.

Once Ben went outside, I waited for Adele to finish the dishes. I wanted to talk to her alone, to ask her what more she had learned about Ben while I was ill. I could scarcely remember what he had told us—only that his mother had died when he was young—and I thought he had said his father was dead, but I couldn't quite remember. Hadn't he said he was twelve when he started working in the woods? Anyway, he certainly had strong survival instincts. I closed my eyes to rest, but his handsome, almost babyish face appeared—he was the only man attractive enough to suit my sister—would it be that bad? But she could not be a logger's wife, living in a logging camp, or even living here with me while he made occasional conjugal visits. That was no life for her. Nor would it be any life for me, and she and I had our future wrapped together since each was all the other had.

I fell asleep before the fire. When I woke, I found Adele sitting across from me with her embroidery. When she noticed I was awake, she said, "You look just like Mother did when she fell asleep in her chair."

I was surprised by her words. She rarely mentioned Mother. I did not think she even remembered her face—she had been so young when Mother died. I knew it was a compliment, yet I grumbled, "I didn't realize I looked that old."

"Barbara, I didn't mean it that way," she said. Then she set her embroidery down, and coming over to me, took out her handkerchief to wipe my matted hair from my brow. "Are you too warm?" she asked.

I nodded so she pulled the blanket from my chest onto my lap.

"I meant you're just as pretty as mother; do you remember how she used to fall asleep in her rocking chair in the evenings?"

"Because she was exhausted; she worked herself to death taking care of us," I replied, yet I was flattered that Adele, who was so beautiful, thought me pretty.

"I think I miss her even more now that Father is gone."

I missed her too, but I dared not say it. I was already ill. I did not need to upset myself further.

"Barbara?"

"Hmm?" I had just closed my eyes, thinking I would be better off asleep than remembering happy times that could never return.

"After Mama died, why did you change so much?"

"What do you mean?"

"You changed after Mama died. I'm afraid now that Father's gone, you're changing again."

My goodness she was annoying. Of course I had changed after Mother died. I had to help Father and look out for her. And of course, now I had changed after Father died. What was exasperating was that Adele had not changed, had made no effort to rise to the occasion by taking responsibility for herself.

"Don't be angry," she said, putting her hand on my shoulder. "It's just, somehow, we weren't as close after Mother died."

"What do you mean? We've lived together every day. We're sisters. How can we not be close?"

"You didn't act like my sister anymore. You wouldn't even play with me."

"How could I play with you? Who was going to do the cooking, and wash Father's work shirts, and hang out the laundry, and a million other things?"

"I would have helped if you had let me."

"You were six years old, Adele. You couldn't help me. All you wanted to do was dawdle about."

"Well, I was only six."

"Exactly, Adele, and I was ten so I had to be the responsible one."

"You were still a child yourself, Barbara."

"I couldn't be anymore. Father needed looking after. You were too young to understand—he was so upset by Mother's death that I had to take over—he didn't know how to raise two girls, even how to cook for us. I did whatever was necessary to keep the household together."

That was the mildest way I could put it. Father had been devastated. He had moped for months. He wouldn't have gotten out of bed to go to work if I hadn't practically pushed him out the door each morning. And all the while, I was just a little girl aching for my mother, and here this great big grown man sought comfort from me because he had no one else—I became his confidant and helper for the good of all of us, and now I was to be reprimanded because I had not played with my little sister—I had made sure she had clean clothes for school, and food to eat, a bath every Saturday night. I had worn myself out until I sometimes wished I were in the grave with Mother.

"Was it so hard on you, Barbara?"

"I didn't have a choice," I replied.

"I asked whether it was hard on you, Barbara?"

"I answered you."

She took her hand from my shoulder and returned to her seat, picking back up her embroidery. She tried to stitch, but the needle fumbled about in her hand. A tear formed in her eye. "We had good times even then, Barbara. Father loved us a great deal. Not everyone is that lucky. I know it's been hard for you, but we've been luckier than most."

"I don't see how."

"We've had each other. I know I can be a ninny sometimes, and I know I add to your responsibilities, but you shouldn't be so hard on me. If you didn't have me, you'd be all alone in the world, and I would be lost without you."

"Don't cry," I moaned.

"I can't help it," she said, but she stopped when the door opened. Ben came inside, carrying another stack of firewood.

"So, are you both ready for our Thanksgiving feast?" he asked, piling wood against the wall, and then rubbing his hands together.

"Yes, I'll help you," said Adele, sniffling as she got up. "We'll let Barbara rest until it's time to eat."

I was glad then—perhaps fully glad for the first time—that Ben was there because he had interrupted our conversation. I did not want to talk about Mother and Father. It only hurt when we did. For a second, I envisioned Adele and me on the floor, crying on each other's shoulders for hours—it might be a relief, but it would be admitting weakness, and if I gave way to despair, I might never pull myself up from it.

I stared into the fire, wishing I were anywhere else, that life could be different in any way. I wished I could go upstairs to sleep, but I had to stay downstairs. I could not leave them alone. Adele was right—we would be lost without each other, but only because we had no one else—the day would come when she would have another since she was beautiful even if she were not as smart or responsible as me. Men preferred ninnies, as she had called herself.

I closed my eyes, tired of listening to her and Ben discussing how to cook the rabbit. I tried to envision what my life might have been if Mother had lived until I was grown—I could scarcely remember my childhood—it was over half my lifetime ago; it seemed like another lifetime. An image from childhood came to me—I was a little girl, not much more than five, and sitting beside an ant hill. I was watching the ants scurry about, even letting them crawl up my shoes and onto my skirt. I did not scream as Adele would have done, but simply watched them with fascination at their industriousness. Perhaps even then, I had had a premonition that I would be like them, always working, never resting. The mind recalls odd moments when it is tired, remembers the most trivial things not recalled in the hectic light of day. I remembered lying in a huge, grassy field, looking up into the sky, searching out the shapes of faces and animals in the clouds. For a minute, I actually felt the earth moving in its rotation, and I sensed how large and magnificent the world was. And although I was such a small child, I felt no fear on that sunny childhood afternoon; I could not remember such a serene, comforting feeling since then—it had been forgotten in the race to survive, just to acquire my daily bread. Why did we always pray "give us this day our daily bread" when every day we had to labor for it? If I truly believed God would provide my bread when I asked, was it possible I would not have to work so very hard? But how could I believe such a thing? It was almost inconceivable that I was now that same conscious being I had been as a child, in a carefree world—when I had bread to play with in the sand, and could build sandcastles for the ants with the bread, and the ants might come and carry me away into their nest, and I could sleep there forever and ever and never have to worry as the clouds swept over Cincinnati, and Cincinnati was a city, so when could I have been in such a field? I had never seen such a field, not unless it was on a picnic when ants always come to carry everything away—I must be falling asleep because nothing was making sense now. "Barbara, you are an ant," said a voice. "Not an ant but an angel," said another voice. "I'm not an angel; Ben is," I told them, whoever they were. I had never heard them before. "Barbara, you are an angel," they repeated together. Who was talking to me? Was I hallucinating again?

"Barbara, wake up. It's time to eat."

Adele's voice jolted me awake. I felt as if I had been struck, shoved back into my body after almost leaving it.

"What?" I asked. I did not understand at first. It must have been Adele and Ben talking, and in my sleep, I had distorted their voices. I opened my eyes, trying to focus, to shake off the strange dream.

"Come to the table. We're going to eat," Adele repeated. "Ben's carving the rabbit now. Do you need me to help you?"

"No, I can manage," I said, still dazed until a log fell in the fireplace, snapping me back to my senses.

All that wood we were using! But at least it was nice and warm.

"Here, I made us coffee," said Ben, pouring me a cup without asking whether I wanted it. Its smell made me ravenous; whether or not my stomach would accept it, I was determined to drink some.

I raised the cup to my lips, wishing I had cream for it. It was still too hot to drink, so I blew on it and set it down.

Ben returned to the table with two plates, one for Adele and one for me. Each plate had a well-cooked slice of rabbit meat on it, and mashed potatoes with butter melting on them, and some carrots Adele said Ben found in the garden and dug out, still edible, to my disbelief but great delight.

I picked up my fork, impatient for Ben to come back with his own plate so we could eat, but the second he sat down, Adele said, "We need to say the blessing."

I bowed my head, and Ben knew enough to bow his, which made me think he must have gone to church at some point in his life, even if he were a logger. Adele made up the prayer, a long one about how grateful she was that God had led us to this new land and given us new friends and that we had a roof over our heads and food to eat. The table was far enough from the fireplace that I started to shiver. I feared the mashed potatoes would turn cold before she finished praying.

"Amen. The rabbit looks so good," she said in one breath, and she grinned at Ben who grinned back, then turned his eyes to his plate. They seemed as pleased with eating rabbit as if it were a delicacy rather than our only option for a meal. Yet I was also thankful to have meat.

I remembered the turkeys Father would cook at Thanksgiving and Christmas, the only times Father would cook. I remembered the many dinners our neighbors had invited us to—meals with cranberries and pumpkin pies. Today, we had only mashed potatoes, rabbit meat, and hard dry little carrots. That was Thanksgiving dinner. Such scarcity was all we had to be thankful for.

I wondered how our neighbors in Cincinnati were faring. I recalled their kind voices, their generosity, how many of them had pressed me to remain there. I had refused their charity since they were not family. I had thought it better to be with family, never imagining we would be more alone in Upper Michigan. I felt homesick for those holidays with friends. If I had not made the mistake of coming here, we might now be sitting around Mrs. Schloegel's long dining room table. Instead, we were alone—well, almost alone.

"Ben," I asked, "when will you be leaving us?"

"Oh, Barbara," Adele said, "he can't go until you're well."

"I'm feeling much better. I think I'll be my old self by tomorrow."

It was a silly thing to say after I had been bedridden for two weeks.

"I really should get back to the logging camp," Ben replied. "Karl said my boss has been understanding, but each day they're short a man, they're losing money."

"You can't go yet," said Adele.

"I'll be fine by tomorrow," I told Ben. "We don't want to keep you from earning money you probably need. We'll manage."

I wasn't sure we would manage, and I wasn't sure I wanted him to leave, but I didn't know how to express that. I was afraid my questioning had just made him decide to leave all the sooner.

"Maybe I'll go the day after tomorrow then, but I promise I'll come check on you every few days."

That would not be so bad. He would not be sleeping here, but neither would we be completely alone.

"You better come," Adele replied.

"You'll always be welcome," I said politely. He had been kind to us. I had probably been wrong about his motives toward Adele. It was best to be on good terms with him now that he would be leaving.

"What shall we do after supper?" Adele asked. "We want to keep Ben entertained while he's here so he won't forget us."

"I'm not likely to forget you," Ben laughed, "but what do you propose?"

I did not like that word, "propose." It gave me the shivers.

"We could play charades," Adele said. "That would work with three people."

I was not about to make a fool of myself playing such a game before a stranger.

"I don't think I'm well enough for anything that active," I said. "I should probably just rest so I can get back to work when Ben leaves."

"Oh, Barbara," Adele said, "Ben and I will do the work tomorrow."

"Ben needs to show me how to shoot that rifle tomorrow."

"Oh, don't worry about that," he replied. "I've three big partridges buried in the snow for you. You'll have enough to eat until I can come back in a week or so when I'll be sure to bring you something more. I'll teach you to shoot then, when you feel better. So let's have dessert now and stop worrying."

"Dessert!" said Adele. "What could we have for dessert?"

He only winked in answer, then collected our plates and brought them to the counter. We both watched as he opened a cupboard and took out a little box he carried back to the table.

"Karl gave them to me. He got them from his mother. He's got such a good heart he could not bear to eat them when he thought they might cheer you up."

Chocolate confections! What a treat! There had been eight in the box, and six remained. That was two apiece! I did not care how my stomach reacted to them—it might be wise to save one for tomorrow, but I knew I would eat both of mine straightaway.

Ben held the box before me, letting me pick the two pieces I wanted before he passed the box to Adele, and then he settled for the ones that were left. One of mine had a molasses flavor, so very rich and delicious I could almost have kissed Ben and Karl too, had he been there. I ate it slowly, letting the chocolate melt on my tongue, rolling it about my mouth, not caring whether I acted unladylike. None of us spoke. We just relished the taste. The second was a chocolate covered nut. Its crunch was satisfaction in itself. I did not expect such another happy moment for the entire winter, so I chewed that nut far more times than necessary, letting the taste linger in my mouth afterwards, refusing to wash it down with coffee.

"Well then," said Ben, smacking his stomach with his gigantic hand. "That's the finest meal I've had in a long time."

"Yes, definitely," Adele replied.

"I think maybe I should go rest some more," I said, feeling my forehead start to perspire. Eating had been all the effort I could muster for the day.

"You do look pale still, Barbara," Adele said.

"I'll carry you upstairs," said Ben.

"Oh no," I replied. I had intended to sit in the rocking chair again, not wanting to lie down right after eating, but before I could protest further, he had his arm around my back and his other arm beneath me. To keep from losing my balance, I had no choice but to put my arms around his neck. For a second, just a second, I dared look into his eyes, but he had such a glorious smile that I had to look away. Adele— her character so much weaker than mine—could not help but be in love with him.

Once he laid me on the bed, I wished he would go back downstairs, but he stood beside me while Adele carried up the blanket and fussed about me.

"If you need anything, just holler," said Ben.

"Thank you," I replied, embarrassed to lie down before a stranger.

"Adele, you can sleep here tonight," I said. "I don't think I'm contagious anymore."

She hesitated a moment, then said, "Oh, all right."

"I hope you feel better, Miss Traugott," said Ben, disappearing down the stairs, followed by Adele.

Once alone, I did not want to think of them anymore, although neither did I want to be alone. I closed my eyes, trying to remember the delicious chocolates, but the wind distracted my thoughts—it was blowing so loudly, making ripping sounds against the roof. I almost hoped it was another storm, so Ben would have to stay longer, but now that I was well, I knew he would leave. We could not expect him to stay—he had to earn a living. I wondered whether he were a good enough logger that he could support Adele, maybe buy a house for them in Marquette, and they would let me stay with them. I longed for such security—for anything better than the uncertainty of living in this cabin the rest of winter.

3

Ben left two days later. When he offered to stay another day, it was difficult not to agree since I still felt weak, but I told him, "No, thank you; we are already under enough obligation to you."

"Miss Traugott," he replied, "the obligation is all mine. Your and Adele's company has been nothing but a pleasure."

He said it as gallantly as a hero in a novel. And then he was gone.

Adele acted depressed after he left. I could not blame her; he had been good company for her while I was ill—better company than I was now. That first day without Ben was a quiet one, each of us feeling the separation from the only person to whom we had felt any connection since our arrival in this harsh land. Yet the bond we felt toward Ben—I admit even I felt it—made me fear how painful would be his loss if he did not return as he had promised.

I soon felt like my old self, up and about, and capable of working as hard as ever. That there was so little work to do only made the solitude all the more trying. The stream now being frozen, I melted water over the fire, which was almost no work at all. The only real task was carrying in firewood. Adele would not gather it alone, but for sheer companionship and from fear of being alone, she came out with me so I had fewer trips to make. The woodpile Ben had left us was truly tremendous, so even if it did not provide us fuel all winter, I could not imagine we would run out before January had ended.

I tried to content myself with little chores, paying meticulous attention to what in our busier Cincinnati life would scarcely have been accomplished—everything from washing the bedding, sweeping the floors, dusting, washing windows, even polishing the rough wood table. But the cabin was like a naughty child, determined to remain cheerless despite my efforts. The gray winter skies did not help matters. Snow kept falling, so I kept shoveling paths to the woodpile until I practically had to walk through a tunnel, the snowbanks being waist high. I now felt constrained, even imprisoned by winter. The paths to the woodpile and outhouse became our only walks, allowing for little exercise. I realized I had not initially made the paths wide enough, because as more snow fell, I could not lift the shovel up to my shoulders to put the snow on the giant banks. Instead, I spent hours chopping down the banks and throwing the snow the few feet away that I could so as to widen the paths, only to have them cave in on me. If the snow continued like this another three or four months, I feared I would be buried in an avalanche from a snowbank in my own front yard.

Of course, Adele was little help shoveling; we only had one shovel, but she never offered to take turns with me. I actually found myself relieved to go out and shovel since her behavior was so unpredictable now; at times she acted gay, humming tunes and prancing about the cabin. At other times, she moped and was despondent if I spoke to her. I knew what both behaviors meant, and I grew nervous as her gay behavior gave way to moping each day, then each week that Ben did not return.

At breakfast one morning, she said, "What will we do about Christmas, Barbara? It's only a couple of days from now."

The question caught me off guard. I had lost track of the days without a calendar, but Adele had apparently been counting them.

"I don't know what we can do about Christmas," I replied. How could she possibly expect we would do anything about it? "We can't go into town to buy presents, and even if we could, we haven't any money."

Rather than acknowledge this fact, she sat glumly for several minutes. Then, her voice cracking, she said, "I wouldn't mind about the presents if only we could have Christmas dinner, for the sake of company more than anything else."

Again I thought of those dinners in Cincinnati, Father inviting the neighbors over, or our being invited to their homes. Yet it was not our old neighbors but Ben whom Adele wanted for company. I did not understand anymore than she did why he had not come—he had said he would come every week, maybe every few days, yet a month had passed now. Perhaps he had wanted to leave all the while he was here, staying only out of a sense of obligation and politeness. Now back with his logger friends, he had apparently forgotten all about us.

Thinking it best to state the facts, even if it made her cry, I said, "I doubt Ben will come. He probably has family or friends to spend the holidays with," and so we did not think only of him, I added, "And I don't think Mr. Smith will come out to see us again, not until spring at least."

Uninterested in Mr. Smith, Adele replied, "Ben has no family, but I suppose he will spend the holiday with Karl's family in Marquette."

"If they can get into town, I guess they won't be coming here."

"Unless," she hoped, "they stop here on their way into Marquette."

On Christmas Eve, the snow fell so heavily I doubted Karl or Ben would make their way to us, especially when we had not seen them for so long. All day and into the evening, Adele dragged herself about the house. I almost wished Ben would come just to please her, but I doubted he would. He was like all men—undependable when a woman needed him.

As dark fell, we sat down to eat the last bit of partridge from the game Ben had shot. We would have no meat now for Christmas Day. I had hoped Ben would come so I would not have to attempt shooting the rifle on my own, but I saw no help for it now. I would go hunting tomorrow. Even if I found no meat, it would be better to be out looking for it than at home watching Adele mope all Christmas Day.

After supper, I suggested we read the Christmas Story from the Bible. It did not take long to read, so I went on to the Baptism of Jesus, then kept reading, thinking we might as well finish all of Luke's gospel just to keep ourselves occupied, but before I got much farther, Adele said, "That's enough, Barbara. It doesn't help any. I don't mean to be ungrateful for what we have, but I wish there really were such things as Christmas miracles."

We went up to bed. Neither of us fell asleep right away; nor did we talk. I could not fall asleep until after she did. I felt tense, saddened by her disappointment, but I knew better than to expect any Christmas miracles—even if Ben did come, it would be an ordinary occurrence. Since Mother had died, I had always disliked Christmas—it only created unfulfilled expectations like those Adele now held in her heart.

In the morning we had pancakes, using the last of our flour. After I did the dishes, I told Adele I was going out to shoot a rabbit or a squirrel or anything I might find.

"But you never did learn how to use the rifle," Adele said.

"I guess I'll learn now," I replied. Then throwing on my overcoat, strapping on the small snowshoes—I had foolishly trusted Ben to take the large ones when he left—and carrying the rifle, I set out into the woods. I could not follow the road, for the snow had blown and drifted over it so I no longer knew where it was. Afraid of getting lost, I walked a straight line from our front door, unsure where I might find game.

I plodded over the snow for several minutes, my overcoat and my exertions soon making me too warm. I realized I was filled with so much frustration that I had not even been looking for wildlife. I had lately noticed I was scarcely even thinking anymore—there was so little to think about, nothing to stimulate our minds—no conversation, no sites of interest, no events. This walk was the most stimulation I had had in days. I was sick of eating partridge. I longed for a good ham or turkey, complete with mashed potatoes, sweet potatoes, and cranberries of course. I would have sold my soul—terrible as it sounds, although now I don't believe it's possible to do—for a thick slice of Mrs. Schloegel's chocolate cake. As I thought about food, I grew hungrier and hungrier until I thought I would starve before I even got back to the cabin. Since coming here, I had managed to eat enough to fill my stomach, but never to satisfy my taste buds. I had not found the rabbit at Thanksgiving very tasty, but of course, I had been sick at the time. I did not know what squirrel tasted like, and the way my walk was going, I did not imagine I would find out.

The cold air did not bother me—the sun was shining, the snow almost blinding as the sun reflected off it—making it one of the few days that had not been gray and overcast. My coat made me hot, tired, and irritable. Finally, I found a thick pine tree to lean up against and rest. I stood there a moment, catching my breath, considering whether I should go back to the cabin. Did I really think I could shoot anything?

If Ben did not come back—and obviously he wasn't—I would simply have to prepare for starvation. I could already see how Adele and I were obviously losing weight. We'd be skin and bones, if not dead, by the spring.

Just then, a squirrel came running across the snow. In a second, another followed. They chased one another, running around a small collection of birch trees some fifteen feet away. They did not appear to notice me.

Quickly, I raised the rifle and looked through its scope. I waited until one of the squirrels paused, clawed against the side of the tree, until his friend would spot him. Then, with all my strength, I pulled the trigger. The rifle bolted backward, hitting me in the eye. The impact jarred my head against the tree. I dropped the rifle into the snow as my hands instinctively covered my eye. I felt warm liquid on my face, and wiped it onto my hand. I was relieved to see it was not blood. I was crying. Then I looked toward the squirrels and cried some more because I had only frightened, not shot them—my supper had run away.

"I didn't want to kill them anyway," I sobbed out loud. "It's Christmas Day. At least they're enjoying themselves. I'm so miserable, but I can't wish them to share in my pain."

I would have sat down in the snow and had a good cry right then, only I did not want to get my coat wet; that would have only made me more miserable. I wiped my tears and looked down at the rifle, cursing how I wished I had never seen the "damn thing"—I was so angry I was shocked to hear myself say an ill word. I wanted to leave the rifle there to be buried by the next snowfall—that's where it belonged since it was used to kill another creature for our own selfish purposes. But Adele and I would starve if I did not find food. What did it matter?

A squirrel's life was of more value than mine. Had I been alone, I gladly would have starved to end my misery, but I could not make that decision for Adele. Damn it, why hadn't she asked Ben to teach her how to use the rifle while I was ill? Why was I always the practical one?

I should bring the rifle home—in case Ben did come and need it to shoot game for us. Damn Ben. Damn him! I couldn't depend on him. What was I thinking? We did not need him. I would bring the rifle home with me, but only so if that bastard showed his face again, I could run him off the property.

I wiped my eyes with my scarf and picked up the rifle. I still did not know where our next meal would come from, but for now, I was going back to the cabin. Tomorrow I might feel better, think better of it, and try again to shoot something. But today I could not extend myself more.

I returned along the track of my snowshoes. With the sun now at my back, and my frustration giving way to weariness, I noticed more of the forest than I had earlier. Halfway home, I passed through a thick clump of pine trees. The ground sloped up a bit beneath them. The snow had not intruded much inside them so some pine needles could be seen on the earth's floor, and among them, some little green plants. Curious to see a sign of life amid so much snow, I stepped closer and was amazed to find the bushes had little red berries on them. They were wintergreen berries, although I did not know their name at the time. I would never again see so many clumped together, yet that Christmas Day, a multitude of them grew around the trunks of the pine trees. But how was I to get them home? I set down the rifle to consider. Then taking off one of my mittens, I knelt down in the snow, now indifferent to my coat or dress getting wet. Carefully, I collected the berries and placed them inside my mitten. I was afraid they might smoosh like a blueberry or raspberry would, but they were hard, perhaps from the cold. I would have tasted one, but I dared not be so selfish, for Adele and I should divide them equally. I did not even know if they were safe to eat, but we had to eat something. I looked them over closely; something had nibbled on a few of them, perhaps a bird or squirrel, so they could not be poisonous.

My mitten was half-filled when I finished picking the berries. I carefully folded over the end of the mitten so I would not lose any and tucked it inside my coat pocket. Then picking back up the rifle with both hands because it was so heavy, I continued home. I felt I had failed in my search to find us meat, but the berries would sustain us at least until tomorrow.

Adele was not at all disappointed by the berries when I reached home. As I poured them from my mitten into a little chipped bowl, she exclaimed, "Why Barbara! They're almost a Christmas miracle! They look like the red beads we strung on our Christmas tree back home."

While drinking the little coffee we had left, we slowly ate the berries, refreshed by their cold yet sharp mint taste. Adele decided to keep half a dozen of hers as a treat for the next day, but I ate all mine. If they were poisonous, I would want them to kill me immediately, and I wanted my stomach to feel full now, whatever hunger pains came later.

That was our Christmas Day. The rest of it was spent sitting and watching the snow falling. Adele suggested we play a wishing game of what we would like for Christmas, and I halfheartedly participated until I was overcome by the boredom of longing for what I could not have. Not long after dark, we went up to bed, to stay warm and preserve firewood.

"It wasn't such a bad Christmas, Barbara. We may not have had much to eat, but at least the berries were a true surprise. I'm sure we can find more if we look hard."

The rifle's backfiring had been my biggest surprise that day, but I did not say so. If I'd had a mirror to look in, I'm certain I would have seen a large bruise around my eye and nose. But if I did have a bruise, Adele never mentioned it.

❅   ❅   ❅

We woke to a pounding sound. It was a few minutes before I realized what it was. Then suddenly, I bolted out of bed. Someone was at the cabin door!

"Hello! Hello in there!" a voice yelled. A man's voice. I threw a blanket over my nightgown and ran downstairs while Adele remained in bed, moaning over the cold and tightening her blanket about her.

I was frightened to open the door—even frightened to look out the window from fear I would be seen. What if it were some criminal, some big rough man who would hurt us? Why had he come to our door?

But before I was all the way downstairs I could see through the front window—for I had forgotten to close the shutters—that there were two men, and by the shape of one in the dim gray morning light, I knew before I opened the door that it was Ben. He had returned! It was about time—when we had been all but sure he had abandoned us for good. When he stood there before me, I could barely restrain myself from running into his arms. Instead I said hello to the stranger with him, whom I knew must be Karl, the man who had been kind enough to bring me medicine when I was ill.

"Hello, Miss Traugott," Ben replied. "This is my friend Karl."

Before he could say more, Adele came downstairs, squealing out,

"Ben!" As glad as I had been to see him, when I heard the joy and longing in her voice, my heart sank.

Ben laughed at her excitement. She ran to within a foot of him, clearly wanting to throw her arms around him, but she hesitated with a yearning look. Ben quickly pushed a sack into my hands and said, "We brought you some Christmas presents. We're a day late I know, but we just got away from Karl's mother. She held us captive this past week, all the while over-feeding us. She sent us home with these treats, but we couldn't eat anymore so we thought you girls might like them."

"Oh, we couldn't possibly," I heard myself politely say, although I badly wanted to see what they were.

"What is it?" Adele asked, taking the sack from my hands. She had to grab onto something if she were not going to grab onto Ben. She laid the sack on the table and began to empty it before I could stop her.

"Barbara, it's an enormous fruitcake, and nuts, oh, so many nuts, and, why, apples, and sweetmeats. Oh, Barbara, it's our Christmas feast after all. There are even some potatoes! And coffee, just when we were almost out." Suddenly, she began to cry, while I stood, staring at the table, my mouth watering over so much bounty. When I tried to thank the boys, I found myself fighting back tears.

"If you're going to cry, then perhaps we should wait to give you these," laughed Ben, pulling two little packages from his coat pockets, while Karl drew out two more.

"Oh no, you've given us enough," I said, but Adele took the package Ben handed her. She quickly pulled off the paper, despite the tears streaming down her face. Inside was a dainty silk handkerchief. A minute later, I found my package contained a similar gift.

"I know they aren't much use to you out here, but women like fine things so we thought they might cheer you up," said Karl. "We bought them in town."

"Thank you," I replied. Mine was a lovely, light blue color while Adele's was pink. "They'll be the prettiest things in the cabin now." But Ben looked at Adele and said, "I'm not sure I agree with that."

"Here, open these too," Karl said. The packages he handed us were larger. They turned out to be little poetry books. "So you have something besides the Bible to read on your long evenings," said Ben. Mine was Longfellow's *Song of Hiawatha*, because Karl said, "It was written about Upper Michigan," while Adele's was *The Courtship of Miles Standish*. The rest of that winter, the rhythms of Longfellow would run through our heads.

"Thank you," I repeated. Adele, unable to restrain her happiness, kissed Ben's cheek so he blushed. Then, feeling confusion over her spontaneous gesture, Adele went up to Karl and politely brushed her lips against his cheek's stubble. I could not reprimand her. I almost wanted to kiss the boys myself—I felt so appreciative.

"I'm glad to see you're both doing well," said Ben as Adele took his hand and led him to the kitchen table. "I've been worried about you. I'm sorry we didn't come sooner, but our logging operations moved about twenty miles from here right after I got back to camp, and then on our way into town, Karl hadn't seen his family in so long, and we wanted to get to Marquette before that last big snow we had a few days back. We had a good time with Karl's family, but I've been anxious to come see you before we go back to logging."

"Can you stay with us a little while?" asked Adele.

"Just tonight, if that's all right, Miss Traugott?" Ben sought permission. "I know you're not used to company, least of all two bears like us."

"It's fine," I said. My voice did not sound very inviting, but I could not turn them away, and if they both stayed, there was less likely to be dallying between Ben and Adele.

"Good," Adele said. "We'll have a real feast tonight."

"I'll put away the food so it doesn't end up in our way or get knocked on the floor," I said, picking up the sack and returning everything into it. A wicked part of me wanted to hoard it from our guests, even if they had brought it; it was all we had to eat, but I could not be discourteous to them. I would ask Ben to shoot me some more game before he left, or at least, have him show me how to shoot properly. But that could wait until the afternoon, after we had done our catching up. I made a pot of coffee so we could visit together.

"So, Karl, you have family in Marquette?" I asked as I waited for the coffee to brew. I did not want him left out of the conversation once Ben and Adele started whispering together, and I wanted to know more about these young men to find out just how respectable they were.

"Yes," he said. "My mother and little sister."

"How old is your sister?" asked Adele.

"Just six, but she's my full sister. I have a stepfather too, but he and my mother have no children together."

"How long have you and Ben known each other?" I asked.

"Only a few months."

"You seem like such close friends," said Adele.

"Like brothers," said Ben, smacking Karl on the back. "At least, he treats me like it since he lets me go home with him for Christmas."

"It beats going home by myself," said Karl. "My stepfather can be a brute, but he won't mistreat my mother in front of company."

"Let's not talk about that, Karl," said Ben. "These girls need some cheering up. Why don't you tell them one of your stories?"

I poured the coffee for everyone and then sat down to listen. I don't remember what Karl's story was, although it was probably something about Paul Bunyan—he always had plenty of those to tell. I don't know that I ever heard anyone tell a story quite like Karl Bergmann. He had us all roaring by the time he finished, and he had a true knack for telling one story that had another story in it, rather like a logger's version of *One Thousand and One Arabian Nights*, not that I ever read that dirty book. But anyway, Karl could tell a story, and I'll never forget how he entertained us, even if now I can only remember one of the stories, as I'll relate in a moment. Perhaps his stories were not as funny as I thought, but in that isolated cabin, any form of entertainment seemed good enough for a king's banquet hall. Adele and I were so starved for friendly voices, and these two men were the only ones who had been kind to us in so long that we would have laughed at anything. Right then, I would have considered even a spider in the chinking of the cabin to be good company.

After his second cup of coffee, Karl excused himself from the table.

"It's out back behind the cabin," Ben said, referring to the outhouse, and Adele said, "Barbara, why don't you go show Karl where it is."

She sent me a glance I had never seen before—a look that told me to go away. I was so surprised that by the time I moved, it had turned into an angry glare.

"You can find it, Karl," I said, getting up to collect the coffee cups. "It's just behind the house."

"Thank you," he said and went outside.

As I carried the cups to the washtub, the room became quiet. It was unsettling after all the laughter. I heard Ben and Adele whispering, but I dared not turn around. I busied myself with washing the cups, as silently as possible, so I might catch a few of their words.

Adele had no right to look at me that way. If Father were alive, he would want me to act as her chaperone. And I suspected from the tone of her voice when she told me to show Karl how to get to the outhouse that not only did she want to be alone with Ben, but she thought I should get to know Karl better. As if I could be interested in a great bearded bear of a lumberjack like that!

When Karl returned, I was relieved to have everything become lively again—he had barely come back in the door before he announced, "That last story I told reminds me of another. Did you ever hear about the time Paul Bunyan couldn't find enough leather to make himself a pair of boots? Well, he—"

And he was off into another story. Paul Bunyan all the time. I came away from the sink and sat back down to laugh with everyone. Then after that story, Karl started another.

"And then there was the time of the big blizzard that snowed all the loggers in, and the men were afraid to go out in it; the snow was coming down a foot an hour. They were all certain they would freeze to death, and not one of those lily-livered cowards would go out to find some game for supper. Then Paul came blazing through the blizzard to the logging camp, and when he saw the situation, although he had just walked back to Upper Michigan from Minnesota, a two hour walk for him, he went right back out into that storm to find some grub for the men. He didn't even stop to tell them they were all acting like a bunch of girls—no offense intended, ladies. The men knew they were cowards, but they also knew Paul could not get lost in that blizzard since he was so tall that with a foot of snow under his feet, why his head stuck up above the clouds so that not a snowflake hit his face, and he could look down into the swirling storm and see the forest and look for game just as easily as you or I might stand in a river and watch for a fish. As Paul walked—"

"Oh dear!" I suddenly remembered. "We have no meat. You boys brought us that fruitcake and all those nuts, but what will I feed you for supper? Ben, we ate the very last meat you shot for us three days ago. We've barely had anything to eat since."

"Then we'll go out straightaway and get you some meat," Ben said.

"Just like Paul Bunyan would do," Karl winked. "Only, I won't tell you the rest of the story then because I don't want to make our processes look inferior to those of Paul. As good a friend as Paul has been to me, he can make a fellow feel a tad inadequate now and then."

"Oh, but both of you don't have to go," said Adele. She obviously wanted Karl to go so she could be with Ben.

"No, Karl, you stay here," Ben said as I watched Adele's face drop. "Miss Traugott and I should go so I can show her how to shoot that rifle."

I had already decided I would not tell him how I had attempted and failed. He would probably only laugh over my sensitivity at not wanting to kill a squirrel. I did not want to kill anything ever, but these men must have meat, and if they could provide for us, I would cook squirrel or raccoon or whatever they made available.

"No, let Miss Traugott rest," said Karl. "I'll go shoot us something."

"Thank you, Karl," Adele smiled to forbid all future discussion of Ben possibly leaving. I had never thought my own sister would turn coquette, but here she was manipulating others to spend time with a man. I was annoyed, but I could say nothing to stop Karl from putting on his boots, and someone had to find us meat; splendid as the boys' treats were, they would not feed all of us, especially not two big hungry men. Yet I refused to leave Ben and Adele alone for one minute while Karl was gone.

"So Ben," I said, planting myself firmly across the table from him and Adele, "what are your plans?"

"What do you mean?" he asked.

I was being bold, but I needed to know his intentions if I were to let him sit and whisper to my sister, as if he were her beau, and especially after his unforgivable month's absence.

"We never had much time to talk when you were here before. You seem like a bright young man. Do you intend to be a logger all your life, or do you have bigger plans?" He might be handsome as sin, but over time, sin loses its glamour, and I doubted Adele would find satisfaction as a lumberjack's wife.

"No place is like the woods," he replied. "It puts your soul at peace, so I guess I have no problem working there the rest of my life."

"You don't have any bigger dreams?"

"Well," he smiled broadly, showing his white teeth, then looking down to admire his forearm, "I guess from the way I'm built, the universe intended for me to chop down trees."

"You're smart enough to do other things, such as being a clerk or a bookkeeper."

"And be locked up in some office all day to crunch numbers? No thank you, Ma'am. Out in the woods, no one tells me what to do, and someday, I imagine I'll be boss of the logging operation and have others do what I say. If not, in time I'll start my own logging company. But yes, I intend always to be a logger. There's better money in it too than being a desk clerk."

"That's ambitious of you," said Adele. "Father always said if a person does the work meant for him, he'll prosper."

Father had not prospered though. He'd had a different job every couple of years, and we had barely made ends meet. He had spent a lot of time trying to figure out what was the work meant for him.

"Karl is a natural like me. Both of us took to logging right away. I've only been at it a few years, but it seems like it's what I was born to do, and Karl's the same. Some things are just meant to be, like he was meant to be a lumberjack, and he and I were meant to be friends, and although we don't have a company of our own yet, I reckon someday we'll be partners in the business."

"He seems like a good friend," Adele said.

"He's got the most loyal heart of anyone I know," Ben replied.

Adele looked down at her lap. I could read her thoughts—she was thinking her heart was just as loyal if Ben would notice. Perhaps she would be loyal to him, but as my sister, she was not being very loyal to me. I knew she would up and leave me at a moment's notice for this lumberjack. And she would regret it if she did. I could just see her, barefoot and pregnant, cooking in a logging camp for a hundred rough, smelly men. Such a life would kill her within a year—she couldn't even fetch water without collapsing on the ground to cry.

"Well, that didn't take long at all," Karl laughed, suddenly opening the door. He displayed a dead rabbit, holding it by its back legs. "Ask and it is given," he said. "Isn't that what the Lord said? So I went outside and I said, 'God, I need a rabbit for Miss Traugott to cook for our dinner, and we're all mighty hungry, so could You make it fast?' Then I walked less than twenty feet from the house before one trotted in my path, and boom, next thing you know, here I am with proof that prayers are answered."

Adele laughed. Ben jumped up from the table to smack Karl on the back. I grimly took the poor rabbit to the counter to skin and cook it. I felt sad. Not for the rabbit, but because my sister had no loyalty toward me—despite her earlier comments that we needed each other now that our parents were gone. Blood was not stronger than love. I felt irritable again, but told myself I was just hungry, and once I ate, I would feel better. I wanted to be cheerful for our company since once Adele left me, I did not imagine my life would have any cheer. Unless Karl—but no, why would he notice me? He seemed a good sort, but he was rough, and even if he wanted my hand, which was unlikely, I would not be a lumberjack's wife.

"Let's read my poem while Barbara makes supper," Adele said.

"Do you need help, Miss Traugott?" Ben asked.

"No, I'm fine," I replied.

"I'll skin that rabbit for you," Karl said. He got up and took it from me before I could object. I peeled the potatoes instead.

Once the rabbit was skinned, Karl was called upon to read aloud *The Courtship of Miles Standish*. I thought it odd he was chosen to read it. Poor Miles Standish, in love with Priscilla Mullins, only to have his friend John Alden marry her—Karl could not help but notice Adele's beauty, but since Ben had seen her first, I imagine as a gentleman, Karl was stepping aside for his friend. I listened for Karl's voice to quiver over some of the lines, to confirm for me that he had feelings for Adele as well, but I heard no quiver. Perhaps all men did not instantly fall in love with my sister.

The rabbit was nearly cooked when Karl finished reading the poem. Our guests were true gentleman, saying I had done a splendid job making supper, although I noticed many pieces of gristle in the meat. Adele had too many stars in her eyes to notice what she put into her mouth.

After supper, Ben produced a stack of playing cards. "I thought I'd save these up for after supper so we'd have some variety this evening," he said.

"Barbara and I don't know how to play cards," Adele replied.

"You don't?" he said in astonishment.

"Actually," I said, "we disapprove of card-playing."

"Oh," said Ben. "All right then." He started to put the cards back into his pocket.

"Barbara," Adele protested. She would actually stoop so low as to play cards to please this man!

"Well," said Karl, "I'd be willing to give *The Song of Hiawatha* a try."

"That sounds nice," I replied before an argument could start over the playing cards.

"Oh, but Karl, you read all of *Miles Standish*," Adele said. "Let Ben read this time."

Ben had a beautiful voice, so I did not object. Yet as he read, I decided while Karl's voice was rougher, it was also stronger and therefore sounded more truthful than Ben's. Nor was I partial to hear a story about Indians—I was very grateful I had not yet seen any in the woods, but no doubt some would come knocking on our door to steal from us the second the boys were gone. The Whitmans had told me the settlers here had had no incidents with the local Chippewa, but I suspected you never could tell with Indians.

For now I felt safe with the boys present, so I tried to concentrate on the poem's odd, appealing rhythm. The descriptions were lovely. When Ben read about summer, I almost felt the warmth of the midsummer sun, as if this miserable winter were long past.

> Heavy with the heat and silence
> Grew the afternoon of Summer;
> With a drowsy sound the forest
> Whispered round the sultry wigwam,

With a sound of sleep the water
Rippled on the beach below it;
From the cornfields shrill and ceaseless
Sang the grasshopper, Pah-puk-keena'
And the guests of Hiawatha,
Weary with the heat of Summer,
Slumbered in the sultry wigwam.

Our fire was warm and crackling, emitting almost enough heat to equal a sultry summer. I felt drowsy, like on a warm summer afternoon. But in a moment, the dream was over. Karl yawned. Ben read to the end of the passage, and then said, "I think I'm ready for bed."

"So am I," I replied. I wanted to keep the image of warmth in my mind, without any other thoughts to interrupt it. I already yearned for summer, although it was months away. Whatever summer brought, I was sure my life would be better then—provided we survived this miserable winter. When winter was over, though I did not know how, I would make sure I no longer lived in this miserable cabin, even though it might be easier to live here in summer than in winter.

"Good night," said Ben as Adele went upstairs. I followed her, but I returned with blankets that Karl spread out before the fire for Ben and himself. We only had three blankets, but I gave them each one for they were such big men, and Adele and I could share ours. The cabin was so warm, the fire crackled so loudly, I did not think any of us would be cold this night. I was looking forward to a good long rest, hoping the boys would let us sleep in, and that they would stay through most of tomorrow. I did not quite understand my feelings toward them—I knew it was not proper for them to be here, yet I felt safe with men in the house. And while I did not want Ben to take Adele from me,

I no longer feared the boys meant us any harm. I would worry about everything tomorrow. I felt so sleepy now, nearly drugged by the rhythmic, lullaby of *Hiawatha*, that I was grateful for my pillow.

But as soon as I crawled into bed, Adele began whispering.

"It was such a nice day, Barbara. I feel so happy."

"It was kind of the boys to bring us the treats," I replied.

"Barbara, they're not boys."

"Well, what am I to call them then? *Ben and Karl* were kind to bring us the treats."

"You know what I mean, Barbara, but you don't need to worry about them."

"Go to sleep, Adele." I did not wish to argue with her. They were barely more than boys—perhaps nineteen or so. If they truly were men, I might have trusted them less.

"Barbara?"

"What is it?"

"I meant it was a nice day because it was like old times. We were so happy and laughed so much today that it reminded me of when Mother and Father were with us."

"That's because it's Christmas time. It's hard to spend our first Christmas without Father."

"Barbara, I mean—I don't know how really to explain it, but I sensed Mother and Father were here, celebrating with us."

"I miss them too," I said. "Now go to sleep."

I was very tired, and now annoyed that I could not remember the rhythm of *Hiawatha* or the exact wording of those lines about summer I had tried to memorize by repeating them to myself after Ben had read them. When one of the boys started snoring, I felt exasperated; he would probably keep me awake—sawing logs like that—as if he didn't do enough of that out in the woods. The deep sleep I longed for would not come now.

"Barbara, no, it wasn't like just missing them," Adele kept blabbering. "It was as if Father were right there beside me—as if I could smell the smoke from his cigars, and somehow I could sense Mama in the rocking chair. I sensed it so strongly I looked over to the chair, and I swear I watched it rocking. That was when I jumped up from the table, using the excuse to get Ben more coffee, even though he said he didn't want any more. I was just so surprised; it was so strange, Barbara, and so—I don't know how to describe it. I just felt so overwhelmed with contentment, as if nothing bad could ever happen to us. Does that make any sense?"

I had no idea what she meant. I couldn't remember her fetching Ben more coffee. I think I would have remembered that since I usually waited on everyone. I don't remember what I replied to her then—I don't remember whether she said anything more. Sarah, since you live in the twentieth century, you might best understand what happened next if I explain it as like the radio suddenly coming on, letting me listen to other people talking. For a minute, I could follow the conversation, although I did not know the voices, but then the reception scrambled so I only heard a jumble of nonsense. I had heard Adele chatting, but I had heard others speaking too, but I could make no sense of the words although it was the second time it had happened. And then I fell into the deep sleep I longed for.

When I woke, I felt oddly disturbed; then after a moment, my last dream came back to me. I had dreamt Karl lay beside me. He nestled his face up against my own, and I had been surprised that the stubble from his beard was not prickly, but soft—even warm and comforting. I felt awkward and shy when he spoke to me in the morning.

We had only toast and coffee to offer our guests for breakfast. I magnanimously offered the boys our nuts, and what little was left from the fruitcake, but they refused anything but toast.

"We'll eat a big supper at the logging camp tonight," Ben said.

"Is it a long walk there?" Adele asked.

"Not so long that there isn't time for another story if you want to hear one," Karl replied.

"Oh yes, please," Adele said.

"I fancy, Miss Traugott, you prefer more serious stories?" he asked.

"Yes, I suppose," I said. "Something with a lesson or a moral to it."

I had laughed previously at his stories to be polite, and because I had enjoyed the company, but not the tales themselves. Frankly, I found Paul Bunyan rather tiresome, but I was not rude enough to say so.

"Well, this here's the most serious story I know about Paul Bunyan," he began.

I sipped my coffee. I hoped the story would not be long—although once it was over, Adele and I would be alone again.

Paul Bunyan and the Spirit of the North

Now this story happened when Paul Bunyan had first become a logger and formed his own logging company. He was young and brash in those days, and his size and strength made him believe he could do just about anything, which he pretty much could, but just about anything is not quite everything as you'll soon hear.

Paul Bunyan's first logging camp was set up near Big Bay, and he thought if he sold enough wood to the new settlers in Marquette, he'd have enough money to buy his sweetheart, Tiny, something pretty to wear. Now, you wouldn't think a man would have to cut down a whole forest to make enough money to buy his sweetheart something pretty, but despite her name, Tiny was no small woman—it would take half a dozen circus tents to clothe her, and she had her heart set on a beautiful white silk dress, and to import that much silk from China would cost a small fortune. But Paul's heart just overflowed with love for Tiny, so with a couple of his closest friends, and of course, Babe the Blue Ox, Paul went to Big Bay and set up his logging camp.

Now, Paul's ax blade could fly faster than any other ax there ever was, because never was there another man who could swing an ax so sure and swift as Paul. So it didn't take no more than a couple of days to cut down a few hundred acres of trees. Paul's men were there to help him, and they could clear an acre for every forty Paul cut, and that was fast work all around so Paul was certain he would have that silk dress for Tiny in no time at all. Before you knew it, there were log piles all over that camp, tall as the Tower of Babel itself. When all the men finally took a break, they felt satisfied looking up at those log piles and thinking how they had accomplished something so impressive so quickly. Of course, being loggers, they knew that to get those logs to Marquette, they'd need a sleigh or a river, and it being spring, it would be a long time before they could use a sleigh, so they piled up the logs alongside a river that would carry all that lumber straight down to Marquette Harbor on Iron Bay.

Now it was powerful warm that year for a spring in Upper Michigan. It was June first and already sixty degrees on the thermometer, and that could create a powerful sweat in a man who's been chopping down trees, so Paul, just to cool himself off, lay down on the riverbank and gently put his hand in the water to scoop some up and cool his brow, and that's how it happened.

"Mother Mackinac!" shouted Paul.

Everyone turned his head to see what was wrong.

"Holy Hiawatha!" he bellowed. And this time, he bolted up into a sitting position as he ran water over his brow.

"What is it, Paul?" asked all the men.

"Well, if Copper isn't King, I'll bet you anything we've made a huge misconception."

"What do you mean, Paul?" they all asked in confusion.

"Why this river's flowing north, not south, not down to Marquette."

Now Paul was right, for it was the Yellow Dog River he was talking about, and that river flows north into Lake Superior rather than south down to Iron Bay. But foolishly, Paul had assumed every river would flow down to Marquette, and while it was a big assumption, you have to remember this land was all unexplored territory when Marquette was first settled, so only a couple of surveyors knew which rivers flowed where.

Well, all the men saw the trouble instantly. There was no way to get their logs to Marquette if the river flowed wrong, and they could not send the logs north up the river, and then down the shore of Lake Superior to Marquette 'cause the waves would be too choppy on the great lake; nor did they have a boat to float the logs down on.

"Paul, what will we do?" they all asked.

"Now, let's just think a minute," he said. "We'll figure out something."

So all the men sat about in a circle, and pondered, and swatted mosquitoes, and pondered, and swatted more mosquitoes. And though it had been morning, soon afternoon passed and the temperature soared up to sixty-five, and all the men exerted their brains so hard that their brows broke out into a sweat just from thinking—nor did smacking their foreheads to kill them mosquitoes help their brains to think.

But then finally, to everyone's relief, Paul spoke.

"Big Mouth Bart," he said, "you've got the biggest mouth of any man this side of the Mississippi, don't you?"

"Biggest in all of North America," Big Mouth Bart replied, and he opened it for all the men to see it was as large as the maw of the whale that swallowed Jonah. "At least that's what Ma always told me," he added. "When I was just a baby, I put the family cow in my mouth and no one could find it for two days. I figured that was just easier than using a bottle to get my milk, but Ma and Pa weren't too pleased when they found out. And I guess they was right, 'cause that cow was so spooked its milk never did taste as sweet afterwards."

Paul let everyone chuckle for a minute. Then he said, "Well, Big Mouth Bart, if you think you're up to it, we'll have you suck up this here river into your mouth, but don't you swallow it, 'cause we'll have you shoot it back out in the opposite direction."

Well, all the men were amazed by this solution, and they wondered why they hadn't thought of it themselves. They all knew that if Big Mouth Bart could swallow that whole river, well then, the problem was solved and their logs would get delivered to Marquette.

So Big Mouth Bart lay down on the riverbank and took a couple of good breaths; then he opened his mouth and began to suck in the Yellow Dog River. In half a minute, you could see the water level drop, and in another half minute, you could see rocks sticking up above the water. As Bart slurped up that river, the men ran into its bed and caught the fish flopping against those rocks—since it was a Friday, that night they held the world's biggest fish fry—and then in another half minute, that riverbed was as dry as the Sahara, and soon the grass started to turn brown and the trees began to droop.

Then Paul said, "Now, Big Mouth Bart, turn around. We got to get this river flowing again before this becomes the Yellow Dog Desert."

So Big Mouth Bart turned around, and when Paul said, "Go!" he spit out that river in the direction of Marquette.

But that river was tricky like a dog, for it flowed along as Paul wanted for about a mile, just until it was out of the men's sight, and then it circled around in the direction it usually ran. You see, that river didn't think the men could see it for the trees, but Paul was so tall he could see ten miles above the trees without straining an eye. When he saw the river change its path, he exclaimed, "Men, that river's got a mind of its own; it's done turned around to flow back the way it was before."

This news saddened all the men, making things look more hopeless than ever. And in another moment, they saw the river come along and flow right back into its old bed, just to mock Paul.

"Now what are we going to do, Paul?" the men all demanded.

"Just let me think about it some more," he replied.

So Paul thought some more, and as he thought, his eyes lit on his giant old ax, and he wondered aloud, "If my ax is strong enough to cut trees, then why can't it cut the earth?"

None of the men knew what he meant by that, but Paul told Pete the Blacksmith to make him a new ax, only even bigger so he could use it to plow up the land.

"Paul, it isn't planting season," said the men, but Paul just ignored them while Pete made him a giant ax blade. Then Paul took that new blade and had a hole drilled in it so he could run a log through and grab it at both ends. Then he tied leather straps to both ends of the log and attached those to a harness he put on Babe. Soon he and Babe were plowing the earth. First Paul plowed into the side of the riverbed; then he started plowing south.

At first that river was hesitant, but it was also curious, and after a little while, it started to trickle into Paul's new trench. As Paul plowed south, he started to whistle to encourage the river. "If music can tame the savage beast," he said, "then maybe it can tame a savage river."

All went well for a few more miles, so that this time all the men thought for sure Paul had figured out how to get those logs to Marquette. But then the river figured out Paul's plan. Pretty soon it realized it was flowing south, not north, and for whatever reason, it did not want to flow south. Nor did it want to run backwards in Paul's trench to return to its old riverbed, so again it decided to circle, up over the side of the trench Paul had dug, and then back to its old waterbed. But that river made such a sharp turn that it knocked over the trench's banks, and as it circled around, it ended up forming a lake.

"This here is the darnedest, most independent river I ever seen!" Paul exclaimed. And for that reason, he named the new lake, Lake Independence, and that name has stuck to it ever since.

Well, Paul was tired by that time as you can well imagine, but there was one other man in camp with a brain, and though his brain was obviously not as large as Paul's, it was just as intelligent. This man was Dutchman Van, and when he told everyone his idea, everyone was certain it would work, for it's a known fact that the Dutch are the smartest people in the world.

"Vindmeel," he said. He did not speak English very well, so at first all the men stared at him, not knowing what he meant. "Vindmeel," he repeated, "like back home in Groeningen." Then he drew a picture in the dirt so all the men would understand. When they finally figured out what he meant, well, they got so excited they started whooping and smacking each other on their backs as if they were certain they had found the solution. For if they built a windmill, the wind would force that tricky river to flow down the trench Paul had dug, whether or not it wanted to because no river is stronger than the wind.

Now when Paul heard that solution, he up and started chopping down more trees to make that windmill. And with all the men joining in, they had it done in six hours. You might think Paul should have been able to do it faster, but a windmill is a mighty display of industrial ingenuity, and none but Dutchman Van had ever seen one in operation so it did take a little figuring out how to build it, and I would say that to have it up and working in six hours was quite an accomplishment.

Once that windmill was built, the men stood about, taking pride in their creation, and waited for the wind to blow.

They waited, and they waited, and they waited.

And no wind blew.

Then Paul thought maybe he should turn the windmill himself since he could easily sit beside it and rotate it with his hand. So he did start turning it, and the river was forced by the windmill to flow in the opposite direction. So the men started pushing the logs in the river and making them flow in the direction they wanted. But poor Paul, strongest man in the world though he was, soon felt his arm get tired from all that repetitive motion, for his muscles were used to the swift blow of chopping down trees, not the circular up and down of windmill turning. Whenever Paul switched arms to rest one, the windmill would stop turning, and that river started rushing right back in its old direction. It's a good thing no settlers were living near that river because they all would have been washed away in the flash floods that Paul caused just by switching off arms. Finally, Paul confessed he could turn that windmill no more, and that river went back on its natural path to the north.

Now Paul looked mighty glum. All the men tried to cheer him up, circling around him and patting him on the leg since he was too tall for anyone to reach his back. They told him not to take it so hard, and that he had done his best. Even Babe the Blue Ox came and laid her head in Paul's lap, but despite the love Paul had for old Babe, not even she could comfort him now.

And Dutchman Van, admitting his own defeat, said, "Vell, you do need vind to make a vindmeel vork."

But no sooner had he said this than Paul jumped up from the ground. And in a couple of swift strides, he had disappeared from sight. All the men were astonished, for they had never thought Paul the type to run away from his troubles, but Van, being the smart one in camp, said, "No, he has an idea."

And that's exactly what Paul had—an idea! He knew he couldn't harness that darn independent river, but he thought maybe he could harness the wind! So if he wanted that river to flow south, he would need the North Wind to help him since it blew from the North to the South, the very direction Paul wanted the Yellow Dog River to flow. Now no man knew where the North Wind lived, but Paul, being smarter than most men, figured it had to be about as far North as one could go, and if it were in Upper Michigan, that meant the very tip of the Keweenaw Peninsula, and Paul also knew Kewadin—for that is the North Wind's name—had to live up high somewhere, and the highest point at the tip of the Keweenaw is Brockway Mountain, so that's where Paul went to find the North Wind. In five strides he reached the tip of the Keweenaw Peninsula, and in a couple more he was atop Brockway Mountain, and sure enough, just near the top of the mountain was a cave.

Now before I go on with the story, I want to warn you not to waste your time going to look for that cave, 'cause it's not there anymore. Kewadin figured if Paul could climb up to his cave, then some ingenuous men might want to come up too, and they would build a road up his mountain, and I imagine some day they will. So after Paul visited him, Kewadin up and moved to Canada. Why, before the North Wind moved there, let me tell you Canada was a tropical paradise, but now it's colder than Upper Michigan, though I know that's near impossible to believe.

But back to my story. So like I said, old Kewadin didn't like visitors. He wasn't an agreeable sort at all, which is why he always sent out the cold winds, though he could have stirred up some gentle warm breezes, if he wanted.

Well, the minute Kewadin saw Paul at the door of his cave, and before Paul's eyes could adjust to the cave's darkness, Kewadin let out such a blast of air that Paul had to grip hard to the edge of the cave not to be blown away. He did lose his hat, and his shirt was ripped plumb from his body, and although his stack of muscles was revealed by the loss of his shirt, the North Wind only laughed out, "Go away, Paul Bunyan. Your strength is no match for mine."

But Paul was so frustrated with trying to get those logs to Iron Bay that he refused to quit now, and he thought sure that first wind that Kewadin blew had just been to toy with him. You see, Paul and Kewadin had never been introduced, yet Kewadin knew Paul's name, so Paul figured Kewadin must have already heard of his mighty deeds, and perhaps he feared Paul enough that he wanted to frighten him away.

Now Paul is the strongest man alive, but like I said at the beginning, he was still young then, and young men are proud and don't yet know their limits, and so Paul paid no heed to Kewadin's words. He figured he would still see whether he could reason with Kewadin, and if he could not, he would come back the next day with the yoke of Babe the Blue Ox to harness the North Wind and make it do his will. So he sat down in the cave to try and talk the North Wind into cooperating.

"What do you want?" Kewadin called from the back of the cave.

"Come out of the darkness so I can see you, and speak to me like a man, and then I'll tell you what I want," Paul said.

And then Paul heard a terrible roar, and a great booming voice warned, "I am no mere man, Paul Bunyan! Tell me what you want."

When the voice spoke, the entire mountain rumbled. Then for the only time in his life, Paul felt fear. A coward feels fear and runs, but a brave man ignores his fear and holds his ground. So Paul did not move, but blurted out, "I want the Yellow Dog River to flow south, and I want you to make it do so with wind power."

"Why should you want the river to change its course?" Kewadin boomed out.

But this time, Paul thought he detected a note of amusement in the voice, and if there was one thing Paul detested, it was not to be taken seriously.

"To get my logs to Marquette's harbor," he said. "The settlers there need lumber for their homes, and I need your help."

And then a tornado broke forth in the cave. It came up so suddenly that Paul found himself surrounded. It whizzed about him like a hurricane, while he was caught in its eye. All around him the wind blew until he grew absolutely terrified. He had thought he might wrestle the wind, and then harness it to do his will, but now he knew he could never grab hold of the wind, while it could grab and throw him about like a puny little grasshopper.

And then from the hurricane broke forth the most terrifying face, so terrible that although Paul tried to describe it later, he admitted there was nothing on earth any man had ever seen that could be compared to it to make understandable its hideous terror. From the mouth of this mighty frightening face blew out the hottest air imaginable, so hot it could melt all of January's snow as fast as a human would melt an ice cube in a frying pan.

Then spoke Kewadin:

"Who are you, Paul Bunyan, to say whether the trees should be cut down, or whether the rivers should change their course at the will of men, or where the mighty North Wind should blow? You, Paul Bunyan, who are so much more than a mere man, should know all the more clearly that this earth is not made to serve man any more than man is made to serve it. Were you there when the flow of the rivers was planned? Could you for all your strength move the mountain on which I live? Can your enormous brain even begin to grasp the full size, depth, and power of Lake Superior that gives life to a million teeming fish and provides commerce for ships throughout the world? Were you the one who pulled back the glaciers to create this lush green land? Were you the one who raised the Porcupine Mountains, or designed the breathtaking Tahquamenon Falls? Do you bring the snows each winter so deep they can bury even a man of your height if you were to stand still long enough? No, Paul Bunyan, do not ask the Spirits of this land to change their natures for your benefit. Our purpose is not to make your human lives easier."

When the voice ceased, Paul found himself shaking. No man or beast had ever frightened him enough to make him tremble before, such that Paul hoped he would never meet Kewadin or any of his kin again; in fact, though he was embarrassed to admit it, he confessed to me that at that moment he was so scared the North Wind might destroy him that he was sweating out a waterfall that ran down the side of the mountain. All Paul wanted then was to return to his logging camp, and he did not care what became of his logs or even whether his Tiny got her silk dress.

And then the North Wind reopened its mouth, but this time it sent out a cool breeze so that Paul's sweat turned to icicles, hanging off his eyelashes.

"Paul Bunyan, because you are the only man brave enough to come to me," said Kewadin, "I will give you one piece of advice. The great Manitou, when he made man, endowed him with one talent beyond all the other creatures, and if you think long enough about it, you will know what that talent is, and then you will know how to move your logs. The answer lies within you."

Then Kewadin closed his eyes and went to sleep.

Paul waited a few minutes to see whether Kewadin would speak more. He was afraid to turn his back and leave, for fear the North Wind should grow angry at his rudeness. But when he realized Kewadin would say no more, he leapt down from the mountain like a child from a step, and in five minutes, he was back in his camp.

He had a strange look about him when he returned, a sort of glow to his face that made everyone step aside when he walked into camp; he spoke not a word to anyone but went straight into his tent, and there he sat for three days and three nights while all the men stared at one another and asked, "How will we ever move all these logs?" and "Has all our work been wasted?" and one or two whispered, "Do you think Paul's gone mad?"

But don't you worry. Paul Bunyan was made of sturdier stuff than that. No, he hadn't gone crazy. But when he came out of that tent finally, several men thought he might have. He came out, ax in hand, and went up to one of those log piles and flew at it with his ax so quick and sharp that chips went flying out into the air and when they came back down, they landed together so perfectly they built a cabin for the men to live in next time they logged in that area.

When the men got over their astonishment, they realized Paul was hollowing out the centers of logs as if to make canoes, yet the men knew he did not intend for the logs to float because he cut off their ends so water would seep right through them.

Paul did all this work so quickly no one could imagine what he was up to until he began shoving together the ends of the chopped up logs. Then he took more logs and stacked them on top of each other until he had a tower, and the logs he had attached to each other he leaned up against the tower.

"Paul, what are you doing?" all the men finally demanded.

"It's a log chute," said Paul. "Look how it works."

Then Paul took his water dipper and dipped it in the river. He picked up a log with one hand, poured water down the chute with the other, and dropped the log in the chute. That log went running down that chute faster than a dog that's gotten into a hornet's nest.

All the men were amazed by the log chute, but they were also all a little slow, so they couldn't see what good was this new invention. Finally, Van the Dutchman spoke up, "Why, we'll build a chute all the way to Marquette to get these logs there."

"Exactly," said Paul.

And that's exactly what they did, and since Paul was so big and strong, they finished it before dark, though Marquette was more than thirty miles away.

Well, that log chute was the first log chute ever built, and it got those logs to Marquette so the settlers could all build their houses. The people of Marquette were so proud of the log chute that they wanted to keep it, and it could be seen for many years after that until the great fire of '68 burnt it down. I remember as a boy that we used to use it as a waterslide into Lake Superior. Let me tell you, it was the greatest fun a boy could have.

And so, Paul Bunyan was able to sell all his logs, and that year, because the people now had lumber, the village of Marquette doubled in size. Best of all, with the money Paul made, he bought Tiny all the silk she needed to make her dress; you should have seen it—why it took a whole steamship to bring that much silk from China, not to mention the 7,777 silkworms who worked nonstop for seven months and seven days to produce it, but it was what Tiny had her heart set on, so Paul got it for her. She was so pleased with the silk that she told Paul she would save it for her wedding dress, and Paul, taking the hint, got down on his knee right then and there and proposed to her. They were wed that winter at the Annual Logging Congress Ball.

The End

"Oh, Karl, that was wonderful," said Adele when he had finished.

"I wouldn't say it was all that serious," I added.

"Oh, Barbara, shush," said Adele. "It was so much fun."

"You didn't like my story, Miss Traugott?" asked Karl.

"I'm sure you did a fine job as a storyteller," I replied, "but I don't think it appropriate to put all that Indian spirit stuff into it. What I mean to say is that I don't think it sounded very Christian." The Indian spirit rather reminded me of the Book of Job actually, and while I did not like Job, it wasn't right to mock him.

"I'm sorry," said Karl. "I meant no offense by it."

"Barbara, it's only a story," Adele sighed.

"I'll do better next time," Karl promised.

"Well, we should get going," said Ben, standing up.

"Oh, I wish you didn't have to go," said Adele.

"Can't be helped," said Ben. "There are trees we need to chop down. But we'll be back soon with fresh game for you."

"We promise not to stay away so long this time," Karl added.

"Right," Ben agreed. "We intend to look after you girls and make sure you get through the winter all right. We'll be back in a few days."

"Good," said Adele.

"Thank you," I said.

I felt tired when they were gone, or rather listless. It was such a contrast, the lonely quiet of the cabin with Adele as my only companion compared to the high spirits we felt when the boys came. But I did not have much time to be lonely, for the boys were as good as their promise; they did not come again to spend the night, but they did appear a couple of times a week. Sometimes only one of them came, but that was enough to keep us from going without company or food, for they were always bringing us small treats, leftover rolls the camp cook had made, a bag of flour, and often a rabbit or squirrel. As much as I hated the isolation of the cabin, I was grateful for these little joys, and as January wore away, I resigned myself to remaining there the rest of winter. Still I wondered whether spring would bring greater hope.

❄   ❄   ❄

And then in February, we did not see either of the boys for five days, and when Karl finally came, he said Ben was ill. Karl stayed only long enough to have a cup of coffee while Adele quizzed him about Ben's health until I think her questioning drove him away. An entire week passed after that without their coming. Finally, Adele said, "Barbara, something terrible has happened to Ben. I just know it. And Karl is afraid to come tell us."

"Don't worry. I'm sure he's fine," I replied. "They didn't come for almost a month just before Christmas, but it all worked out in the end. You'll see."

"But now we're such better friends than then, Barbara; I can't imagine Ben would stay away unless he were seriously ill."

"If something happened, Karl would come tell us," I replied.

She was silent then until we went to bed when she put her arm around me and started to sob. "Oh, Barbara, I don't think I can bear it, not knowing. If anything happened to Ben I wouldn't want to live. I—"

"Don't be silly," I snapped, and moved across the bed to shake off her hold. "You hardly even know him."

"I love him."

I could say nothing to that. I had already known it. I had feared it. Yet I had not been prepared to hear it spoken.

After a few seconds, she repeated, "I love him, Barbara. Always. I love him. With all my heart."

What could I say? She was lovesick. She was lost to me. If I disapproved, it would only push her into his arms sooner.

In the morning, as I made breakfast, we heard a knock at the door.

Adele ran to open it. By the time I turned to look, she had her arms around Ben's neck.

"I'm so glad to see you. I've worried so much," she exclaimed.

He only laughed while Karl sheepishly grinned at me. "Hello, Miss Traugott."

"Hello," I replied, concealing my pleasure at seeing them both.

"Come outside," Ben said. "We have a treat for you."

I instantly imagined a nice rabbit, but that kind of treat the boys could have brought inside. Before I reached the door, Adele screamed with delight.

Two horses were in front of the cabin, hitched to a beautiful red sleigh with silver runners sparkling in the morning sun.

"We're going to take you girls for a ride," Ben said, "and we have a real treat in store for you when you see where we go."

"To Marquette?" asked Adele.

"No, even better," Karl replied.

I could not imagine anything better than going to Marquette, but I was glad just simply to get out of the suffocating cabin. Had I been wise that day, I would have insisted they take us into Marquette to stay permanently.

The boys breakfasted with us. All the while, Ben teased Adele as she pestered him with questions regarding where we were going in the beautiful red sleigh. Laughing, he made up fantastic tales of how the sleigh would fly us through the air to Bombay, or it would float over Lake Superior and down the Great Lakes to Atlantis. Karl laughed and joined in, verifying that Santa Claus had gotten a new sleigh, so they had bought this old one off him, then flown clear to Sheba to have tea there with the Queen. They were all so merry I could not help joining in their laughter, but when the time came to go, my heart sank inside me. Wherever we were going, I knew it would not be so wonderful as the tales from *The One Thousand and One Arabian Nights* I had read as a little girl, secretly under my bedcovers in case Father should catch me with such a fantastic book. Even then, I had known flying carpets and genii were ridiculous, but I had been young enough to find pleasure in them.

Still, as we set off in the sleigh, I tried to keep up my spirits. I allowed Karl to tuck me under the buffalo robe beside Adele, and I did not protest when he sat beside me with Ben beside my sister. Soon the horses were dashing over the snow, whisking us along, faster than I had thought possible, nearly as fast as a train it seemed. At this speed, we could have been in Marquette in under an hour had we wished. But I did not care where we went; I was simply enjoying the cool air blowing on my face, and I imagined it being the warm breath of desert wind, as though I were on a magic carpet, soaring over the sands of Persia. I could have nodded off to sleep, the sleigh's motion had such a steady smoothness. I did not know where we were going until Karl hollered, "Here we are." In another minute, Ben pulled the sleigh up beside a cliff.

"Where is here?" Adele asked.

"Wait and you'll see," said Ben.

He jumped out of the sleigh to help Adele down. Karl got out on the other side. He intended to help me down, but I did not know him well enough, so I let Ben help me as well, although I could have managed on my own. The snow was crunchy under my feet. It felt like a warm day—just at the freezing point—so the snow had started to melt on its surface.

When Karl heard the snow crunch beneath our boots, he said, "It won't be long now until spring. We're two-thirds of the way."

Two-thirds. Only two-thirds? It was almost mid-February. Could I bear another two months?

"Oh, we're farther than that," said Ben. "It's only five more weeks until the equinox."

"In Upper Michigan, spring doesn't come until another five weeks after the equinox," Karl replied.

Already seven weeks had passed since Christmas—each day since then had seemed never-ending, yet now, Christmas did not seem so long ago.

"Come along," said Ben, taking Adele's hand.

"But how am I to walk?" she asked.

"We won't walk far," he replied.

He had taken her hand so naturally, as if he were in the habit—he apparently had been when I was ill—but I had never seen him bold enough to do so before me until now. I stood for a moment, watching them walk away from me, before Karl said, "Miss Traugott, are you coming?"

"Where are we going? I can't walk in this snow."

"It's only a few feet," he said, leading the way.

We walked up to the cliff and then around its side. There, coming down the cliff, gleaming in the noontime sun, was a huge sheet of ice with icicles like stalactites hanging from its bottom, reaching to the ground.

"We can go in through here," said Ben. Before I understood what he meant, he disappeared between two of the enormous icicles. Adele followed him without a second thought.

"It's a frozen over waterfall," Karl said, "and there's a cave behind it. It's not even cold in there."

I had never dreamt of such a thing. Compelled, feeling like Ali Baba, I stepped between the icicles, being careful not to slide on the ice floor, and entered the cave.

I had expected darkness inside, but instead I was dazzled by the sunlight that still shone through the breaks between the icicles and the dazzling white and blue glow, almost like glass, that the sun refracted through the ice.

"It's amazing!" I said. "I—I can't believe it!"

Ben laughed. "Miss Traugott, I never thought I would get that much emotion out of you."

Instead of being annoyed by his remark, I replied, "What do you mean?" and I laughed, half-embarrassed by my idiosyncrasies.

"You never seem to get excited about anything," said Ben. "I thought Adele would like this treat, but I wasn't half sure about you."

"It's like nothing I ever saw before," I replied.

Then we were all silent. We were listening. I could hear little cracking sounds where the warm sun melted the ice. My senses were dazzled by the dim dripping sound of water, the sparkling shades of white and blue and gray—I never would have thought that gray could sparkle, and inside the wall of ice, water bubbled and moved about as the warm sun penetrated it. The cave floor was also ice; apparently, the waterfall had carved a little pool beneath it that flowed back into the cave rather than joining the river that ran through the forest. I was walking on ice, slightly nervous I might slip, but surprised by its strength. As I walked, I saw streaks of white and blue water move accordingly with the pressure of my feet. I had never felt so—I would almost say, connected to the earth, but amazed is the only word, if any word can describe the experience.

And then something queer happened—I felt a jolt to my forehead, as if I had been struck by a stone. My head seemed to bolt back a couple of inches, but I did not fall over—instead, it was almost like what is called déjà vu—I felt I had been here before, at least in this situation, inside a great hall with these same people—only the entrance to the cave was the doorway to a great balcony, and I could look out over the sands of a desert—the sands of time, I curiously thought—and I felt that time stretched on and on forever. I felt dizzy, overcome with some forgotten knowledge I could not quite grasp, yet remembered once knowing.

Karl circled his arm around my back.

"Are you all right?" he asked.

"Yes, fine. I just thought I was going to slip."

"Barbara," said Adele, "your face is pale as if you're going to faint."

"No, I'm fine," I insisted.

"Do you want to go back outside?" asked Ben.

"Yes, please," I said, reluctant to leave the cave, yet fearing to remain. "I'm sorry. I think the air is just a little stale in here."

I wanted to see that vision again, whatever it had been, that desert, and Karl and Ben and Adele, dressed far differently, like people from the Bible almost, yet people I had known only perhaps in a different time. Yet how could I have? I had not known Ben and Karl even three months. And there had been something more—I had felt as if I knew what was about to happen, only—but the memory was gone. I felt so frustrated by my inability to remember. But how could I remember something that had never happened in my lifetime? I was so confused. Was something wrong with me?

I felt like crying as I stepped from the cave. A large rock was by the river. Karl quickly brushed the snow off it and insisted I sit down. It was cold to sit on, but I did not argue. I still felt dizzy.

"Are you going to be all right, Barbara?" asked Adele.

"Yes, I just need a minute. I'm not sure what happened."

"We haven't finished the surprise yet," said Ben. "We brought ice skates for you girls, but I don't think you should skate, Miss Traugott, if you're not feeling well."

"I'll be all right in a second," I said. "I don't want to spoil everyone else's fun."

"I'll go back to the sleigh to get the skates then," said Ben. "I won't be gone but a minute."

"I'll go with you," said Adele. Ben again took her hand as they returned to the sleigh. Karl stood beside me, not knowing what to say. I still felt a little weak. I breathed in the cool air until my eyes felt moist. I had not noticed how beautiful the snow was, so very white that afternoon. The pine trees along the river were so powerful, soaring to the sky, their silent winter sleep so sublimely peaceful. They might have grown here for decades, without ever having been seen by human eye. The land looked so quiet and unexplored, so timeless.

In a couple of minutes, Ben and Adele returned. I stood up, not wanting to be fussed over. Adele sat down on the rock while Ben helped her with her skates, which were too big for her so he stuffed them with rags. Then he put on his own skates, and Karl put on his. I feared if I tried to skate, I would fall over, but I let Ben put the skates on my feet. I was relieved Karl had not been the one to help me.

Ben waited for me to stand up, to make sure I had my balance. Then he took Adele's hand, leading her onto the ice. I was left with Karl.

"Do I just walk in them?" I asked.

"You want to push your feet forward, so you're sliding."

I was still standing in the snow, so he told me to walk until I reached the ice, which I managed without losing my balance. But once both skates scraped the ice, so did I.

He bent over to help me up. I had no choice but to let him.

"Now, just lift your foot slightly and then as you bring it down, glide into it," he said once I was standing up again.

I did as he said while he balanced me by putting his hands on my waist. I found it harder to concentrate then, but somehow, we managed to move forward.

"I'm not going to pull you over?" I asked.

"No, don't worry."

But I was worried. I was afraid of falling down and just as afraid of what liberties he thought he might take since I had let him hold my waist.

"I think I need to watch you first," I said.

"All right. Can you stand still?"

"Yes."

I did not know whether I could, but I would use all my might if it kept him from putting his hands on my waist again.

I watched him take a few steps or glides or whatever he called them. Then he started to skate backward—just to show off—I think perhaps that was his way of flirting with me. I didn't care how many treats he had brought us at Christmas. I was not going to be his, or probably not any man's.

"Barbara, come on! It's such fun!" shouted Adele. She and Ben were linked arm in arm, skating down the river as if they were born to do nothing more—and she never once on skates before!

"Now you try," said Karl, returning to my side. Before he could touch me, I gave my right foot a good push forward. Somehow my left foot followed. My feet came together, and I sailed clear halfway across the river. I even managed to stop without falling.

"Bravo!" cried Ben. He and Adele skated up to me. Turning around, I found Karl already at my side.

"Very good," said Karl. "I thought for a minute you would fall over, but you kept your balance. Just try smaller steps to be safe."

But I could not turn around now without nearly toppling over; Ben had to steady me and push me into the curve of my movement.

"I don't think this is for me," I said.

"You're doing really well," Ben replied.

"Let me help you," Karl said.

I restrained myself from wincing as his hand reached toward me. I stepped back. "No, I don't think I want to try anymore."

"Barbara, don't give up yet," said Adele.

"I just feel tired," I replied. I wasn't tired, but the odd feeling from the cave would not leave me, and Karl made me uncomfortable. "I didn't sleep well last night. Maybe some other time."

I doubted I would ever learn to skate, although I did hope the boys would bring us here again—so I could go back inside the cave. But I did not feel strong enough to do so right then. I would have to rest. I would enter it some other time.

I managed to glide slowly back across the ice, Karl at my side in case I should lose my balance. I was extra careful so he would not have to catch me if I fell.

"I'll help you take off your skates then," he said when I sat back down on the rock.

"No, I can manage. You go enjoy yourself."

I sounded as if I were giving orders, but I did not mean it that way. I just didn't know how to talk to young men. Karl looked disappointed, and I did pity him a bit—it must be hard to see your best friend have a beautiful girl, when even a plain one was not interested in you. But it was not his fault I was uninterested. "Thanks for your help," I said. "I did enjoy myself, but I am tired, and I don't want to spoil your fun."

"If you get cold," he replied, "you can always go back inside the cave to warm up. At least there's no wind in there."

"I'll do that," I said, forcing a smile.

So I sat and watched them. I did get cold, but I did not want to go into the cave alone. I wanted time to think about what had stirred in me before I reentered it. So I sat on that rock until my whole body ached from the stillness and the cold, and even then, I remained until the sun started to set. Finally, Ben said, "We better head for home."

They skated back toward me and then pulled off their skates. Soon we were all piled back into the sleigh. I felt content, despite not having skated, and I was looking forward to a warm fire when we got home—it would not hurt to burn a little extra wood—February was half-over. I felt my spirits had lifted that day, despite how odd I had felt. Then Adele turned to me and said, "Oh, Barbara, why can't you ever enjoy anything?"

Karl let out a little snort. I did not know what to say—I was too astonished to defend myself.

How dare she? How dare she say such a thing to her own sister, and in front of these strangers?

I had wanted to enjoy myself—I just wasn't as good as other people at doing trivial things like skating. I had spent too much of my life working to have learned how to be amused.

I was grateful to be sitting on the very end of the sleigh. I could look out at the snow and up at the moon without anyone seeing the tears slide down my cheek. Why couldn't I have enjoyed myself? It had been a relief to be out of the cabin, but I had felt so afraid. It had been that cave—it had frightened me—I had been cooped up in the cabin all winter, and then I was afraid of being cooped up inside that cold cave—that must have been it. But no, I could not blame the cave or the cabin. I was never happy. I had not been happy all my life it seemed, and no one liked me. Even Adele, my own sister, found me nearly intolerable. How could I bear it any longer? How could God have taken my father from me and brought me to this miserable land when He knew how little joy had already existed in my life?

Hardly anyone said a word as we drove home. We went more slowly now. In the moonlight, the snow looked blue. I remembered a Christmas picture I had once seen, of Bethlehem with the star shining above it, and all the earth had looked blue around it, and I had told my father it was a silly picture because it did not snow in Bethlehem. I had been critical and unable to enjoy the picture's silent beauty. And now I remembered my vision of the desert—it had appeared blue—I understood now that sand or snow could look blue in the moonlight—I had thought the picture had reflected snow, but it was only sand. My tears stopped; the sleigh felt as if it were floating on something blue, perhaps a cloud rather than snow or desert sand. I felt peaceful, sleepy; I imagined my father being there, holding me.

The sleigh gave a little jolt. I opened my eyes to find we were back at the cabin.

Ben and Karl climbed out of the sleigh and then helped Adele down.

"Do you want to come in and eat something?" she asked the boys.

I was grateful when Ben said, "No, we have to get back to the camp. We have an early start tomorrow morning."

I climbed out of the sleigh by myself while they had their backs to me. Then I shook each one's hand and said, "Thank you so much."

"We'll have to do it again sometime," said Adele.

"If we can borrow our friend's sleigh again," said Karl.

I was too tired to stand out in the cold and discuss it, so I went inside. I left the door open behind me, assuming Adele would follow. But by the time I had the kerosene lantern lit, I realized only Karl had followed me inside, and he had shut the door behind him.

For a moment, I was afraid—had he sought this moment alone with me?

"How about I start a fire for you before we leave?" he said.

"Oh, you don't have to. I can do it."

"No, you're tired, Miss Traugott. Let me do it."

"All right," I said. "Thank you."

I went to the cupboard and occupied myself with pretending to put things away, as if I were too busy to talk to him. But when I could think of nothing more to do, and Adele still did not come inside, I understood; Karl had not come in to speak to me—he had not wanted to interrupt a private conversation between Ben and Adele. For a moment, I thought of going outside to interrupt them, but then I felt indifference, almost resignation to her loss. I sat down in Adele's rocking chair while Karl remained crouched before the fire, poking at it, though it blazed nicely. We sat there in silence; I felt everything was all right after all. Ben was a nice young man—he would treat my sister well. That was more important than money. She was lucky to have found him. I felt sleepy, and though I fought against it, my eyes finally closed.

I snapped awake when the door opened. Adele had entered. She looked at Karl a moment. Then he said, "Goodnight," and went outside, apparently thinking I was asleep so he need not bid me goodbye. Adele latched the door behind him, and then she leaned back against it.

"I'm tired," I said before she could speak. "Let's go to bed."

She could tell me about her engagement in the morning, when I was thinking more clearly.

"All right," she replied, but she still leaned against the door.

I pushed myself out of the rocking chair and wearily climbed the stairs. I was asleep before she came up to bed.

PART III

1

Three days passed. During that time, I kept replaying in my mind Adele's words, "Oh, Barbara, why can't you ever enjoy anything?" Rather than be angry now, I grew distressed because I knew the words were true; I did not enjoy anything; I was always too full of fear. Adele could find pleasure in the simplest things, while I—in the same miserable circumstances—could scarcely sustain a minute of happiness. I wished I had tried harder to ice skate, if only because it had gotten me out of this wretched cabin. If the boys took us again, I was determined to do better; perhaps if it had been warmer, I would have enjoyed myself—but that was just an excuse, and had it been any warmer, the ice would have been melting so we could not skate.

Of course, I also wondered what had been said between Adele and Ben when we returned home that night—I had thought maybe he had asked her to marry him—but she said nothing, and I was so angry with myself that I was not up to questioning her. I felt I needed to understand why I found so little joy in life, and I could not bear to think my joy would be lessened if she left me. But after a couple of days of berating myself, I noticed Adele was more quiet than usual—

she was always quiet for a day or so after she saw Ben—quiet in a contented sort of humming way. But now she seemed to be moping, and he had not been absent long. I had wondered whether they might be secretly engaged, but she would not mope if that were the case. I wondered whether she might be angry at me—angry because she felt guilty about leaving me, yet anxious to leave because she found my company intolerable. Finally, I could not bear the extended silence any longer.

"I imagine Ben and Karl will come again any day now," I said.

We were eating supper. She did not even acknowledge I had spoken. I had been looking at my plate, but now I raised my head to see her staring at the floor. I waited a full minute. Then I could not stop myself.

"Won't you speak to me at all?" I asked. "Am I that awful to be around?" I could not believe our sisterly bond had become so frail.

"Barbara, I—"

She was trembling. Was she ill and only keeping it from me so I would not worry? What would I do then? Should I apologize for my outburst?

"They're not coming back."

"What?"

I did not comprehend at first. Then like a bolt of lightning, fear gripped me; it welled right up in my chest, then into my throat, choking me. It was only late February—winter would last another month, probably two considering what I had heard about Upper Michigan winters, and I had already learned the winter was as bad or worse than I had been told. Would we have enough wood? What would we eat? I had not succeeded in shooting anything with the rifle. Why had I allowed myself to rely on men, men who were mere strangers? And now they had abandoned us.

"They're not coming back," Adele repeated.

"Why not?"

"They're moving to another logging camp."

"What do you mean? Their whole camp is moving?"

"No—just—just the two of them—Ben says he can't come here anymore—it upsets him too much."

"Upsets him?" I was so astounded I lost control of my tongue. "Of course, it upsets him to be parted from you—he's like a sick puppy, he's so in love with you, but you could—" But I could not say it, could not say they could get married. I knew I should be happy that they loved one another, but since I could never enjoy anything, I found it impossible to wish her happiness with him. But why did they not get married? They were just tormenting each other by staying apart.

"No," she nearly whispered, the blood flowing from her cheeks. "It's not like—it's not love."

"What?" I said in astonishment.

"He can't love me."

"Can't love you? Why else is he always here?"

"I thought he loved me; part of me still thinks he does, but he just can't accept love—just can't let it into his life. I don't know why. I love him. I'd die for him."

She started to sob so loud it shook me with fear. It wasn't even sobbing. It was wailing. I couldn't stand it. I jumped up. We never showed affection to each other, but I tried to put my arm around her shoulder to make her stop.

"Don't. Don't," was all I could say. I didn't know how to comfort her. I just wanted this horrible moment to end.

After a couple of minutes, she reached into her pocket for her handkerchief to blow her nose. I drew my arm away, then just stood there, not knowing what to say.

"I don't understand, Barbara. I just don't understand." She wiped her eyes, only to break into another sob.

"What happened?" I asked. "What did he say to you? I remember you stayed outside with Ben after Karl and I came inside." I did not tell her I had suspected a secret engagement—how had I been so wrong?

She got up and went to the water bucket for a drink. Then she went to her rocking chair, leaving her supper untouched. I sank into her kitchen chair and waited—waited to hear why we had been abandoned to winter's cruelty by two men I now thought equally cruel.

"Adele, what did Ben say to you?" I repeated after she blew her nose. When she finally spoke, she sounded as if she were in a trance.

"He said, 'It's no good, Adele. I just can't be with you. I don't know why. I can't explain it. I just know I can't.'" And then still another sob burst forth.

I was too impatient to wait for her to get a hold of herself. "Why can't he explain it to you?" I asked. "He couldn't possibly have said only that. He has to have a reason! You have a right to know after he's been leading you on all these months!"

She closed her eyes. To rein in my frustration, I got up to poke the fire. I was okay for a moment, but then I gave into anger and threw the poker on the floor. She did not even act startled. She opened her eyes but remained silent. I went back to my chair. I was enraged. Like a man, I took my fist and pounded on the table.

"I'll never be able to understand it!" I shouted. "Never."

"Barbara!" Adele cried, shocked by my behavior. "It's not your heart that's broken!"

I restrained myself from lashing out, "But I'll starve because your heart is." I could not hurt her like that, not when she was hurting. I wanted her to be angry like me—that would be better for her anyway. "How can you not be angry?" I asked. "Can you understand it? Can you understand how a man who obviously loves you can suddenly abandon you like this?"

"I don't know," she sighed. "Maybe. I'm trying to."

"Maybe? If maybe you can understand it, then he must have given you some reason."

"No, he didn't give me a reason—he just said it didn't feel right for him to be with me. I know him better than you do, Barbara. I know he's a good, kind man. I think he's just afraid to trust people. He's never had anyone he could trust—except Karl; he did tell me he trusts Karl."

"Karl? Why would he trust Karl and not you?"

"I'm not even sure it's that he doesn't trust me, Barbara. I think maybe he doesn't trust himself—I think he's afraid to get close to people, afraid even of being loved, as if he doesn't believe it's possible that anyone could love him."

"Why? What's wrong with him?"

"I—he just—he told me things about himself that I don't think he ever shared with anyone before. I feel as if I would be breaking his confidence if I told you."

"You don't need to keep his secrets. How can you defend him after he's treated you this way?"

"I don't understand why he feels the way he does, but I know he doesn't want to hurt me. He doesn't understand it himself—he told me that. I know it's not because he wants it this way—he just can't help how he feels. I know if he were able to, he would love me forever."

I seethed inside. I breathed in through my teeth. If Ben were present,

I would have slapped him. I almost wanted to slap her. She was such a fool to make excuses for him. He had lied to her, led her on, amused himself until he grew tired of her. I didn't want to believe that, but what other explanation could there be? He obviously had no concern for her feelings. How could she have been so stupid not to see it? I had suspected it all along—I should have just come out and warned her—but I wouldn't blame myself for this—she would not have listened to me anyway—she would have only told me that because I was unhappy, I did not want anyone else to be happy. I knew that was how she saw me, but it wasn't true—not totally. I wanted both of us to be happy, but I also wanted us to survive. She would have run off with that scoundrel given the chance, but wasn't she better off with me? Wasn't I the only one she could depend on, the only one willing to protect her, despite all the trouble she caused me?

And then she burst out crying again. I loved her, but I could not comfort her then. I buried my head in my arms on the table, and again I wondered how God could have allowed us to fall into such degradation.

I heard her blow her nose. Then the rocking chair squeaked and her footsteps approached me. I did not want to face her. Did she realize we would probably starve now? How could I even care about her broken heart under these circumstances?

"Barbara, I'm not upset for myself," she said. She put her hand on my shoulder to comfort me. I was surprised. She was the one hurting, and usually far more selfish than me. I didn't need her comfort, but I raised my head and stared into the fire as I listened to her. "I'm crying more because I know he's hurting, and I want to comfort him, but I don't know how. And even if I did know, I don't think he would let me."

I wanted to tell her to cry for herself—she was the one who had been mistreated; she was the one who would starve before winter was over.

"Barbara, perhaps I shouldn't tell you this," she said, "but I love him so much I can't bear for you to think ill of him. Please don't say mean things about him—that's like putting a bullet through my heart. Try to feel kindness toward him, or at least to forgive him because he didn't mean to hurt me. I've been hurting for three days, but now that I've told you, I find I don't have any anger toward him."

I wiped my own tears with my sleeve. I did not understand where her tenderness came from. She must be withholding something from me. If she would tell me everything, then perhaps I could understand—then perhaps I could go to Ben and try to make things right. But I wouldn't know what to do until I knew the whole truth.

"Adele, there must be some reason for why he feels that way. Are you sure he didn't tell you anything more?"

"No, he didn't give me any real reason, but I think I understand a little from what he told me before—things he told me when you were sick or later, when we were outside together alone when he would come to visit. I did keep some things from you because he told them to me in confidence."

"Tell me now, please," I begged.

"Barbara, he told me—" Her voice faltered as if what she were to say was so awful she could barely speak it. "When he was a little boy, he said his father used to beat him horribly—even to the point of breaking his arm one time. That's why he left his father when he was only twelve, because he couldn't take his father's abuse anymore. I know lots of children get beaten, but Barbara, we don't know what that's like—we can't know what that did to him. Father was always kind to us, even if he weren't overly affectionate. No one ever raised a hand against us. One day, Barbara, while you were ill, Ben and I went for a walk, and I told him how much I missed Father, especially since you were sick because Father had always cared for us during our illnesses. As I started to tell him how good Father had always been to us, I was surprised because he started crying. I didn't know what to say then. I asked him what was wrong. He said he had never known anything like a father's love. His mother was the only person who had ever really been kind to him, and she died when he was little; he had always tried to be kind to people, but he had never received any kindness back until he met Karl and then us, and he felt he was trying to be kind to you and me just in hopes we would be kind to him. He said that until he met me, he had even quit believing in God. His mother had taught him to read the Bible before she died, but he had always concentrated on the parts about God's anger, and he felt if God were supposed to be like a father, then God must always be angry like his own father. He had never actually read the Twenty-Third Psalm until that first day he was with us and I asked him to read it; then he said something shifted inside of him—he suddenly realized God might actually be loving and good—that the Lord was his Shepherd, guiding him down the path to good, and perhaps the Lord had even led him to us that night of the storm so he could realize what life was really supposed to be like—that life could be a blessing. Can you imagine going for years, not feeling as if you had ever known any kindness? Barbara, his father actually killed his dog. His father got drunk and angry one night and flew into a rage and beat Ben and when the dog tried to protect him, his father killed it. Ben left that night after his father fell asleep because he feared that otherwise his father would kill him next. Barbara, how can I be angry with him after he went through all that?"

I tried to comprehend all this—to see Ben as a poor abused little boy—but he was such a large, powerfully built man that I found it hard to have sympathy for him. He had probably just exaggerated his sufferings to get sympathy from my sister, to manipulate her, to make her fall in love with him—but if that were true, why had he abandoned her now? Much as I wanted to hate him, I had to admit I did not believe he had ever been anything but a gentleman in her company, at least until the night he had abandoned her.

"Adele," I said, "his childhood was over years ago. I don't see how the way his father treated him has any bearing on how he treated you. I just don't understand." But to some extent I did understand—I was still angry with Ben, and no one had ever been unkind to me—but I had often felt my father had loved Adele better, no matter how much I tried to please him. I understood why Ben would be kind to people in hopes they would be kind to him. I had done everything I could to win Father's praise and approval. Adele had done nothing, yet I had always suspected he loved her best.

"Ben should love you all the more," I said, "because you were kind to him. And I know he does love you—it was written all over his face whenever he saw you. I thought he wanted to marry you."

"He never made me any promises like that," said Adele. "He never mentioned marriage."

"He didn't need to. It was implied by his constantly coming to see you—by the way he always looked at you. He wronged you by leading you on. You wasted your time. If he hadn't been here—you could have—well, Mr. Smith was interested in you, but Ben scared him off, and—"

"Really, Barbara! Mr. Smith!" she spat out the name.

She would be lucky to get Mr. Smith now, or any man, after Ben had ruined her chances, and Mr. Smith had probably destroyed our reputations in town. Although I had momentarily softened toward Ben, now my anger rose up as I realized he may have destroyed our lives, or left us to starve at the very least. I could not listen any further to Adele defending him. I had to get away from her. I felt as if I could walk all the way to Marquette at that moment, snow or no snow. I got up, threw on my coat, and went out the door, slamming it behind me. I knew that would upset her, but I had to go before I said worse words I would later regret.

It was still early in the evening—now that February was almost over, the days were getting longer. Even after we ate supper now, we still had a little bit of daylight. Last night, there had been a full moon, so I imagined it would be light enough for me to see if I decided to walk into town and never come back. But I knew I would not do so, even if Marquette had only been a mile or two. I would not leave Adele behind, and she knew I wouldn't. I could not be that heartless—not when she was hurting so much—even though since she had met Ben, she had never once given thought to what I might want.

I did pity her. She must be embarrassed to have fallen in love with a man who could cast her off so easily without even feeling the need to give an explanation. It didn't really matter what his reasons were, or how badly he had been hurt in his past. Let Adele feel sympathy for him. I had to figure out how we were going to survive—and it was partly my fault we were in this situation—I had allowed us to become dependent on the boys as our providers. But before I could do anything, I decided I would walk off my anger.

Since the night of the storm when I had discovered Ben, I had always made sure we had enough firewood so I didn't have to go out at night. I was afraid the dark would prevent me from seeing a bear or wolf, even though they should be hibernating. I was so scared to be alone in the forest that even in the daylight I doubt I could have walked to town. I wished now I had brought the rifle with me—I could barely shoot it, but it would have made me feel safe.

What a fool I had been to think two women could live in a cabin by themselves all winter? Why had I not thought about such dangers the day we came? I had been frightened all along, but more frightened to admit my fears than to be logical and sell the property and find work in Marquette or return to Cincinnati. I had been afraid of what people would think—afraid I would be looked down upon for working, and for not having a husband—and especially afraid I might have to ask for charity from others. Any of those things, I now knew, would have been better than Adele and I starving to death. My false pride had put us in this situation—not Ben or Karl. As the older sister, I was supposed to be the responsible one, and I had failed in every way—from finding us a reasonable living situation, to not forbidding Adele's involvement with a young man who might be a gypsy's son for all we knew.

And now, because I had already made so many wrong decisions, I saw no options before me. I wanted to cry to God for a solution—but He would not answer me. I would only end up with a face of frozen tears. And then I heard a wolf howl, and trembling, I turned around and ran back into the cabin.

Hardly a word was spoken between us when I went in. Adele looked as if she wanted to speak to me, but I was too upset to talk. I grumbled about the cold, and how numb my hands felt, then stood before the fire with my back to her. Only when my hands were too warm to bear the heat any longer did I go to clear the table. We had hardly eaten anything off our plates, which was good—we had no one to bring us more food, but at least we would have leftovers tomorrow.

When I had cleaned up everything, I looked over to where she sat, staring into the fire.

I was afraid to talk to her. Afraid she would cry, afraid I would cry, or lose my temper again. It was too much of a shock, all this. I figured I would feel better in the morning, so I muttered, "I'm going to bed. I'm really tired."

Then I walked past her and went upstairs. I listened for a few moments to see whether she would follow, then gave up and crawled into bed. I thought about shouting down to her to put out the fire—after all, who would chop wood for us now? But I decided it was better just to leave her alone and that I should sleep on the situation. By morning, I might be over my anger enough to figure out how we would survive until the snow melted and we could get back into town. Then I would sell the place and work in town—whatever was necessary so at least we wouldn't starve.

Adele sat up late that night. She started to sit up late every night—burning far more firewood than we could afford, but I did not reprimand her. I should have been worried, but I no longer had the energy to be upset. If we were lucky, we might have an early, warm spring. I almost did not care anymore. During the day, I busied myself with what work I could find about the cabin. We both made excuses to go outside alone, more to be away from the constant pressure of each other's company than from a need for water, firewood, or fresh air. Even when I wanted to talk to her, I did not know what to say. I knew she needed time to grieve. I had never been in love, but I knew how it felt to lose someone, for I had still not allowed myself to grieve for Father. I understood that Ben's absence was like a loved one's death for her.

Days passed as she moped about the house. Some days, sharp

words nearly fell from my tongue, words of frustration more than anger, because she would sleep late and do nothing to help me. If I had let my anger take verbal form, it would have been to curse Ben—after all, Adele was my sister, and I loved her. It hurt me to see her in pain so deep she could not speak of it, and I hurt more because she felt I was not someone easy to speak to, but I did not know how to change that now.

One morning I went downstairs to make breakfast while she was still in bed. As I walked past the rocking chair, my eye caught a slip of white paper peeking out from beneath the cushion. I instantly suspected she had hid it there. I heard the bedsprings creak, so I dared not look at the paper right then, when she might catch me, but I was desperate to know what it was. We only had a few pieces of paper, which we kept in the back of the Bible, so if she had written down anything, she would have kept it there, or in one of the books Ben and Karl had given us—how I hated during those days when she would sit for hours reading *The Courtship of Miles Standish*, knowing full well it reminded her of Ben. She had only slid a piece of paper under that cushion to hide it from me; there could be no other reason. But her trick had not succeeded; even if she now hid the paper away somewhere else before I could read it, I would find it and learn the truth of what it contained— perhaps it was a love letter he had written, or something perhaps that would make me understand what had happened between them.

When she came downstairs, I tried to act nonchalant and not look at the chair cushion. However, when she was not looking, I kept glancing over to make sure it was there. She had not yet noticed it was visible, or else when my back was turned, she would have slid it farther under the cushion, or hidden it in her dress.

By mid-afternoon, I could barely stand my curiosity. After an hour of trying to think of some way to get her from the room, I finally said, "Adele, you look tired. Why don't you go upstairs and rest?"

"I am feeling a little sleepy," she said. "I think it's just because it's such a cold day."

"Go take a nap," I said. "Now that March has come, we need to be careful; our bodies get confused when we have a warm day, then a really cold one."

"Maybe I'll just lie down for an hour," she replied. "That couldn't hurt."

Determined not to glance at the slip of paper, I followed her face as she stood up. She really did look a little pale, and she shuffled her feet as she walked to the stairs.

"Have a good sleep," I called after her. I remained in my chair as I heard her lie down on the bed. I waited until in the stillness of the winter afternoon, I heard her breathing grow gentler so I knew she was asleep.

Then, slowly rising from my chair, stepping gingerly to avoid creaking floorboards, I crossed to the rocker and quietly pulled the paper from beneath the cushion. As I touched it, I realized it wasn't just paper—it was a photograph. On the back was writing, but first I turned it over—yes, it was Ben with all his glorious blond hair—even in black and white, he looked a very Adonis. How could anyone so beautiful be so cruel? How could she help but to love him, no matter how he tortured her?

Hard knowledge—hard to know he had given her his picture—hard to know she had not confided in me. Even harder to think she had probably sighed over the picture every minute I was not looking, making herself all the more lovesick for him. He would not have given her the photograph if he had not had intentions toward her; he had broken his promise, even if that promise had not been spoken; he had proclaimed his love by his constant attentions to her.

The back of the photograph was signed "To Adele. Love, Ben." That was proof right there that he loved her! But most horrible of all, scribbled in her own tiny handwriting, so I could barely read it, were verses she must have written since he had abandoned her. While I had been outside, trying to chop wood to keep us warm, worrying what we would eat, she had been sitting inside, obsessing over him.

> My beautiful Apollo,
> I tremble at your sight, for you are almost a god to me.
> You are the beautiful light in my life of darkness.
> You are the promise of warm summer in my cold winter.
> My golden-crowned Apollo, you fill my heart with warmth.
> You are the splendor of my life.
> If not quite a god, you are the gift God put in my life
> A sign of His Love for me,
> His assurance of the Love to come in the next life
> When nothing will separate us.
> We spent only a few days in each other's presence,
> Yet that is only a foretaste of the happiness
> We will know in the lifetime where we shall never part.
> I love you. I love you.
> I will always love you.
> I love you purely and wholly and unashamedly.
> Thank you for your presence.
> Your love will keep me warm through the winter of life
> Until we meet in Paradise.

I wanted to cry out in frustration—how could she write such a thing? I wanted to toss it into the fire. But destroying his photo and her love dirge would not destroy the pain eating at her heart. Why couldn't she reconcile herself to his loss and admit he had betrayed her? She needed to be angry at him. Then she could go on with her life. I had anger enough for both of us, but my anger could not ease her pain.

I sat fuming, reliving in my mind the whole situation from the day she had first met Ben. Only when I heard the bed creak upstairs did I quickly jump up from the rocking chair and shove the photograph back under the cushion. I returned to my kitchen chair, and quickly started working on the quilt I had put off finishing for fear my only task would be completed, and then I would be bored all winter long. As I waited for her to come downstairs, I tried to control my anger—I made excuses for her. I told myself she would not have hidden the picture except that she feared my disapproval. I should have been a better sister, easier to talk to. And now she apparently had no self-control over the burning love she felt for Ben; she was ashamed of her infatuation, but she had no one to help her sort it out. That sorry verse was her attempt to release her pain by putting it into words. I did not know how to talk to her about it—but I would try to be kinder to her. And as soon as I could, I would get her out of this cabin, where his memory only made the situation worse.

I did not know what I would do when we got to town—probably sell the cabin and live on the money until we found work. It did not matter how we lived in town. We would manage. We just had to get out of this cabin. Once we were in town, Adele would meet other men, men just as handsome as Ben—well, I wasn't sure that was possible, but almost as handsome, and certainly wealthier—men who were able to appreciate her, to take care of her. Maybe Mr. Smith could still be won over to buy the property, and to offer me a fair price if Adele would have him. But no, she wouldn't have to stoop to that. She was a beautiful girl—hopefully she would not keep crying and ruin her looks. She would find a good man—I would find her a good man. I would take the time to look around for a goodhearted one—one who would let me live with them. After how Ben had mistreated her, she would be relieved to find a man who truly loved her. That was what I wanted. For her to be happy. I would find her a husband to love her. It was partly my fault that I had not stopped her from becoming attached to Ben. Once in town, I would be wiser. It could all still work out for us. It was not too late yet—after all, we were still alive. In a few weeks we could make it into town. We wouldn't starve that soon.

When Adele came downstairs, I pretended to be busy sewing my quilt. I did not glance up until I realized she was standing motionless before the fire. When I raised my head, I saw how pale she still was.

"Barbara."

Her eyes told me she had something more to tell me.

"Barbara, I—"

At first I thought she would cry. Instead, she took a minute to catch her breath. Then she came and stood beside me, again putting her hand on my shoulder, as if she were trying to draw on my strength.

"Sit down, Adele. Then tell me." I tried to sound gentle, but it came out like an order; I winced at the harsh sound of my voice.

She sat down at the table. I waited patiently. After a minute, she took the far end of my quilt in her hands.

"You've always done such beautiful work, Barbara. You used to sew all the time at home. I always found it comforting to see you sewing, sitting in Mother's old chair, so that it felt almost as if I had not lost her at all. Barbara, I know we've had our differences, but you've always been like a second mother to me, more so than a sister."

"You're my little sister, so I've tried to take care of you," I said.

"I know you have. You've always done the best you knew how."

A tear slowly trickled down her cheek. I was relieved when it did not turn into hysterical sobbing. I hoped the worst was over now—that her healing had begun.

"What do you need to say, Adele?"

This time my voice did sound gentle, although I felt very impatient, anxious to hear she was ready to quit being foolish over a boy she had scarcely known.

"Barbara," she began, her voice hesitant, yet rushing forward with the words, "when Ben came—I—I was just missing Father so much, and Ben seemed to understand. I don't know why, but I just couldn't talk to you about Father. I don't mean to be critical of you, Barbara. You know I love you, but sometimes you can be so stern, and I was afraid that if I did talk to you about Father, you might break down, and I didn't think either of us could bear that."

"I understand," I said gently.

"You're not being stern now, Barbara. I appreciate that. What I'm trying to say is that when Ben came, it felt as if we had a family again. Not like Father was here—no one could ever replace Father—but Ben, and Karl to a lesser extent, felt like family. Maybe only because they were the only ones who came to see us, so I probably depended on them too much, but—"

She hesitated. To encourage her, I said, "I know what you mean—I was always glad when they came to visit. It sort of brightened the day."

"Really? I didn't think you liked them that much, but they were so kind I was sure you would grow to like them—and—and—"

Her tone revealed that all she had just said was only a prelude for what was to come.

"Barbara, there's a good reason why you should like Ben."

"Yes, he helped take care of me when I was ill."

I knew that was not the reason although I hoped it were nothing more. I felt afraid to learn what reason she meant.

"Not just that, Barbara." She took a deep breath. "When I said Ben was like family, well, it's because he is family."

Did she mean what I thought? Oh, but—they couldn't possibly have gotten married while I was sick. How else could he be family? She had not been out of my sight more than a few minutes at a time except during my illness.

"Barbara," she said, "you know this cabin was Uncle Shepard's."

And then I understood before she could finish.

"Barbara, the night you found him in the snow, Ben had purposely been coming here. He thought this was his cabin now because he had just learned his father was dead. Barbara, Ben is Uncle Shepard's son. He's our cousin. His mother was our Aunt Marie. You know he told us his mother died when he was little, and that his father was abusive to him—Uncle Shepard was a cruel man. Ben said he wore down Aunt Marie's spirit until she could take it no longer and died, and then after Uncle killed Ben's dog, Ben feared he would end up dead too if he stayed here. He didn't see his father again after that, but when he heard in Marquette that his father was dead, he came out here to see the cabin. It really belongs to him. I know Uncle left it to Father in his will, so legally it's ours, but if Uncle hadn't been so hateful, he would have left it to Ben."

"All this time that Ben stayed here," I wondered aloud, "he never said a word of this to me!" But it made sense, for he had so easily found the second pair of snowshoes that first day, and later, he had known where Uncle kept his bullets. "But didn't Ben resent having us in his home?" I asked.

"No. One day he nearly let it slip that his last name was Shepard, but you didn't seem to notice. He sensed you didn't like him, so he didn't want you to feel obligated to him by telling you the truth. He understood we had nowhere else to go, so he wouldn't stake his claim to the cabin."

All this time that I had been angry at him, we had been in his debt—living in his home, living on his charity. That made me even angrier—that I owed an obligation to the man who had broken my sister's heart. But why did any of this matter? Cousins marry. What difference did this make? It did not explain why he had abandoned Adele.

"If it's Ben's cabin by rights, then we'll leave so he can have it," I said. But I said the words in anger. I wanted to leave, but I wanted to sell the cabin. If we let Ben have it, we would have absolutely nothing; how would we live?

"No, Barbara. He doesn't want it. It's ours for the rest of our lives if we wish, or we can do whatever we like with it, even sell it. That's what Ben wants."

If he were going to be so stupid as to let us have the cabin, then I would sell it. I would get whatever money I could for it. Then we would move far, far away, far from Ben and all this wretched land.

"But I still don't understand," I replied. "Why won't he come again? He's our cousin. Did he really love you, or was it just some sort of family affection?"

"He did love me, Barbara. I'm certain of it. He even told me he loved me, but he also said he could not be with me, even though he could not explain why. I can't understand it except that maybe he would rather be in the woods chopping down trees than stuck in a cabin with me. I don't doubt at all that he loves me, so it hurts so much that it's almost unbearable at times. I constantly ache, as if I'm breaking apart inside. I never believed people could die of broken hearts, but now I know they can."

"But you won't, Adele."

"I don't know, Barbara. I'm not sure how I'll go on. I feel like I want to die."

"I need you," I said. "That's a reason."

She moved her chair beside me and laid her head on my shoulder. It should have been awkward, yet part of me wanted to reach up to stroke her hair—only if I had, my quilt would have dropped on the floor. For a moment, I did close my eyes; I remembered as a little girl how Mother used to brush and braid our hair; once after Mother's death, I had tried to brush Adele's hair, but she had shouted no and run to hide under her bed. Tears now welled up into my eyes. I had only sought to comfort her over Mother's loss, but I felt she had rejected me, even though she had simply not wanted to be unfaithful to Mother's memory. She had not been able to bear being comforted over Mother's loss, just as now I could not bear to discuss Father.

We are so foolish in this life, so afraid to show how much we love by letting ourselves mourn. In those days elaborate rules existed for what we should wear to express sincerity in our mourning, and at different points in the grieving period, different pieces of clothing, different shades of dark colors were appropriate, as if grief could be locked into a timeframe. Since then, mourning has become even more inhumane, a funeral a few days after the loved one's death, and then we are expected to go on with life. I never did allow myself to mourn for

Mother or Father. But that winter, Adele mourned for Ben, and even I felt pain at the loss of a family member I had never really known. As winter came to its end, each day I found my blood boiled less when I thought of him.

After a moment, Adele went back upstairs, and I went to see about making us something to eat. We spoke no more of Ben.

I left Adele alone to mope after that. I hoped she would rid herself of enough grief that by spring we could go into Marquette and start over. In the weeks that followed, somehow I managed to feed us, to melt snow for us to drink, to find berries to eat, and even some meat, as I will explain. All that time, I had to encourage Adele to eat. And often, I found myself thinking of Uncle Shepard.

When we had first come to this miserable, isolated cabin, I had often wondered how Uncle Shepard could have chosen such a life. Now I realized he had created his own misery, and then surrendered to it. For whatever reason, he had isolated his family in the woods. He had driven his wife to death. Then rather than go to town with his son, he had brooded about his cabin, making life a nightmare for Ben and himself.

In his sulking, self-hatred, and the intensified guilt he must have felt over his wife's death, Uncle Shepard had taken out his own misery on his son, forcing his son to abandon him as well. He must have been a horrible man, to drive away everyone who loved him. When I had first learned that he left Father the cabin, I had thought perhaps he felt some affection for my father, and even for his wife's nieces, but leaving us the cabin had only been a last act of hatred against his son. Yet I pitied him. I did not know what had caused Uncle to be so cruel, but part of me identified with him—I often feared I would also drive away those who loved me—that I would succumb to an equally lonely end.

I was terrified Adele might marry and leave me, and so I had tried to control her relationships with men, but apparently, that had only hurt her more. I could not keep her from loving anyone. If I did, she would grow angry and leave me anyway. I had not known what to do when Ben was here, and I did not know what to do now. I could not figure it out. For the first time that winter, I began to pray sincerely for an answer.

Adele barely ate in those days. She repeatedly said she was not hungry, so when I did find food for us, I would end up eating two-thirds of it before it spoiled. I could see she was losing weight. Two weeks had passed since the boys had abandoned us, and we had had no meat after the first couple of days. And the bread they had last brought us had grown so hard it was nothing but crumbs now. After a few days of nothing but snow to eat, I went out with the rifle. Somehow I managed not to have it backfire and knock me over again, but I always missed my targets, and I never saw anything more substantial than a dove or squirrel. Never a deer—though I could not have dragged it back to the cabin had I been so lucky. Then one morning, I saw a rabbit sitting beside the cabin while I was at the woodpile. I watched it a moment before it disappeared down a hole in the snow. I became determined to catch it. I rigged up a crate Ben and Karl had once brought supplies in. I placed a stick beneath it to hold it up. I found a dry crust of bread to put beneath it, and I tied a long string to the stick. I had placed this contraption just a couple of feet from the rabbit's hole, and I thought my idea quite ingenious. But my work was only partially done. One evening as dark fell, I sat behind a tree in the numbing cold for three hours, waiting for the stupid rabbit. And he was stupid, because eventually he appeared, and he sniffed about until he saw the bread and went under the crate. Then bang, I pulled down the crate, grabbed the rifle by my side, went up to the crate and shot him. He shrieked like a baby—the sound would haunt my dreams for the next two nights—but at that moment, I was so hungry I did not care. He was fat enough to feed us for three nights—that was all that mattered.

I brought my prize inside the house and began to skin him.

When Adele came over to the counter, she cried, "Oh Barbara, stop!"

"Why?" I asked.

She said, "I can't bear to hurt something after I've been hurt so much."

"Well, he's dead now so it can't hurt him anymore," I told her. "Go sit down and I'll tell you when it's time to eat." She went upstairs, sobbing. I ignored her. She did come down when I called her to supper. She looked unwilling to eat, but I sat down and started chewing. After a few minutes, Adele picked up her fork and joined me. Whatever it took, I was not going to let my sister die of starvation. If I could just get her to live through each day, we would make it until spring. Surely something better would come then.

One morning, I told Adele that soon we should be able to walk into Marquette. A month had passed since we had seen the boys—March was nearly over, and a couple of different times, we had watched the snow melt in the late afternoon sun. Just the day before, it must have been forty degrees, and while we could not yet see the road to the cabin, patches of grass were visible around the tree trunks, and some low spots in the yard had become pools of slush. Once the road was accessible by foot, we would walk into town. It would be a long, tiresome walk, but we would do it. Our few possessions would be safe in the cabin since we had seen no one all winter, except Karl and Ben, and I doubted anyone else would come this way before I asked Mr. Smith to come collect our trunk. We would ask the Whitmans to put us up until we sold the cabin. In the meantime, I would pay them whatever I could and look for work.

But when I told Adele all these plans, she said, "Barbara, I don't think I can do all that."

"We don't have any other choice," I replied. "Even if we sold the cabin, we couldn't afford to buy a house in town, and if we don't work, soon all the money from the cabin will be gone to pay rent at the boarding house."

"I'm sorry, Barbara. You can do what you like, but I won't go to work in Marquette."

"You won't have to work long. We'll find you a husband," I said. I saw no reason to tread softly around the topic. She would get over Ben once she was around other people; plenty of men in Marquette would take an interest in her.

"No, Barbara," she repeated.

"What do you mean 'No'?" I demanded. "What do you intend to do then? Live here by yourself, hoping Ben will return? I won't have it."

"No, I won't stay here. Barbara, I know you don't understand, but I still love Ben. I can't marry any other man. I don't feel he wronged me—the entire world might say so, but I know in my heart that was never his intention. He is good, Barbara. So very good that if he could marry me, I know he would. But I won't have any other husband."

"How can you say that? How can you say that when he—"

"Shush, Barbara," she said, silencing me for the first time in her life. "What I mean is that I now understand no man can fulfill the aching in my heart, not even Ben. I love him. I'll always love him. But if he came back now, I'm not sure I would marry him, even though I'm certain he loves me. That last night we were together, he told me he loved me. I thought then that he only said it to comfort me, but the more I think about it, the more I'm certain he meant it. Now I find that his love has freed me; it's made me realize I don't need anyone's love to be free. Barbara, do you remember in Catholic school when we had to read St. Teresa of Avila's *Life*? I remember her saying something about how she could never love anyone who did not love God more, and that no person could replace God for her. I know Ben and I will always love each other, and I know in Paradise we will be together again, but for now, I think having known Ben's love was enough—enough to teach me that loving another person is not enough, and I think—no, I know I love God more."

Her words frightened me, although I was not yet sure why. My voice cracked as I asked, "What do you mean?" I had never heard her talk like this. I could not understand it.

"When we get back into town, I want to speak to the bishop. I'm going to ask whether he will let me enter the convent. I want to be with God and to find ways to bring others to Him, so they can know the comfort I've found in Him."

"Become a nun," I gasped, unable to fathom it. A dozen questions ran through my head. I did not know which to ask first. She had always said her prayers and read her Bible. I knew she was a good Christian, but I had never suspected she would make such a choice. She wasn't thinking logically—she needed—I didn't know what she needed, but she couldn't do this. It made no sense. And by her joining a convent, we would be parted. I had feared a man taking her, but not God. After all I had lost, did God hate me so much that He would take my sister from me, the only person I had left in the world?

"I don't understand, Adele. You can't go hide in a convent. I know you hurt over Ben, but—"

"No, Barbara. It has nothing to do with Ben anymore. I love him, and I can't love any other man, but it's not because of Ben really. It's because God wanted something more for me; what happened with Ben was God's mysterious way of bringing me to that understanding. You've always protected me, Barbara. But I don't need to be protected, and I don't need a husband to take care of me. I can take care of myself, or at least, I can rely on God to take care of me. And there are other people who need love. By knowing Ben, I've learned how to love, but not so I could love just one man. So I could love all people. I want to spread love—I want to do my Father's work. I—I don't think I have any choice. It's what I'm meant to do. It's why we had to come here, and why I met Ben, and why I had to learn this hard lesson. My heart still hurts over Ben, but I know it will soften now. I know the reason for it all."

I wanted to scream, "But what about me?" She wanted to give love, but I feared losing the only love I had left. The tears welled up in my face. My throat choked up, and I tried to repress a sob. I would have begged her not to make this choice if I could, but I found myself unable to speak.

A log broke and fell on the fire, nearly extinguishing the last of the flames. I swallowed the lump in my throat, then muttered, "I better go get some more wood."

I stood up and slid my boots onto my feet. I did not bother to put on my coat and gloves. I just wanted to get out of the cabin and away from Adele. I loved her too well to tell her what I thought of her self-sacrificial delusions. I did not want her to shut herself up in a convent because a man had rejected her. Yet the glow in her face as she spoke told me she had her heart set upon going to the convent, just as firmly as she had set it upon loving Ben. I could not keep her from loving Ben, so how could I keep her from loving God?

What would happen now? She would not marry—she would not have a family or a home. I would have no one to be with, unless I went with her to the convent, and not even God would want me for a nun—a sorry nun I would be with my temper. If God wanted her for His own, didn't He realize He must figure out what to do with me? Did He not care at all about me? Would He really abandon me to loneliness?

I skinned my hand as I tried to lift a log from the woodpile. I watched warm blood flow from the break in my skin. Having nothing to wipe it with, I bent down and clutched a handful of snow to freeze my hand and stop the bleeding. Then I just stood there, listening to the warm spring wind as it shook the trees. I felt my skirt blow against the woodpile, my bleeding hand grow numb from the snow it clutched. I stood until I shivered and knew I should go inside before Adele worried about me.

I felt all the weight of the world upon me. As soon as I resolved myself to one tragedy—be it my father's death, our life in this wretched cabin, or Ben abandoning my sister—another blow always struck me. I had survived all the other blows, but the blow of being separated from my sister—the blow I had always feared most—I did not think I could bear this one.

Exhausted, I lay my head on the woodpile. I knew I should go back inside, but my heart was breaking. She was my sister, not my lover, but I now understood how her own heart had felt like breaking over the loss of Ben. I wished I could cry just to feel relief—to let all the pain and frustration of the last several months come forth, but the hurt was so deep I could not force my tears to come.

Then I heard, at first lightly, then boldly, the sweetest bird song—I would later learn it was a whippoorwill's. The song was all the sweeter because it was the only voice, other than Adele's, that I had heard in weeks. I raised my head, transfixed by its beauty, nearly intoxicated by its singing. My thoughts reverted back to my school days and a dramatic reading I had once performed. I had forgotten most of the lines, but I knew it was from Keats' "Ode to a Nightingale," and that it could aptly be applied to the whippoorwill.

> The voice I hear this passing night was heard
>   In ancient days by emperor and clown;
> Perhaps the self-same song that found a path
>   Through the sad heart of Ruth, when, sick for home,
>   She stood in tears amid the alien corn;

I remembered Ben reading to us from the Book of Ruth; I had equated myself with Ruth, alone in an alien land, without friends, the snowbanks replacing the corn that surrounded her. I could remember no more than this most melancholy part of the poem, yet the whippoorwill's song felt cheering, and deep down inside me, a little voice said, "Remember that Ruth found her happiness."

It was nearly spring. Soon we would go to Marquette. As frightening as it was that my sister would leave me to enter the convent, could it truly be any worse than this long lonely winter? And she might change her mind. She had been through so much, and being cloistered in this cabin had separated us both from the real world. Once we were back among people, she would probably change her mind. I was almost certain she would. I breathed deeply, and asked God to help me. Then

I picked up a couple of logs and walked back to the door.

When I returned inside, Adele and I did not resume our conversation. She was sitting in the rocking chair—the fire had gone out—I would need to light another match, and there were only half a dozen left, but I did not reprimand her for not protecting the fire until I returned. As I bent down to lay a log in the fireplace, she stopped me.

"Don't, Barbara. I feel terribly warm."

"It's freezing in here," I said.

"I—I don't think I'm well."

I stood and went to feel her forehead. She was burning up.

2

I sent Adele straight to bed. I was frightened by how hot she was. I brought her up some water with snow in it to try and cool her off, and I carried up a snowball to rub against her forehead. She drank the water, but she ate nothing the remainder of the day.

I dared not sleep beside her, for if I got sick, I did not know how either of us would manage. In the morning, I found her delirious, muttering nonsensical words—I listened closely, expecting to hear Ben's name, but she might as well have been speaking a foreign language—her words were completely incoherent. All that day I sat beside her, mopping her forehead with snow wrapped in a towel to lower her fever. I prayed to God she would be all right. I had prayed yesterday that He would somehow resolve my situation, but losing my sister could not be the answer. I promised God I would not argue with Adele about going to the convent if He would only let her live. That night I could not bear to be parted from her. I lay beside her, feeling how hot she was—knowing her situation must be dangerous for the fever to last so long. I did not sleep, too worried and continually disturbed by her restless thrashing. In the early morning hours, she finally lay still, but the fever remained; I think she was utterly exhausted, all color had left her face now; her lips were starting to look gray.

Then I panicked. I dared not leave the cabin, yet I was more afraid not to get help for her. She would need medicine. Karl had brought medicine for me when I had been ill, but now no one would bring us supplies. If only Adele could have held off getting sick a couple of more weeks, we might have been back in Marquette.

But I had no time to debate or bemoan the situation. Glimpses of the road were now visible through the snow. If I were careful, I could pick out the road's path between the trees. If I only walked a short distance, I might come to where the road was clear, up out of the valley where the cabin was somewhat hid. We were only a couple of miles from the main road—if I could reach there, the snow might have melted enough for the road to be clear, so that someone might pass by on the way into town. I had to go now; I could do nothing for her if I stayed here; she would only get worse if I waited. I had no idea how long it would take me to reach Marquette, but even if I walked all day, I might get a doctor to come overnight. Surely within twenty-four hours, if she only lasted that long, she could have medicine.

Quickly, I penned a note stating I had gone to Marquette to fetch a doctor. I placed it on the chair beside the bed where she might see it; I doubted she would regain consciousness, but if she did, that would give her hope. Then I threw on my coat, gloves, and boots, and debated a minute whether I should take the snowshoes, but seeing how much slush was around the cabin, I decided they would be no practical use. Before it was fully daylight, I was off on a desperate mission, determined to reach town. No other reason than to save my sister could have made me walk through those snow-filled woods alone, but once resolved, I would not turn back.

I did not quite know where the road was. I only vaguely remembered in which direction it lay. Two miles is a long distance in the snow, especially when it crunches beneath your feet. A couple of times, my foot broke through the snow and got stuck so that I had to pull my foot from my boot, then reach down and dig the boot out of the snow; I tried to balance myself so I did not get my stocking wet, while fretting about the precious time I was losing. By the time I got the boot back on my foot, I felt hot from the exertion—it must have been forty degrees. My coat only made me sweat, so I took it off and carried it with me, which only encumbered me more. I cursed myself for being so possessive I could not just leave the coat on a tree when my sister's life was in danger, but I had no money to buy a new one if it were lost, and it was not quite spring yet.

I was so full of anxiety that when my foot again sunk into the snow, I jerked it out so quickly that my foot slipped out and I lost my balance, plummeting me face forward into the snowbank. The cold on my face stunned me, and I quickly jumped up when snow slid down my blouse. I was so hot, and sticky from sweating, and having my blouse now wet only made me more miserable. But I picked myself up; I could cry later, but for now, I had to continue on.

I trudged. That's the best word to describe it. The snow was little more than slush in many places, and when I came to what I thought was the road, I could see large mud puddles, little bodies of water that had apparently thawed and melted, then frozen over again at night. As I skirted my way around them, I could see they were thawing again in the morning sun, and if I stepped on them, I would land my boots in the water—some of the frozen puddles looked a foot deep along the hillsides.

I was growing tired and wanted to stop and rest, but there was nowhere to rest. I could not sit in the snow, and to lean against a tree would mean standing in a puddle. I thought I must have walked my two miles to the main road by now. I had seen nothing other than trees and once a squirrel, which made me wish I had brought the rifle—but that would have been extra weight to carry; hopefully, I could find food in town—I had forgotten to bring any money! How could I have been so stupid? And I should have brought the rifle because it was almost spring—the bears might be coming out of hibernation. I had not seen one all winter, but now, when I most needed to get to town, one was bound to appear—if I were attacked by a bear, my journey would do Adele no good. Even if I managed to climb a tree in my skirt, the bear would only wait below for me, and no matter how much I hollered, I was too far from civilization for anyone to hear me.

I was unsure whether I was even going in the right direction, and after the first hour, I had to stop because I could barely breathe anymore. I found a tree where the ground was dry around its trunk with little dead bushes sticking up about its base, including a wintergreen berry plant with two berries that I ate. I had not even eaten breakfast in my urgency to get to town—had I eaten, I probably would have had more strength, but I had not thought of that at the time. I looked up at the sun to check my progress. It was still morning, the sun not yet in the center of the sky, but neither was it in the east—it was in the west! I could not have been walking so long that it was two in the afternoon! No, it had to be more like ten in the morning, and that meant—I was going in the wrong direction! Somehow I must have circled around and started to head south, rather than north toward Marquette.

Panic gripped me. If I turned north now, I did not know how far east or west I was from Marquette. I might walk past the town until I reached Lake Superior's shore. Then if I kept walking along the shore, not knowing if I had missed the town, I might be heading toward or away from Marquette. I would have to backtrack my steps, although that would be wasting time.

I thought about backtracking just to the cabin, then going inside to see how Adele was. By the time I got there, she would have been alone for several hours. Even if I only backtracked enough to where I could see the sun in the east as it should have been, I had no idea how long that would take—I had thought I was walking a straight line all this while, but the trees and hills I had skirted had apparently thrown me off my intended straight line. What should I do? Just keep walking and hope to come across someone? What if I only got lost deeper in the forest, farther and farther away from civilization?

"Barbara, stop and think," I told myself. "You have to do something. Anything is better than just standing here. Even if you end up going farther from Marquette, you might find someone if you just keep walking."

But if I were far from the road, I would see no one because no one could go where there was not a road—even if I found the road, it was unlikely anyone would come this way for days or weeks. I was so tired and cold, and my whole body had a sticky, sweaty feeling. If I did not keep moving, I might be trapped out here in the dark before I reached town. That now became my biggest fear—that if I did not return to the cabin now, I would find myself lost in the woods overnight. Even if I found the right direction, I would have wasted so much time I might not make it to town before nightfall. If it snowed, my footsteps might be covered, or the snow might melt enough that I could no longer distinguish them. Then I would be lost. Then I might starve in the woods and poor Adele might die in the cabin. I had better go back, at least to see how she felt; if she were going to die, better I be with her than she be alone. Even if all I could do was mop her forehead and moisten her lips, it was better than abandoning her. And maybe tomorrow she would be better—and if not, I could try again—tomorrow the snow might have melted enough for me to see the road.

Admitting defeat, I retraced my steps. Each minute, I felt worse, as if I had failed my sister, who was all I had in the world, and if she were sick enough to die, it was my fault. My fault for bringing her to this wretched land, and now my fault for being stupid enough to get lost in the woods. Why hadn't I paid attention to the sun from the start? If Adele died, I would die too—from guilt and loneliness.

"Why God? Why?" I cried out. No one would hear me anyway, not even Him. "Why did all this have to happen? Why did you make me so stubborn and so stupid that I got us into this situation? Why?"

I kept asking myself those questions over and over, blaming myself for everything. I hoped Adele would live to reprimand me as I deserved. I was not worthy of such a good sister as her—not when I had always been so hateful, so mean and petty toward her. She was right that I had pushed her away after Mother had died. I would give anything now to relive those years. I would do better if given the chance. And my poor father—I know he had appreciated all I did around the house for him, but I had never done it with a cheerful heart. Instead, I had always been stubborn, and selfish, and now my selfishness was destroying everything I loved. God knew I had not deserved anything He gave me. I had not even been grateful for Adele's companionship, so now He was taking her from me.

"Please, God," I begged. "Please. I love Adele. I can't bear to lose her. I don't care if she goes to the convent, just so long as you save her life. I promise I'll treat her better. I promise I'll be good. I'll be kind to everyone if only you'll do this one thing for me. I love her, God, and she's all I have. Please. Please."

I started sobbing. I sank down in my knees in the snow—half praying, half in despair. There was nothing more I could do. I knew I should get up and keep walking, but I didn't even know which direction to go. I blamed myself for everything that had gone wrong. It was all my fault, and all I could do was hope God would be merciful to me.

My inner voice of blame was so loud that I am still amazed I heard the childish laughter. I looked up with a start. There, standing about a hundred feet in front of me was a little girl in an old-fashioned hoop skirt. She looked straight at me and laughed again. At first, I thought she must be laughing at my appearance, my hair a mess, my clothes wet, my blouse half untucked from my skirt, my face sweating, my enormous winter coat dragging behind me in the snow. But I was only self-conscious a moment. No little girl would be alone in the woods! Her parents must be close by!

"Hello!" I shouted. I started to run toward her in the crunching snow.

She stood still until I was no more than fifty feet from her—then she let out another laugh and ran.

"Stop!" I cried, fearful I would lose her. "Stop! I need your help!"

She was a foolish little girl. She thought it was a game to run from me. My sister's life was in danger! What was wrong with her? Hadn't her parents taught her any manners?

She kept running. I shouted, "Stop!" until my throat was hoarse, but she ignored me.

She disappeared down a hill. I ran all the harder once she was out of sight. When I came to the top of the hill, she was nowhere to be seen. The hill only had a few scattered trees on it, so I could see to its bottom seventy feet below, yet nowhere could I spot her.

"Where did she go?" I moaned. The trees were not thick along the hillside, but possibly, she might be hiding among them. I started slowly down the hill, hoping to catch sight of her, trying not to panic that I had lost her. What confused me most of all is that I saw no footprints for her, although perhaps she was small enough not to leave an impression on the hard snow. But had she run down the hill at all? Yet I had definitely seen her head this way. I did not know where else she could have gone.

"She has to live around here," I told myself. But where? In what direction? Had I only gotten myself further lost? Was I just wasting time chasing after a silly little girl when my sister needed me at home?

Halfway down the hill, I decided to turn back, angry that the little girl had run away, but angrier that I had been foolish enough to seek help from a child. Yet I had only taken a few steps back when I heard her laughter again. "Please, this isn't funny!" I cried, turning around. "I need help. My sister is sick!" I still did not see her—there was nothing but the empty hill and a few scattered trees and—there was a team of horses, and then a wagon, and then a man came into view around the bottom of the hill!

I was so stunned I could only stand there and stare. Could it be Ben or Karl, or even Mr. Smith, coming to check on us? But I did not know where I was, or how far from the cabin, so it might be anyone. And it did not matter who it was! I ran down the hill, shouting, "Help!" before the wagon could disappear.

The driver heard me right away and stopped his horses. By the time I reached the bottom of the hill, he had gotten down from his seat and walked a dozen yards toward me.

"Hello," he said, as I stopped and tried to catch my breath.

"Please help," I gasped. He looked kind. That was all I could think at the moment. I struggled for words.

"What's wrong?" he asked.

"My sister's sick. She needs a doctor."

"Where is she?"

"At home. In our cabin."

He looked surprised and said, "I didn't know anyone lived around here. Where is it?"

"I'm not sure. I'm lost. It's a couple of miles that way I think."

I pointed in what I hoped was the right direction, but I was so disoriented I might have been pointing anywhere.

"Only cabin I know of in that direction is old man Shepard's, and I hear he died last fall."

"Yes," I said. "He was our uncle. We're staying at his place. Please, my sister has a horrible fever. I was trying to get to Marquette for help."

"Well, you're going in the wrong direction," he said.

He was wasting time telling me that. "Please," I panted.

"Better get in the wagon. I think that road is snowed over, but we can probably get most of the way there."

"But it's this way—" I said, pointing up the hill.

"Trust me. I grew up in these woods. I'll get us there," he replied.

I was too tired to argue. I wanted so much to sit down that I let him hand me up into the wagon. I figured even if we went in the wrong direction, it would be faster if we had to circle back later than if I kept walking now. I really had no idea where the cabin was, but there was nothing I could do now. I had to trust him. I had no other choice.

The road we went down was free from snow, not even wet—it had to be the main road past our cabin that I had somehow missed. I felt relieved that it was clear. If we could get back to the cabin, it would not take long then to get into town.

The man glanced over at me a couple of times as we traveled. Whenever he did, I turned my face away, ashamed by my appearance. I knew my eyes had to be red, my hair a mess, my face covered in sweat. He must have seen how nervous I was, for he didn't ask any questions.

Whenever I saw him turn his head away, however, I would glance at him, wondering who he was, wondering how he could just drop everything to help me. Would I have done that for someone? I who always had a million things on my mind, always anxious about getting something done? He was like the Good Samaritan who put others before himself. I told myself I wouldn't cry, but I felt like I should. He was like an angel, sent by the Lord when I was crying for help. It was a silly thought—being in the cabin all winter had made me practically delusional. He was just an ordinary man, doing his Christian duty. Once we were in town, I would probably never see him again. It did not matter. My heart was grateful. I sniffled a little. I felt like crying, but I would not cry in front of him. I would wait until we reached town, until I knew for certain Adele was safe.

We rode about twenty minutes. Then he halted the horses.

"If we walk in that direction," he said, "we should come to old man Shepard's cabin in about ten minutes."

Ten minutes. I couldn't believe it. If I had gone in the right direction, I would have come to a cleared road in ten minutes! Instead I had wasted more than three hours. I could have been in Marquette by now if I had—

"Will you take us to Marquette?" I begged. "We don't have much money, only a few dollars, but it's yours if you'll help us. My sister's all I have in the world. I can't bear to lose her."

He looked annoyed. Should I offer him Uncle's rifle for his trouble?

"I don't need anything for doing a neighbor a favor," he said.

"You're just lucky I came along when I did."

"I—thank you." Words could not express my gratitude. I felt all my life I had said the wrong words, and I had better not say anything more now to upset him. I could not take that risk this time.

As I trudged beside him in the snow, I realized I had actually been lucky—had I not gone in the wrong direction, I would not have met up with him, and if I had walked into town, I would have had to bring someone back out with me, which would have taken many more hours. Instead, he was going to take us both into town. Why, in just a couple of hours, Adele could see a doctor! And I wouldn't have even met this man, if not for that little girl.

"Did you see a little girl?" I suddenly thought to ask him.

"No, when?"

"Just before I met you. I was chasing after her, calling to her for help, but she only ran away from me."

"What did she look like?" he asked.

"She wasn't very old. Maybe eight. She had dark brown curls, and she had a hoop skirt on, an old fashioned looking one, like girls used to wear before the war."

He smiled and nodded, as if he thought me crazy or hallucinating.

"You did say no one else lived around here, didn't you?" I asked.

He only pointed through the trees. "There's your cabin. We'll have your sister in my wagon and on the way into town in ten minutes."

Overjoyed, I pushed away the nagging memory of the mysterious little girl. "What were you doing out here?" I asked him. Then the old fears rose in me—maybe he would not have good intentions once he got inside the cabin. But I had to take my chances.

"I'm a landlooker," he said. "But my folks used to own some property around here. I'm thinking about selling it this spring, so I came out to have a look at it. I didn't know whether the roads would be passable, but I thought I'd give it a try."

"I'm glad you did," I said, and then, I was so relieved to be back at the cabin, I broke into a near-run through the snow. He kept a steady stride without running and reached the door only five seconds after me, just as I opened it.

I raced upstairs. Adele was still lying in the bed, her forehead still warm, but she had quit sweating. I took the cloth, still damp from the morning, and mopped her forehead. Then he was beside me.

"I'm Samuel, by the way. Samuel Stonegate," he said, as he leaned over my sister.

"I'm Barbara Traugott. And this is Adele."

"She's awful pale. I'll carry her. You bring down the blankets. It looks like she needs a doctor pretty bad."

I did not argue. The wagon could have carried our trunk and all our belongings back to town so we would never have to return to this miserable cabin, but I did not worry about those things right then. It would have taken at least an hour to pack everything, and Adele might not have an hour to spare. The cabin could burn down with everything in it for all I cared.

Samuel picked up Adele and carried her downstairs. He set her in the rocking chair while I gathered up the blankets, a pillow, and an extra pair of her clothes since she was in her nightgown. I set the blankets on the table and went to the cupboard where I had hidden our few remaining dollars. I stuffed them in my pocket.

"Are you ready?" he asked.

"Yes," I said. I left my coat behind since I had to carry the blankets. By the time I gathered them back up and managed to shut the cabin door behind me, he was halfway to the wagon, but I could not expect him to wait. I doubted Adele weighed much more than a hundred pounds, but that was enough for anyone to carry a quarter mile through slushy snow.

I followed behind him, trying to step where his feet had made a path in the snow, but his stride was longer than mine. I marveled to see him walk so quickly through the snow, never faltering despite Adele's weight. Again I wanted to cry at the relief I felt that he was helping us. I couldn't imagine any man being more kind at that moment—not Ben or Karl, or even my father. I thought of my father then, and how I had once followed him through the streets of Cincinnati, unable to catch up with him. For just a second, Samuel reminded me of father, when Father was young and strong and would carry me. But I had no time to be nostalgic now. I raised my head from concentrating on stepping in his footprints and saw Samuel was at the wagon already, waiting for me to come and spread out the blankets before he could lay Adele down.

I quickly stepped forward, and in another minute, the blankets were spread, and Samuel laid Adele gently on them. I tucked a pillow beneath her head while he tucked another blanket over her.

Then he took my arm and easily hoisted me up onto the seat before climbing up on the other side.

"Where am I going to take you when we get to town?" he asked as his team started down the road.

"The Whitmans' boarding house," I replied. "We've stayed there before."

He nodded. "They'll take good care of you."

It was slow going on the bumpy roads, but they were dry in most places. Samuel drove carefully, nearly inching the wagon wheels over holes and rocks that had been carved out by winter. It must have been three hours back to town, but I did not complain or fret. Adele made not a sound all that while, but whenever I looked back at her, she was breathing steadily. I was no longer afraid, only grateful that Samuel had come along, and even grateful for the strange little girl who had inadvertently led me to him. The ride into town was so long that I doubted even if I had found the road, I would have reached town by nightfall. Everything had turned out for the best, and Adele would see a doctor before dark.

❄   ❄   ❄

We arrived at the Whitmans' boarding house just before suppertime. I had fretted half the way into town about how to explain our return to Mrs. Whitman, but Samuel handled everything. He carried Adele from the wagon into the house and right up the front hall stairs while shouting, "This girl is ill. We need a room immediately!"

As he reached the upper landing, Edna came scurrying out from one of the bedrooms. She took one look at Samuel carrying Adele, glanced over her shoulder at me, and opened a door at the hall's end to let us into an empty room.

"My parents aren't here right now," she said, "but this room should be fine."

"Thank you," Samuel replied for me. He took care of everything from that point. Once he had laid Adele on the bed, I started to tend to her. Edna, at Samuel's orders, went to get wet cloths and water, and the dear girl also brought some tea and medicine, although I would not give Adele anything but water until the doctor saw her. I turned around to speak to Samuel, but Edna said he had passed her on the stairs, on his way to fetch the doctor. He was a real treasure—having forgotten his own interests to tend to my sister's needs. I felt so grateful. In twenty minutes, the doctor arrived, and while he examined Adele, Samuel waited in the parlor so he could give the doctor a ride home— at least that's the reason Samuel gave Edna, although the doctor's walk home would not have been more than fifteen minutes. When Edna whispered to me that Samuel was waiting downstairs, I felt surprised by his attention, then realized that like all other men, he must be attracted to my sister—even now, as pale as she was, she was still pretty. Perhaps he fancied himself some sort of hero, some prince come to restore Sleeping Beauty to life, and her love would be his reward. But that would be better than her going to the convent. I did not care what she did now—so long as she lived.

The doctor said Adele's fever had started to diminish, and he gave me medicine to help bring it down further. He admitted he could do nothing else but wait for the fever to break. For the next two days I waited, waited as she hallucinated, as she moaned, as she called for Father or Mother, and once for me when I momentarily let go of her hand. To my relief, never once during this time did she call out Ben's name; I would not have known how to explain it to the doctor or the Whitmans if she had. I also did not know how to explain Samuel's behavior. The day after he brought us to town, he went back to the cabin and fetched all our belongings—how he managed to lift that gigantic trunk into the wagon by himself I could never imagine. I was grateful, but I thought it odd that he kept stopping by to inquire how Adele was; he would sit in the parlor for an hour or two, waiting for word of Adele's health. Edna told me of his visits since I would not leave my sister's side. Mr. Whitman sat with Samuel in the parlor long enough to smoke with him—I don't know what they talked about. I was concerned that his frequent visits would make the Whitmans think he was more than just a kind stranger to us.

At dusk on the second day, Adele's fever finally broke. The instant she opened her eyes, I felt her forehead. Thank God it was cool.

"It's all right now, Barbara," she said. Then she drifted back into a peaceful sleep. All this time, I had not left her side. Now Mrs. Whitman said, "Why don't you rest, dear? Edna and I will sit with her and let you know whether anything changes."

I did not want to leave Adele, but finally I consented to a nap if they promised not to let me sleep longer than an hour.

Relieved that Adele was out of immediate danger, I felt as if I could sleep for a week. Edna took me to her own bed, and I slept there soundly throughout the night. They did not wake me as promised, but I could not be angry with them. They feared I would become sicker than Adele if I continued to strain myself.

When I woke in the gray of early dawn, I immediately went back to Adele. Poor Edna had slept in the chair beside Adele all night while I had occupied her bed. I woke Edna and sent her to her own room, then sat beside my sister, thankful to see her beauty had not been lost. When I looked out the window, the sun was rising over the village of Marquette, spread out below. Nearly six months ago, we had come here—the very first day winter's snowflakes had fallen. Now only little patches of snow were scattered here and there. Winter was over. Whatever lay before me now, I had survived to see the spring.

After a couple of hours, Mrs. Whitman came and persuaded me to eat some breakfast. I had refused all food but some tea and toast up until then.

"She'll be fine now, dear," she said in a motherly tone. I had thought Mrs. Whitman almost uncivil before, but now she was only kind. She took me downstairs and fixed me some eggs and a slice of ham. Then she sat beside me, sipping her coffee, while I ate.

"I fed the other boarders before I came to fetch you," she said. "I didn't think you would want to make conversation with strangers, and I sent Nathaniel off to our son Jacob's house so you wouldn't have to be bothered with all his questions."

"Thank you," I said. She had not even requested payment since we had arrived, but I would pay her back every penny for her kindness. "I don't know what we'll do now," I said. "We can't go back to the cabin to live. I'll find work, and then, I'll pay you for—"

"Hush," she silenced me. "Don't worry about that."

I was tired of being stubborn. I courteously accepted her Christian kindness, but I would not accept any long-term charity. "I need to go see Mr. Smith about the property," I said. "He was interested in purchasing it last fall—maybe he still is. I might as well go see him today. There's no sense in wasting time."

Then the dining room door opened.

"Adele!" I cried, jumping up as she entered with Edna.

"I'm fine, Barbara," she said. "Just hungry."

Mrs. Whitman and Edna went to fix Adele breakfast. I was left at the table with my sister, to tell her how we had gotten into town and all about Samuel Stonegate's help and the Whitmans' kindness.

"I'd like to thank Mr. Stonegate myself," said Adele.

"He's stopped by several times to check on you," I said. "I'm sure he'll be by today."

In my heart, I felt jealousy surging again. I did not want him to come, but I kept this to myself because his presence might help her forget Ben, whom I blamed for her illness.

Adele said little during breakfast. I told her I was going that day to see Mr. Smith about the property. She said she would just sit in the parlor and read a little. She promised to go back to bed if she felt tired.

I went upstairs to dress. Since Samuel had brought us our trunk, I had all my clothes, and I made certain to choose my very best to see Mr. Smith. He had been very rude at our last meeting, but I thought him greedy enough that he might still be interested in the property, and perhaps he might still take an interest in Adele. He would not be the ideal brother-in-law, but he was preferable to a convent—although I had promised God that if Adele got well, I would not interfere with her religious calling. But neither would I interfere if Mr. Smith wished to court her.

And so I got myself all dolled up, even putting on my mother's earrings. Despite a winter in the wilderness, I think I did quite a fine job of making myself up. I did not have Adele's charms, but I was a mature and intelligent woman, and Mr. Smith, being a sophisticated man, might think my intelligence fair compensation for my lack of beauty. He would bargain with me for my property, perhaps for my sister's hand, perhaps even for mine—that seemed unlikely, but it depended on how badly he wanted the property. He should count himself fortunate with either of the Traugott sisters. I left the boarding house, feeling certain I would persuade Mr. Smith to be agreeable.

I marched downtown, determined to do what was best for Adele and me. I opened Mr. Smith's office door, and not even waiting for the clerk to look up, I said, "I am here to see Mr. Smith, please."

"I'm afraid Mr. Smith is out until next week," replied the clerk. "He's away on his honeymoon."

Then I just stood there. I had never imagined such a possibility. I had figured it might take some wheedling to rekindle his interest in Adele, but I had not considered he might no longer be available—how could he be so fickle? Six months had not passed since he had been so captivated by Adele's beauty.

"Thank you," I said. "Goodbye." I tried to depart with dignity, although my impulse was to run from the office in shame. What should I do now? I might still sell Mr. Smith the property when he returned—but I knew my ulterior motive had been to convince him to marry Adele.

As soon as I was back in the street, I cursed myself. "Barbara Traugott, you old fool!" My anger turned to pain. Quickly, I walked around the side of the building where no one would see me. Then I laid my arm against the brick wall, hid my face, and gave way to tears.

I had nothing! Absolutely nothing. Not even my sister—she was going off to her damn convent! I was completely alone in the world. Barbara Traugott might as well be dead for all anyone cared.

How many times now had I cried since we had come to Upper Michigan? Why had it all been so hard? Would I ever find an answer? Would I ever know a moment of happiness? "Why am I always so frustrated in everything I try to do?" I asked. "God, I can't do it anymore. Tell me what to do now. Change this for me, or change me so I quit making these same mistakes over and over. I don't care what you do; just don't make me have to go on like this."

It was a desperate cry. I knew God wouldn't hear it. He never listened to me. But if I had not been afraid of someone hearing me, I would have shouted it out loud to let go of all my frustration. Instead, I held it in so that my stomach twisted into a knot. The only solution I could imagine was to join the convent with Adele since no man wanted me—but God wouldn't want me either.

"Barbara."

My name spoken. A hand on my shoulder. At first, I was surprised to be called by my first name, but not at all alarmed. Before I even turned to look at him, I somehow knew it was Samuel.

"Barbara, why are you crying? What's wrong?"

He was a stranger. I could not tell him. I was ashamed to speak.

"Breathe," he said. "Breathe. Then you'll be able to tell me."

I obeyed. I stopped crying. I swallowed to relieve my dry throat.

"Now, tell me what's wrong."

I lowered my eyes. I could not explain to him how I was a failure, how every time I tried to fix things, I only made them worse.

"It's okay, Barbara. You can trust me."

I shook my head. I was afraid to tell him. I never trusted anyone.

"Come, I'll walk you back to the boarding house," he said, taking my arm. I let him lead me. I felt too weak to resist. As we stepped onto Front Street, I was mortified when he tipped his hat at a well-dressed lady. "Good day, Mrs. Henning." Once she had passed us, he said, "That's Mrs. Whitman's sister."

"I know," I said. I remembered how snobbish she had been at Sunday dinner the day Mr. Smith had driven Adele and me to the cabin.

"I work for her husband," Samuel added.

"Oh," I said, without interest. I did not feel up to making small talk with him. We walked in silence the rest of the way. I was afraid of what the passersby would think to see me on the arm of a man, but I was more afraid to pull away—I felt he was holding me up now. I was afraid I would collapse back into tears if he were not there. Mercifully, we only passed a few children playing in their front yards. Nor was anyone sitting on the front porch when we reached the boarding house. I was grateful no one saw me return with Mr. Stonegate—unless Edna were peeping through a window—I sensed that like me, she felt alone, and longing for—what I could not say.

I wanted Samuel to leave me at the front walk, but he walked right up the steps and onto the porch before he released my arm. Then he took off his hat and held it against his chest as I turned the doorknob.

"I hope your sister is better, Barbara. I hope everything is well for you. If there is ever anything I can do, please never hesitate to ask me."

"Thank you, Mr. Stonegate," I said, then stepped inside and closed the door. I shut it quickly because his face reflected that he wanted to say more. He was obviously worried about me. I was so embarrassed. I had made a complete fool of myself.

As I turned toward the stairs, I glimpsed Adele in the parlor, sitting at the writing desk. I wanted to go upstairs and bury myself under my pillow, but she looked up when she saw me. "Barbara, I've been writing my letter to the bishop, requesting permission to join the convent in Sault Sainte Marie. It's the closest convent to Marquette. I know it's still far away, Barbara, but you can always come visit me on the train."

"I'm not feeling well," I said, unable to discuss the convent right then. "I'm going upstairs to lie down."

"I hope you didn't catch my sickness," she called after me.

"No, I think I'm just tired," I called back, relieved that she did not follow me.

I went to bed. I did not get up for supper, and I was glad no one came to fetch me. I did not sleep, just lay awake in a daze, my mind too overwhelmed by everything to function properly. When Adele came to bed, she said no one had come to call me to supper because they assumed I needed to catch up on my sleep after staying up with her for several nights. I told myself I needed to rest. It had been a long winter. Once I was rested, I would be able to figure out what to do.

I lay in bed most of the next day. In the late afternoon, Adele came into the room to tell me she had carried her letter to the bishop. He had promised to contact the Mother Superior of the convent to arrange things for her. In the meantime, she would write to our parish church in Cincinnati for proof of our having made the sacraments there so she would have all the necessary paperwork to enter the order of the Ursuline nuns. I was miserable, but I did not protest her decision.

By suppertime, I found the solitude of my room intolerable, and although I doubted company would please me any better, I went downstairs to eat.

Everyone welcomed me at the table. Mr. Whitman politely inquired after my health. I told him I was fine and assured everyone I had not been ill, only exhausted, and I felt better now.

"Mr. Stonegate stopped by this morning," Edna said, "but I told him you were sleeping."

Before I could reply, Mrs. Whitman said, "Why didn't you tell us you were courting Mr. Stonegate?"

"Barbara, why didn't you tell me?" Adele asked in astonishment.

"Did it just come about then?" asked Mrs. Whitman, equally surprised Adele did not know. "My sister said she saw Mr. Stonegate walking you home yesterday."

"He seems very smitten with you, the way he keeps stopping by," Edna chimed in.

I was completely caught off guard. What was I to say? Why had I let Samuel walk me home yesterday—if I had been in my right mind, I never would have permitted it. And why did that Mrs. Henning have to be such a busybody, going about spreading rumors?

"Barbara, tell us how it happened," Adele said.

I was too embarrassed to explain—I could not tell the truth—that he had found me in tears yesterday—then they would ask why I had been crying. Before I knew what to say, the front door creaked open.

"Oh, who is that now?" groaned Mrs. Whitman. As she rose from the table, Mr. Stonegate appeared in the doorway.

"Pardon me," he said, his hat in his hands. "I didn't know you would all be eating."

"It's all right," Mrs. Whitman smiled.

"Have you had supper, Mr. Stonegate? You're welcome to join us," said Edna. "You can have that empty seat beside Miss Traugott."

The only empty chair just would have to be beside me!

"Thank you," he replied. I would have thought him enough of a gentleman to excuse himself, but he did not offer the slightest protestation to Edna's invitation. He simply pulled out the chair and sat down beside me, then took the bowl of mashed potatoes Mr. Wainscott passed him.

"So Mr. Stonegate," Adele began before I could stop her, "or should I call you Samuel now that we are to be brother and sister?"

"Excuse me?" he replied.

"Oh, don't dilly-dally, young man," Mr. Whitman actually giggled. "The young lady here has told us how it is. When's the wedding date?"

I would have thought Mr. Whitman, not being a woman, would have had more tact than to pry into other people's romances, but apparently his wife and daughter were a bad influence on him.

Samuel looked to me for an explanation, but I could only turn my eyes to the slice of ham on my plate.

"Nathaniel!" Mrs. Whitman said. "Now see what you've done! The poor girl's blushing!"

"Nothing to be ashamed of," her husband replied. "Love's the most natural thing in the world. I think it's splendid these two young people have found each other."

"Yes, it is," Mrs. Whitman said.

I could feel Samuel's eyes probing me. I tried, but I could not raise my eyes higher than his shirt buttons.

"Mr. Stonegate, I'm—I'm sorry. I don't know why—"

"Miss Traugott," he interrupted. "May I speak to you in private?"

I was terrified. I didn't think he would display anger before the others if I explained it at the table. But I could not be alone with him! I was too embarrassed to speak before everyone—but if I went into the parlor, I would have to come back later and explain it again, explain it twice! And he was more likely to be angry if we were alone.

I found myself getting up from my chair, leaving the room, letting him follow me into the parlor. What else could I do? I was a mouse caught in a cat's claws. As Samuel closed the parlor door behind us, I heard Edna giggle. Then I was alone with him.

"Mr. Stonegate, I'm so sorry," I began. "Apparently Mrs. Henning—"

I stared at the floor, but I sensed how close he was standing. Then his hand was on my chin, slowly lifting it up toward his face, to an enormous smile.

"Miss Traugott, I had not dared to hope. Yesterday when I took your arm, I was afraid you would think I was being forward, but—"

"Not at all," I said. "It was just that Mrs. Henning—"

"Miss Traugott, I think you're lovely. I haven't much to offer, but I can give you a roof over your head, and perhaps I can relieve some of the loneliness I imagine you feel since I understand your parents are gone and your sister intends to leave you. The Whitmans have told me everything. I hope you don't mind—I have been very inquisitive about your situation. I feel somehow akin to you; my own parents died of pneumonia the winter before last. I've been miserable ever since, but when you allowed me to help you, well, I started to think you might need me a little, and I began to hope—perhaps foolishly—that I still had some chance for happiness in this world."

"There is always hope," I said, unsure where the words came from, but unexplainably feeling a strong, sudden urge to comfort him. His hand was still on my chin—I could feel it trembling there, hesitating to draw it closer to his own face. Then he said, "Miss Traugott, will you marry me?"

I could not speak. He interpreted my silence as a "yes." Then he kissed me as if I had promised myself to him; in my heart, I had. I did not know it until that moment, but it felt right to me, as if it were meant to be. For a second, I remembered again walking behind him as he carried Adele to the wagon, and I sensed it would be my life to follow him from then on. But still I could not understand.

"I love you, Barbara," he said, holding me closely to him. "I don't know how it happened so sudden, but I do. I think I loved you the moment I saw you running down that hill in the snow. Anyone so devoted to her sister, any woman with that much love in her—I knew that was the woman I wanted for my wife."

My head was pressed against his chest. He was warm, and I was safe. I knew he was wrong about my character—I did not deserve his admiration or love, but rather than disillusion him, I decided I would make myself worthy of that love. I need not tell him my faults. I was safe with him. I didn't understand it, but I just knew in my heart I could love him and have that love returned.

Never before would I have believed it, but now I accepted that someone could love me, despite my many imperfections. A great enveloping feeling of peace flowed through me as he held me closely for the longest time.

Finally, he said, "We should go eat before the food is cold. Now there won't have to be any explanations."

That is how I found what I had thought I never would find. He meant so much more than just someone to take care of me, even more than someone to love me; he was someone I could love.

If this story were only mine, I would end it now, like Cinderella's, with us living happily ever after. Of course, I did not live "happily ever after," but neither was the rest of my life a tragedy as I had often feared. From that day on, I always had some degree of contentment to fall back upon, no matter how hard my lot.

Once back in the dining room, Samuel pulled my chair out for me while everyone stared at us, not daring to ask what had been said until Samuel took his seat.

"Barbara," he announced, and although I blushed, I was pleased, "has agreed to be my wife."

A commotion of congratulations followed, and by the time they were all given, the food was cold, but we ate it cold and scarcely noticed. I looked about the table, seeing myself surrounded by glowing faces. For the first time in my life, I felt life was full of good, and I realized all these people rejoiced in my happiness. Had I not been so stubborn and afraid when I first came to Marquette, I might have found such happiness sooner. It no longer mattered how long I had spent in that miserable cabin, or how long I had been unhappy; now good had come to me, and the past was almost as if it had never been.

"Oh, you'll have to have Mrs. Montoni make your wedding gown," Edna said. "She made my sister-in-law Agnes' wedding veil."

"Oh, Barbara, you'll make such a lovely bride," said Adele.

"But I have no money for a wedding dress," I replied.

"I do," said Samuel, "and Mrs. Montoni does beautiful work. I don't care what the dress costs so long as my Barbara is happy."

That was the first time he called me his Barbara. I felt I did not care about anything now so long as my Samuel was happy.

❊   ❊   ❊

Two days later, Mrs. Montoni came to make my wedding gown. Edna fetched me from upstairs. "She's brought over all kinds of fabrics for you to choose from," she said. "Oh, she'll make you such a beautiful dress."

When I went into the parlor, I was stunned to see so many types of cloth, from cottons to silks and satins, and delicate beads for trim, and the most shimmering lace to make the veil. Edna fussed about the room, shutting all the curtains, locking the parlor door, moving the chairs so we could spread out all the fabrics. Adele and Mrs. Whitman marveled over the beautiful cloths, while I stood in disbelief that such elegant material should be on my person. I found myself on a stool in the middle of the room, stripped to my undergarments, decorated like a Christmas tree as Mrs. Montoni measured, draped me with fabrics, then sewed them together to determine what would look best. I let the other women choose what the dress should be made from. They were so excited about it—I was more excited to think how pleased Samuel would be to see his wife look beautiful—if only for our wedding day. I tried to imagine the unimaginable marriage ceremony—I dressed in white—he so handsome—maybe not as handsome as Ben, but I did not care. To me he was the most handsome man in the world, and I the luckiest woman. I preferred his brown eyes and straight brown hair to any blue-eyed, golden-haired Adonis.

"We appreciate your coming over," Mrs. Whitman told Mrs. Montoni. "I know you would rather be home since Karl and Ben are visiting."

"Oh, it's all right," she replied. "They were going out for a walk anyway. I love having them, and I appreciate that they feel dutiful enough to come visit, but those two boys are only really happy when they're out in the woods; they get restless when they stay more than two days."

As Mrs. Montoni spoke, all my joy changed to concern for Adele. I looked over to see her face fall. Quickly, so no one would suspect we knew the boys, I said, "Are Karl and Ben your sons, Mrs. Montoni?"

"Karl is," she replied. "Ben is his logging partner. They spend so much time in the woods that I haven't seen them since Christmas, but they've come now to stay a whole week, so I'll have plenty more time to see them before they leave."

"I bet you're glad to have them home," said Mrs. Whitman.

"Oh yes," Mrs. Montoni said. "They're such good boys. I've only known Ben this past year, but he's just as good to me as Karl. I know Kathy sure looks up to them both. Kathy is my daughter," she said to me. "I was going to bring her today, but she insisted on going off with them."

"I'm surprised neither of them is married yet," said Edna.

"I don't think you have a chance there, Edna," Mrs. Whitman laughed. Edna frowned. My heart ached for her—she was plain like me. I wanted to tell her that if a man could love me, there was hope for her. But I was more concerned for Adele. She looked nervous, and her legs were fidgeting about.

"I wish Ben and Karl would marry," said Mrs. Montoni. "They'd make good husbands."

Adele stood up and walked to the door. To protect her from embarrassment, I said, "Adele, you look pale. Why don't you go lie down?"

"I will," she said.

I would have gone after her, but I couldn't when I was in my undergarments and Mr. Whitman or Mr. Wainscott might see me.

"Do you want me to go up with you?" Edna asked her.

"No, I'll be fine. I don't think I'm sick, just tired."

As Adele closed the door behind her, Mrs. Whitman explained to Mrs. Montoni, "Poor dear, she hasn't been well. It can't have been good for her, being cooped up in that cabin all winter."

I feared Mrs. Montoni might then realize we were the two girls Karl and Ben had brought food to at Christmas, but she did not say a word. If she knew who we were, perhaps she had decided not to speak of it—or perhaps the boys had not mentioned us to her because she had intended the food for them, and they did not wish to hurt her feelings by telling her they had given it away—they had always been sensitive like that—well, except when Ben had abandoned us—but I wouldn't think about that now. I was getting married—I would not let anger over the past steal my joy. I thought about trying to find out from Mrs. Montoni if she knew anything about Ben's past, maybe even later going to her house to explain everything to her, to see whether she could understand Ben's behavior. But then I told myself it did not matter now. He was gone, all but forgotten. I would rather Adele went to the convent than be with someone so fickle.

As soon as Adele had gone upstairs, Edna said, "Barbara, it's so splendid you're getting married. I'm so excited for you."

"I remember my first wedding," Mrs. Montoni sighed.

"You've been married more than once?" I asked, not because I was interested, but to distract myself from my sorrowing sister, for whom I could do nothing.

"Yes, Mr. Montoni is my second husband. He's a good provider, but my first husband, Fritz, was the great love of my life." Then she smiled and said, "Make sure Samuel is yours, dear."

I nodded out of respect to her. I did love Samuel, but was he really "the great love of my life"? I felt my love for him was built more on gratitude that he would have me than true love for him. After all, I barely knew him. Would he end up being no more to me than what Mr. Montoni apparently was to his wife, "a good provider"? That was really all I had ever thought of a man as being, but it would be nice if he were my great love.

"Mrs. Montoni, what was your first wedding like?" Edna asked.

But before Mrs. Montoni could answer, someone knocked on the door. Edna opened it only slightly, in case it was a man, but it was her sister-in-law, Agnes, holding her youngest daughter, Sylvia, while tiny Mary toddled in behind her. The little girls were two and four years old, and quite curious about seeing a bride prepare for her wedding. When Mary saw me, with white silk draped about me and lace adorning my hair, she froze as if she were struck by a thunderbolt. "Oh, you're beautiful!" she gushed. "You're a beautiful bride."

"Mary, she isn't a bride yet," Agnes laughed. "She's just getting fitted for her wedding dress."

"She's beautiful," Mary insisted.

I thought Mary would not think me beautiful if Adele were in the room—I could never compare to my sister—yet I was pleased by her compliment. I was overwhelmed with happiness to have all these women here with me, sharing in my joy. And at least one man thought me beautiful, so beautiful inside and out that he wanted to marry me. He might be wrong about my beauty, but I would do my best not to deceive him by becoming the good wife he deserved.

Agnes pulled Mary over to the sofa and set Sylvia down on the floor. From her immense coat pockets, she produced two rag dolls. "Now girls," she told her daughters, "you must play quietly here by the sofa. You wouldn't want Mrs. Montoni to stick a pin in Miss Traugott because you distracted her, now would you?"

Both shook their heads "No" then set about playing wedding, although both dolls were obviously female.

"Mrs. Montoni was just about to tell us about her first wedding," Edna told Agnes.

"Oh, there isn't that much to tell," Mrs. Montoni said. "Fritz and I got married in a little church in Boston. We didn't have much money—neither of us had been off the boat from Europe that long— he had just come over from Saxony a few months before, and I had emigrated from Ireland with my family not many years earlier. But we managed despite how poor we were, and my mistress at the house where I worked as a maid bought me a beautiful veil for the wedding, even though I couldn't afford a wedding dress."

"You made me such a beautiful veil for my wedding," Agnes smiled. "I have it safely put away, but I confess sometimes I take it out and put it on to look at myself in the mirror—but only when Jacob isn't home; he would just laugh at me. I don't take it out often, though; I want to save it so Mary and Sylvia can wear it for their weddings."

"It should last until then," said Mrs. Montoni, "but if not, I'll make them each one when the time comes."

"Oh, Miss Traugott, Mr. Stonegate is going to be so pleased when he sees you," Edna repeated.

I don't think I heard what was said next. I was too busy playing model as Mrs. Montoni cut material and draped and pinned it, and cut more cloth and sewed and hemmed it. I truly felt I would be a beautiful bride; I just hoped Samuel would stay pleased with me after the wedding. We barely knew one another, and I feared he had made rather a hasty step in asking me to marry him. In my heart, I felt a little ashamed my marriage prospects were so minimal that I had said, "Yes" to my first proposal. I had heard a woman should say, "No" twice before she said, "Yes," but I doubted Samuel was sophisticated enough to know such proprieties, and I did not want to lose him. I was also afraid he had only asked me because he was himself desperate and no other woman had wanted him. I wondered why he had not already married. He was twenty-three after all, a whole year older than me.

"Miss Traugott," said Mrs. Montoni, when she had removed the pins from her mouth, "I think any man who saw you right now would kick himself for not having asked you to marry him."

"Apparently, no other man was smart enough," Agnes laughed.

"Most men aren't smart when it comes to love," said Mrs. Whitman.

"No, they go for a pretty face and take no thought to whether a woman can cook and clean," Mrs. Montoni said.

"A woman can do more than cook and clean," said Edna.

"Of course she can," replied Mrs. Montoni. "Most men just don't want her to."

"If you find the right man, he'll appreciate you for more than keeping house," said Agnes, turning to her mother-in-law. "Jacob loves me for who I am, not for what I can do, and I have you to thank for that."

Mrs. Whitman smiled and patted her hand. "I'd like to take all the credit, but Nathaniel had something to do with it. For all his frustrating little ways of leaving messes around the house, he always respected me, and he taught Jacob to do the same."

"I have the best father and brother," Edna smiled, "but after them,

I would say Barbara is getting the best man in town. In fact, I'm a little jealous."

"The right man will come for you too," I said. My words did not express all I meant, but I hoped she would take them to heart, for she must realize I was no more beautiful or good than she.

"Yes, Sam is a good man," said Mrs. Whitman. My heart glowed to hear him praised, although her calling him Sam made him sound so common when I thought him so uncommonly good. "If the women in this town had any common sense, one of them would have snatched him up long ago; he has a tender heart, and someday he'll be a patient father. But most young girls run after the handsome wicked men, just like the young men run after the pretty faces. I imagine most of the girls in this town are in love with Ben Shepard—Edna included."

Edna gave her mother an ugly look. I felt myself tremble. Agnes said, "Ben certainly is handsome, but he doesn't fit the 'handsome, wicked men' criteria."

"No, there isn't a mean bone in his body," Mrs. Whitman replied.

"Still, I know what you mean," said Mrs. Montoni. "I'm not sure why, but I don't think Ben's the marrying type. I love him like a son, but I'm afraid he's a bad influence on Karl in that respect. I want to get Karl married off so I can see my grandchildren, but he seems to want to stay a bachelor like Ben, and Kathy's too young to give me any grandchildren for another dozen years at least, and who's to say I'll last that long?"

"You just said you'd make Mary and Sylvia's wedding veils," Agnes reminded her, "and they're several years younger than Kathy."

"Ben is handsome," Edna said dismissively, to deny any attraction she felt for him, "and he is kind, not wicked, but I do think him unsteady. I don't think he's so horrid he would take to gambling, but somehow I've always equated him with Valancourt in Mrs. Radcliffe's *The Mysteries of Udolpho*."

"Oh, Edna," moaned Mrs. Whitman, "it's talking about all those silly books that keeps you from finding a husband."

"Any man should be proud of my reading," she replied. "At least I have a brain, and that's more than many men can say."

"You're right, Edna," said Agnes. "The right man will respect you for your intelligence."

"But, Edna," her mother said, "no one knows what you're talking about—like with that Valiant-hearted fellow I mean."

"Well, they should. They would have fifty years ago, so I'm surprised you don't, Mother."

"When I was your age," Mrs. Whitman replied, "young ladies were taught it was a sin to read novels. Your Grandmother Brookfield would have been horrified to catch me reading one. Only when Mr. Hawthorne's *The Scarlet Letter* came out did she read a novel, and only then because she felt it had a strong moral lesson in it."

"Grandmother Brookfield," said Edna, "might have been a Methodist, but she acted as old-fashioned as her Puritan ancestors."

"Be respectful of your forebears, dear," Mrs. Whitman said.

"Let me explain what I mean about Valancourt being popular fifty years ago," said Edna, ignoring her mother, "by quoting Mr. Thackeray."

"Thack-a-who?" laughed Mrs. Whitman.

"William Makepeace Thackeray, the author of *Vanity Fair*." Edna rolled her eyes as our faces all went blank at the mention of this unknown book. "This is what he said about Valancourt and Mrs. Radcliffe's *The Mysteries of Udolpho*, which was published in 1794: 'Valancourt, and who was he? cry the young people. Valancourt, my dears, was the hero of one of the most famous romances which ever was published in this country. The beauty and elegance of Valancourt made your young grandmammas' gentle hearts to beat with respectful sympathy. He and his glory have passed away.'"

"I guess they have," laughed Mrs. Whitman.

Edna just scowled.

"Marriage isn't like in those old romances," said Mrs. Montoni. "Sometimes it's just dull, and it can be a lot of hard work, but if you have a man kind enough to put you first at least half the time, as I'm sure Samuel will, then you'll find it's not that difficult, and quite satisfying."

"I just hope I'm not making a mistake," I said. "I don't want to disappoint him."

"I'd say that's a good start," replied Mrs. Montoni. "You want to do everything you can to please him."

"But don't let him play lord and master," Mrs. Whitman said. "Treat him as your equal, not your better, and make it clear he must treat you the same."

"Sam will treat you that way," Agnes said. "I don't think you have to worry about that."

"Be grateful for all his virtues," Mrs. Montoni added, "and overlook his little faults. Concentrate on appreciating him, and then the love will grow. That's the best advice I can give you. I wish I remembered it more often myself. I hope you'll take it to heart, dear."

Then Mrs. Montoni said it was time for her to leave. She had everything measured and cut and laid out, so she would go home now to sew the dress. I thanked her with all my heart, and I extended her advice to appreciate my husband by appreciating all these women who shared my happiness even though not one of them was my kin. I realized Adele was not, nor ever had been, all I had in the world—I had simply needed to open myself to others. And while I missed my mother more than ever in the days leading up to the wedding, I had suddenly found a host of women to be like mothers and sisters to me.

When I went upstairs, Adele was sitting and looking out the window. "Did they say anything when I left?" she asked. "Did they say anything more about Ben?"

"No," I replied. "No one suspects anything. Don't think about it anymore."

"I'll be glad when I've gone to the convent," she sighed.

I knew it would be best to stay silent, but still I said, "Adele, you can't hide from the world in a convent. That's no answer—that's only running away."

"That's not why I'm going, Barbara."

I waited for her to explain. I waited for her to convince me that she felt a legitimate calling to serve God. But instead, Edna came upstairs to tell me Samuel was there.

I went down to the parlor. As soon as I saw him, I found myself overflowing with more words in a half hour than I had said to him since the day we met. I told him all about my dress, and how kind everyone had been to me, and how excited I was to get married. He laughed gently, finding pleasure in my joy, so I kept talking, feeling I was free to say anything to him because I had found someone who valued me as I always should have valued myself.

❄   ❄   ❄

I want to make it clear that my happiness at this time was not only because I was getting married or because I had found a man to love me and share my life. My happiness came when I realized my own power, my own worthiness to be loved. Had I said, "No" to Samuel—his asking me to marry him was so nearly unbelievable to me that I am still surprised I did not say, "No" out of fear—but had I said, "No" I would have denied my happiness, thinking myself unworthy. At that time, I was only just awakening to what life could be. I learned I deserve happiness—that each one of us deserves it—and we can find it within ourselves by believing in our own worthiness and allowing good into our lives. A change had begun in me—slowly the old nagging, scornful, self-deprecating Barbara, who had always acted out of fear, was being transformed into a woman who loved herself, and could extend that love to others. Even now, that change, that continual expansion of my own knowledge and self-appreciation continues, and life is all the more wonderful for it. I do not know how better to explain it to those of you still in human form. I only promise that whatever your present pain, it will pass away, and it will pass away more quickly if you open yourself to the good that wants to come to you.

3

The wedding was set for June. Until then, Adele and I remained at the Whitmans' boarding house while Samuel prepared his home for me to become its mistress. Samuel knew how I hated the cabin, so he had immediately taken matters into his own hands to sell it and divide the money from the sale between Adele and me. Within a couple of weeks, he found a buyer who offered quite a bit more than Mr. Smith—enough to pay the Whitmans for their hospitality and to leave a nice little nest egg over for Adele and me to split. Adele, however, refused her half since she was going to the convent, so I put her share away, thinking I might need it when the children came—until then, I had never imagined being a mother, but now life was full of wonderful possibilities.

The day before the wedding, Samuel went out to the cabin to tidy it up, and to fetch Uncle Traugott's rifle, which he wanted to keep for himself. He had suggested I go with him, but I excused myself, saying I had to have one last fitting for my wedding dress, although I could have found time to do both. I just could not bear to see the cabin again.

And so that afternoon, while Samuel was gone and Adele sat in the parlor with her embroidery, I walked to Mrs. Montoni's house so I could try on the dress and she could make any last minute alterations. I had seen her the day before at the boarding house, and she had mentioned that Karl and Ben had left town, so I did not hesitate to go visit her. The fitting went fine; Mrs. Montoni promised to bring the dress to the church early in the morning so I would have plenty of time to get dressed before the ceremony. I thanked her and started back to the boarding house. That was when I saw Ben and Karl.

They were walking down Superior Street like the best of friends, as they were. They stopped outside a saloon, which I would later learn was owned by Mrs. Montoni's husband. I, being a lady, wanted nothing to do with saloons, and I found it hard to reconcile that a good woman like Mrs. Montoni was married to a saloonkeeper. But in those days, Marquette was filled with so many saloons catering to the miners, loggers, and sailors that the most self-respecting Christian woman could not avoid walking past one.

I crossed the street, just as Ben went inside the saloon. I hoped Karl, who waited outside, would not see me. I had no such luck.

"Miss Traugott!" he called out. I pretended not to hear him, but before I had walked far, he crossed the street.

"It's so good to see you, Miss Traugott," he said, stopping in front of me. "I tried to tell Ben we should go out to the cabin to visit you before we moved away, but we just haven't had time."

I knew this was just an excuse. For a moment, I felt like going into the saloon to give Ben a piece of my mind, even if he were my cousin, but Karl had done nothing to deserve my wrath.

"We don't live at the cabin anymore," I said. "We've moved to Marquette."

"That's funny," he replied, "because we're moving up to Calumet.

Logging season is over, but Ben has a cousin up there doing carpentry work, so we're going there to help build some houses for the summer."

"I wish you well then, Mr. Bergmann," I said and tried to pass on, but he kept speaking.

"It's good to see you, Miss Traugott. What's the chance we would meet like this on the last day I'm in Marquette? But how did you happen to get into town?"

"My fiancé brought us to town. I'm to be married to Mr. Stonegate tomorrow."

"You don't say! Why, my mother did say she was busy making a wedding dress. Any chance it's for you?"

"Yes," I said. I did not care any longer whether Mrs. Montoni learned the boys had been visiting Adele and me—she was too good to think ill of us, and if anyone should be ashamed, it was Ben, not Adele.

"And how is Miss Adele?" asked Karl. I was surprised his tone did not reflect concern for her. Had Ben not told him the truth about the situation—how he had jilted my sister? It was difficult to believe Ben would not have told his best friend. But I found I did not care. Instead, hoping Karl would pass the information on to Ben so he would feel guilty, I said, "My sister is taking the veil. She will be leaving next week to enter the convent in Sault Sainte Marie."

"Oh," said Karl. He stood silent for a second. I imagine he was considering how he would break this news to Ben. I felt sorry for Karl—rather caught in the middle as I was—but I don't think he ever fully understood the situation as I did—not that I really understood it myself.

"Well, I wish her all the best," he said, "and congratulations to you, Miss Traugott. I know Mr. Stonegate is a deserving man."

"I could find none better," I replied.

Then a shout of "Karl!" came from across the street. I did not have to look. I knew Ben's voice all too well.

"Good day, Mr. Bergmann," I said. I pushed past him before he or Ben could stop me. For a moment, I almost turned back, to reprimand Ben for how he had hurt my sister, to tell him he should be ashamed to have led her on as he had, to break her heart so she felt she had no other choice but to take the veil. I wished Samuel had been with me at that moment. I had not told him a word about Ben and Adele, but had I, he would have—but what could Samuel do? He was a good, gentle man, and I doubted there was a single man among all the mighty lumberjacks in Upper Michigan who could thrash Ben Shepard. I remained afraid to tell Samuel about Ben and Karl—he might question my and Adele's virtue at letting strange men stay with us—just like Mr. Smith had.

Perhaps someday I would tell Samuel, but not until we were safely wed. For now, I was thankful I had escaped speaking to Ben, for the tongue-lashing I would have given him would have caused a spectacle in the street.

❆   ❆   ❆

When I got back to the boarding house, I sat in the parlor with Adele. I dared not tell her I had seen Ben and Karl. In the last few days, I had started to feel guilty about my getting married while her heart remained broken, but had I expressed this to her, she would only have told me to stop being foolish. I had already begun to miss her. I sat with my face hid in a book I did not read, wishing there were some way I could still convince her not to go—to live with Samuel and me.

A little before suppertime, Samuel returned. I felt nervous when his wagon pulled up in front of the boarding house. Tomorrow was our wedding. I wanted to run and greet him, but I shyly stayed in my chair, pretending I had not noticed his wagon. Since Adele remained bent over her needlework and did not see him, I was able, when he entered, to raise my eyes in surprise.

From behind his back he pulled out a tremendous bouquet of the most delicate, oddly shaped flowers I had ever seen.

"Oh, Samuel, they're lovely," I said, standing up to accept them. "What are they?"

They were puffy and white with bright pink streaks running through them.

"Lady's slippers," he said. "I thought they would make a beautiful wedding bouquet."

"Oh, Barbara," said Adele, coming near to look at them. "They're so perfectly delicate, just like your wedding dress."

"Just like my beautiful wife," Samuel smiled. He spoke in that certain tone that melted my heart. I did not feel like a delicate flower, but I was pleased by the comparison.

"Thank you," I said, lowering my eyes to hide my embarrassment over the compliment.

"I wish you could have seen them out in the woods," he said. "First I saw a couple by the side of the cabin, but when I went to pick them, I noticed practically a field of lady's slippers behind the cabin—at least a hundred I bet, just scattered perfectly with the baby ferns. These don't even begin to represent how beautiful they were all together. I never saw anything so naturally beautiful, except for you," he said, giving me a peck on the cheek.

Still embarrassed, I excused myself.

"I better find a vase to put them in so they'll keep until tomorrow,"

I said. As I disappeared into the kitchen, I wondered why I still felt so uncomfortable around him when he was such a sweet man—perhaps because I still didn't believe I deserved that sweetness, especially not when my sister would never know it. Samuel was not handsome like Ben, but I was glad to have him, and he was far more than Adele had.

I had hoped to find Edna in the kitchen so I could ask for a vase, but the room was empty. Through the window, I saw her and Mrs. Whitman hanging laundry on the clothesline, so I searched through the cupboards on my own. I felt sad then, although I knew I had every reason to be happy since I would be married tomorrow. It would not always be so, but that day, I still loved my sister better than Samuel. Adele was the only one I had who remembered the old days, who remembered my childhood and Father and Mother, and I would miss her. But I knew I had to let go of the past now—I had longed all winter for Father, but now a wonderful man had come to take his place.

As I filled the vase with water and arranged the lady's slippers, I regretted not having gone to the cabin with Samuel that day; we could have spent more time getting to know each other before the wedding. And looking at those beautiful flowers, I could only imagine what a whole field of green ferns and pink lady's slippers would have looked like—the sight of them had given Samuel such pleasure; I wished I could have shared that pleasure with him. I had missed an opportunity to experience joy because I had allowed my hatred of the cabin to control me. If I had gone, neither would I have seen Ben and Karl and upset myself. These flowers seemed representative of all my past life—all the opportunities I had lost because I had refused to let them into my life. I had lived in continual anger at God for giving gifts to others that I had always seemed to be denied, but now I realized I had been the one continually denying good to myself because I had been convinced the world was a place of pain, not joy.

If I had never gone to that horrid cabin, I might never have met Samuel. Now I could no longer resent the long, solitary winter. I could not change the past, but I could remember how it had taught me strength as I strove to make a better future.

"Oh, look at the beautiful flowers!" said Edna, coming into the kitchen with a basket of laundry, followed by Mrs. Whitman. When I explained that Samuel had just brought them, both women went into the parlor to insist he stay for supper. What a meal that was with so much joking among the Whitmans and the boarders about what my married life would be like. Even Adele laughed when Edna started suggesting funny names for my babies, names from her old books like Grandison and Laurana, Zanoni and Emila—it was the first time Adele had laughed since the skating party with Ben and Karl. Her laughter made me believe everything would now be all right.

I honestly don't recall much about the actual wedding ceremony. I remember Mr. Whitman taking my arm to walk me down the aisle. The next thing I remember is standing on the church steps, receiving congratulations from a flood of people I did not even know, but Samuel had many friends in town, which made married life easier for me, for no one ever said anything but good about him, and all his friends' wives instantly adopted me as one of their own, insisting I join their sewing circles, quilting bees, church bazaars, and Fourth of July picnics. We had the wedding dinner at our house—prepared by several of his friends' wives. That was the first time I had seen my new home—it was the first time since I had left Cincinnati that I had felt at home.

Our friends all ate and laughed and wished us joy, then politely left us as it grew dark. Only Adele remained behind, for Samuel had agreed she could stay with us that week until she went to the convent. When bedtime came, Adele kissed me and told me to be happy, and then Samuel led me to our room.

He was gentle with me that night. It was the first time I had been held since Mother had died. Not even Father had ever held me—we rarely expressed affection in our family—but it was safe to do so with Samuel. Why he loved me I still could not fully understand, but I did not doubt it, and as the years went by and children came, our love only grew.

I should have been completely happy, yet I still wished to keep Adele with me. The evening before she was to leave, as we were eating supper, and without Samuel's permission, I said, "Adele, you don't need to go to the convent. You can stay with us until you find a husband. You will find one, you know."

"Barbara," she replied, "I don't want a husband. I'm no longer concerned with the ways of this world. I must go about the Lord's business."

What did she mean by that? Had she truly had a calling from God? I still could not believe she was doing anything except trying to hide from her pain—pain she could not hide from.

After supper, Samuel went outside to feed his horses, so Adele and I had a few minutes alone while we washed the dishes. Again, I tried to speak to her.

"Adele, Ben is not worth giving up your life."

She set down the dish she was wiping. Then she boldly looked me in the eye and said, "Barbara, I know you love me, and I know you want what is best for me, but you have to believe I know what is best for myself. Did I love Ben? Yes. Do I still love him? Of course. I'm not a fickle person. Once I love someone, that love does not die. I don't know why he left, but I'm sure he had his reasons. I wish him well, but I'm not going to the convent to run away from my pain. I'm going because I have found I cannot base my happiness on earthly things, not even human relationships. If Ben came to me today and asked me to be his wife, it would not change my decision to serve the Lord."

"But I don't understand," I said. "You were never that devoted to God before."

"You never saw the inside of my soul, Barbara. I always loved God, but I loved you and Father and then Ben more. Now I have learned that I must put the Lord first. In my heart, I know Ben loves me, and he would be with me if he could, but for now, the Lord has set different paths for us. It does not matter because I know Ben and I will be together again when the time is right. That is enough for me."

I wanted to tell her she was crazy and delusional, but Samuel came back inside. I went to sit with him in the parlor. Adele went upstairs to bed, saying she needed to rest before the long train-ride tomorrow.

I sat all evening with Samuel, hardly saying a word. I had always held my pain inside—I had never revealed my feelings in front of anyone except the day Samuel had found me crying outside Mr. Smith's office. But somehow Samuel sensed when I was hurting, and once we were in bed, he pulled me into the warm nook of his arm, and said, "My Barbara, tell me what is bothering you."

I was afraid to tell him, but we were married now, and I thought perhaps he could convince Adele not to leave. I told him everything—how Ben had lived with us in the cabin while I was ill, how he and Karl had frequently visited us, how Ben had led Adele on, how he was our cousin but had not wanted to claim the cabin, and finally, how he had jilted Adele and broken her heart. I told Samuel that Adele was only going to the convent to hide from her pain, and I begged him to talk to her because maybe she would listen to a man.

I sobbed against his nightshirt as I spoke, and all the while he said not a word, only stroked my hair, and then wiped my eyes dry with his fingertips. When I had finished speaking, Samuel gently crawled out of bed and returned with a glass of water.

"Here, drink this," he said.

"Will you talk to her?" I asked when I was able to speak.

He sighed. "I'm sorry you're hurting, Barbara, but Adele is a grown woman, and I'm sure she knows her own mind."

"But the things she says," I replied. "That Ben loves her and she knows someday they will be together again—it's all so nonsensical."

"No," he said. "We don't know that. If she feels close to him still, who are we to say otherwise? We don't know what that relationship was like, or why there was such a bond between them, and there must have been a strong bond for her to take his leaving so hard. I don't know Ben Shepard that well, but I've never heard a hard word spoken against him in this town. If he made a mistake or if he left her, I'm sure he did not do it lightly. I wouldn't doubt whether he hurts as much as she does. We just have to trust that in time it will work out for the best."

"I would like to believe that," I said, "but I don't know how. I don't know whether I can even believe that God cares about us. I can't believe there's any meaning or order to life at all."

"Barbara, I don't wish to change your mind if you don't want it changed, but since you trust me enough to share your sadness, there's something about my own family that I want to tell you."

I was afraid to hear that. Did he have worse skeletons in his family closet than I did? But I remembered how Edna, Mrs. Whitman, and Mrs. Montoni had all spoken well of him. I could not believe any ill of this man—but neither would I have believed it of Ben when he had been so kind. Yet I felt I must trust my own husband.

Samuel took a deep breath, obviously nervous about what he had to say.

"Do you remember how you told me about seeing that girl you saw in the woods the day we met?"

"Yes," I said, surprised because I had not thought of her once since that time.

"She's my sister."

It took me a few seconds to understand what he said. If she were his sister, why then had I not seen her again? Where was she? Why hadn't she been at the wedding?

"I don't understand," I said. "I didn't know you had any siblings. Is she living with some relatives, or—"

"No," he said firmly.

"But I thought you said your parents were dead, so she can't be living with them."

"My parents are dead."

"Then where does she live?"

"She's also dead."

My mind filled with complete confusion.

"She's a spirit, a ghost if you will," he said. "She's often—well, not often seen, but she has been seen by me anywhere between Marquette and the woods near your uncle's cabin. They're known as the Stonegate Woods because they belonged to my family. When my parents first came to Marquette, right when the town was first founded, we had a place out in those woods. I've seen my sister in those woods several times because that's where she died."

I stared at him in disbelief; it made no sense to me. I wanted to believe him because I loved him, but I was shocked by his words, fearful he had lost his senses.

"Let me start at the beginning," he said. "My sister died when she was only eight years old. She was five years older than me, so I barely remember her, but I know it was her you saw from the way you described her, the old fashioned hoop skirt, the dark curls, her size. She—I suppose I should tell you her name—Annabella—Annabella Stonegate. And I know it was her, not just because of how you described her, or because I remember how she looked, or even that there's a picture of her taken at Christmas just one year to the day she died, for she died on Christmas. I know it was her because since she died, I've seen her many times."

And then he paused, waiting for my reaction. All I could say was, "I thought ghosts were people who had done something evil in life and were being punished."

"Oh no. Well, maybe in some cases, but I think with her, it's because she died so young and unexpectedly, and she left behind work she never completed."

"Is that what your parents told you?"

He sighed.

"My parents never believed I could see her. When I got older, I began to wonder myself whether she had just been in my mind. But then you told me you saw her—and then I felt—well, it wasn't the only reason, but I felt we had something in common, something that connected us, as if she had led us to one another. As if she intends for us to be together. I was feeling so lonely that day we met—it was actually one year ago that day that my parents had died, died within hours of each other from pneumonia, and it seemed so odd that your sister should be ill like they were. But I hoped I could do something to help save your sister's life, even though I had been unable to save my parents. I had felt that day as if I didn't know how I could go on when I was so lonely, but when I saw how much you loved your sister—how you were willing to walk all the way to town for her sake—I knew then I would love you, and I felt my sister wanted me to love you. I felt you must have a great love in you if it were warm enough to make me feel love again."

I smiled at him, encouraging him to continue, although I knew I did not deserve his kind words. I sympathized with his pain, but I was also frightened by what he was telling me, especially frightened that I had been able to see his sister. "How did she die?" I dared ask.

"That's what fascinates me most about how you and I met. Annabella died when she was lost out in the woods. I think maybe she knew you were lost, and she did not want you to share her fate, or for your sister to share the fate of our parents; I think she was protecting you, leading you to safety by guiding you to me."

"She died lost in the woods? She must have been so frightened."

I had been so frightened myself that I could not imagine the fear a small child would have felt.

"She died on Christmas Eve," he said. "Our nearest neighbors, the Ridges, lived a mile away. They had two little girls, Virginia and Georgiana, who were my sisters' only playmates. That afternoon, my sister set out through the woods with Christmas presents for her two friends. It had barely snowed yet, and there was a worn path between the houses. One of my parents had usually accompanied her in the past, but they thought if she went alone, they could prepare her surprises for Christmas morning. Besides, she knew the path, and they made her promise to return home before dark.

"She stayed at the Ridges' house for the afternoon, and then just before dark, she started toward home. I don't think Mrs. Ridge ever forgave herself for not noticing how hard it had started to snow that afternoon. The path must already have been covered by the time my sister left their house.

"My parents waited until a little after dark, then went out to look for her, but by then, it was too late. The snow started pouring down, and my sister's footsteps, being so small, were quickly buried in the drifting. My father nearly went mad that night. He and Mr. Ridge searched for her until well after dawn, until finally my mother went out looking for them and left me alone in the house. By that point, she was just as terrified that she would lose her husband to madness as that her little girl would not be found. Finally, she found my father and brought him home while Mr. Ridge promised to continue searching. I remember that Christmas morning, my parents sitting beside each other, Father with his head on the kitchen table, Mother with her arms around him. I remember them weeping, while I sat in the corner, frightened, not understanding what had happened.

"At some point that morning, the cabin door was suddenly kicked open. First I heard my mother shriek. Then I saw an Indian come inside. It was Chief Kawbawgam, the head of the local Chippewa. For a moment, I was terrified he had come to hurt us. Then I saw that he was carrying my sister in his arms. He had found her in the snow, frozen to death, lost halfway between Marquette and our cabin."

"Oh, Samuel," I said. "I'm so sorry."

What more could I say? Wanting to comfort him, I kissed his hand, and added, "I'm sorry you lost your sister, but I'm here for you now."

He smiled. "You mean to comfort me, Barbara, and I love you for it, but the reason I'm telling you all this is because I didn't lose her. She is alive, and I have seen her many, many times. Just days after I saw her carried dead into the house, she appeared to me. I was only three years old, so I did not yet comprehend that she was really dead or that death is supposed to be something final. I don't know how many times I saw her after that before I said anything to my parents—I just assumed that they saw her too. Then one day when my mother found me outside talking to myself, she asked me what I was doing, and I replied, "Playing with Annabella." My mother grew very angry with me and told my father. He warned me not to tell lies, but I insisted I was telling the truth. When they saw I was serious, they tried to explain that I could not see Annabella because she was dead. Only then did I start to wonder why I never saw her in the house, only outside near the woods, and why she did not sleep or eat with us. When I kept insisting I could see her, they took me to the doctor in Marquette. He told them I was having delusions, and it would be best if we moved into town where it would be less lonely and I would be distracted from such strange thoughts. I quit seeing Annabella after that. When I mentioned to my parents a few times later how I used to see her when we lived in the woods, they told me to stop talking nonsense, so finally, I kept it to myself, and as I grew older, I began to wonder whether I hadn't imagined it all.

Then after my parents died, I started coming into the woods again. I was grieving so deeply for my parents, and although I hadn't thought of it in years, I remembered how I used to see my sister, and I wondered whether if I came into the woods, whether I might see her again, or she might bring me some sign from my parents. I saw nothing when I went into the woods last year, so all this past winter, I thought I should give up hope. But then this spring, I decided I would try one last time. That was the day I met you, and although I didn't see my sister that day, you did, Barbara. I was surprised when you asked me about it, and it was all I could do to contain myself and focus on getting your sister back to town because I knew then that I hadn't imagined seeing Annabella. The funny thing is, I never felt any grief over her death, not like I did over my parents, maybe because I was so young when she died, but I think it was also because she's always been there, watching over me. Please tell me you understand, Barbara—that you don't think your husband is mad."

"Samuel, I don't know what to say. It's so unbelievable."

"But you do believe me?"

"If anyone else told it to me, I wouldn't, but I—well, I did see her myself."

He seemed content with my reply. He held my hand for a moment, and then said, "Barbara, the reason I'm telling you all this is because you seem ashamed of your sister's love for Ben Shepard. Yet somehow I trust your sister's intuition; she is a simple—perhaps an honest person might be a better way to put it—I don't think she lets her mind get muddled with anxieties that the rest of us find difficult to stave off. And I believe there are things we all know on a level beyond our mere human understanding. If Adele believes Ben loves her, then I imagine he must, whatever his reasons for not being with her. And I think you, rather than being upset about it, should feel comforted that she has this inner knowledge to give her peace after all the pain she felt previously."

I did not know what to say. I felt Samuel was just so very much the most perfect man in the world, to understand me so well, to tell me what my own heart said was true if I had only been open to listening to it. Again, I felt he was so much more wonderful a man than I deserved, and this spirit child, his own sister, Annabella, had brought us together, so how could I argue with him? I argued with myself still that I must be insane to accept such beliefs, but gradually, I did come to accept them.

Epilogue

The events of the rest of my life are really of little account for this story. Adele did go to the convent in Sault Sainte Marie, where she remained until her death many years later. Samuel and I lived happily together and had four strong, healthy children—three boys to carry on the Stonegate name, and my baby girl, Ruth, who was your own mother, Sarah, named after the biblical mother whose story had comforted me; just like Ruth, I had been a stranger in a strange land, yet found a man to love me and bless me with children. Of all the blessings I received, it is my husband and children for whom I am most grateful, and also that I lived to a ripe old age, to see my children bring their children home, to prove God's never-ending love. I know I seldom showed that love I felt, but it was there in my heart.

My Samuel passed away in 1900, from heart failure, after twenty-six years of marriage. That was far too soon for me—I wished I could have spent twice as long with him, and I missed him every day, grieving for him deeply.

A couple of times a year, I took the train to Sault Sainte Marie to visit Adele, and these visits comforted me, making me realize I had not lost her. Now and then, we would speak a word or two about the winter we had spent in the cabin, and occasionally, she would say something like, "The first time I heard Ben read from the Bible was the first time I think God's Word really stirred in my soul." I would not comment on these statements, but like her, I had come to understand that winter as the beginning of my own spiritual journey.

Then one morning, in 1901, I opened *The Mining Journal* and read about a terrible accident that had happened in a logging camp near Chassell. I felt faint when I saw the name—Ben Shepard. He had died instantaneously when a tree fell on him. I did not know how to take it—I found it hard to believe him dead when he had been such an expert woodsman and so strong that he could have out-logged Paul Bunyan, and he was not that old yet—only forty-seven.

I did not know whether Adele would read the paper, but I wanted to be the first to tell her, or to be there to comfort her if she already knew. Immediately, I took a train to the Sault, fearing news of Ben's death might cause all her old pain to well up again.

At the convent, I was shown into the visitors' room. I had not let her know I was coming, yet she did not act surprised to see me.

"Hello, Barbara," she said simply. "I was expecting you."

Not knowing what she meant, I said, "Adele, I'm afraid I have bad news for you."

"You have news, but it is not bad," she smiled. When I must have looked puzzled, she said, "Barbara, I already know."

"About—about Ben?"

She nodded.

"Did you read it in the paper? How terrible for him—to die from a tree falling on him."

She looked a bit startled when I mentioned how he had died. For a second, I thought she had somehow misunderstood me. But then she said, "No, I didn't read it in the paper, and no one told me. I didn't know how he had died."

Now I was more confused.

"Adele," I said. "I'm talking about Ben. He's the one who is dead."

"Yes, I know," she replied. "I know because he came to me yesterday, in the early morning hours. He stood right at the foot of my bed. He was there when I woke."

I stood up in dismay, feeling I should be frightened. But after a second, I realized I felt very calm.

"Sit down, Barbara. Don't be alarmed," she said gently. "It's not impossible, although you may choose not to believe it. But really it makes sense, for he could not come to me after that day of the skating party—he could only come to me now when his life was over and his mission on earth complete."

I found I believed her—just as I had believed Samuel's story that his sister lived on. That Adele had seen Ben was not so strange, considering his death had been unexpected like Annabella's.

"He spoke to me, Barbara," Adele said once she saw I was past my initial shock and able to listen. Later, I was surprised I was not also shocked by these words, but now, as she spoke, everything seemed to make perfect sense, and she rolled out her words, like a red carpet is unrolled, making way for a great king, as if all that she said were right and as it should be. "When he came to me, Ben told me it was time for him to leave, but he would be waiting for me. Perhaps it was the only way he thought I would recognize him after so many years, but he appeared to me as if he were only nineteen again, his face more innocent and boyish than ever, yet his whole being looking more strong and radiant than before. His locks of blond hair were a literal halo the way they glowed, lighting up the entire room. I felt bathed in a warm, golden light. He gazed fondly at me—he did not even actually speak—I only felt his words in my heart. I don't know how else to explain it. I knew he was at peace—and that there was peace between us. All these years, I had still occasionally doubted myself, wondered whether it had only been a self-delusion of mine that he had loved me, but now I understand it was all meant to be, all planned long ago, so we would learn lessons from the experience to point us toward our individual life's work. And when we have completed our experiences, we will be together again. He told me to be patient, Barbara, and that the time would yet come when we would be together."

I was speechless.

"Barbara," she said, her face beaming with light, "it is absolutely true what the Bible says—Love does go on Forever."

Her face was so radiant I could not speak. I stood up and kissed her cheek. Then I pressed her hand and simply said, "Thank you. Thank you."

She had provided me with indescribable comfort. I was stunned; I felt almost disembodied as I stood up. As I walked back down the hall of the convent, I clenched my face as I passed a couple of the nuns, but once I was in the stairwell, where no one could see me, I let out a little sob, a cry of relief. I missed Samuel. For a year I had held my grief inside. Now I could release it. I knew I would see him again.

❄   ❄   ❄

Adele and I never again mentioned Ben's name between us. After she passed away, I went to the convent to collect her few belongings. Among them I found the photograph of Ben, with the poem she had written on its back. She must have hidden it from the other nuns, for I can't imagine she would have been allowed to keep it with the declaration of love it contained. Not knowing what to do with it, I brought it home and stuck it under my dresser scarf. Then I promptly forgot about it until the day you, Sarah, found it while cleaning my room. That day I considered telling you the story of Ben and Adele, but I held back, afraid you might not believe me. I don't think even then, after so many years, I understood the story well enough to tell it, which is why I have waited to communicate it to you in this extraordinary way.

I don't know whether I have told the story properly even now. I have tried to be truthful about everything, even truthful about the times I did not behave as I should. It was most important I be truthful about my shortcomings to demonstrate how I had let my fear limit me. I have had to hold back now from laughing at myself as I remember that frightened young woman I was. One of the most important lessons I learned during my life was just how safe I always was—I wish all people could understand that—that no matter what happens in life— truthfully, we are always safe.

Part of my fear came from the way the world was in those days— it was more limited, people were more isolated. There were no high-speed trains as now, no automobiles; the streetcars you already know as something of the past did not yet exist. We had no telephones or radios, or the many other forms of communication still to come that you will soon marvel over. In the last century, the human race has concentrated largely on improving communication. Using that communication to understand one another is part of humanity's evolution, and understanding one another will expand our possibilities. The universe is always expanding. We must reach out toward that expansion of ourselves rather than allowing our fears to limit us. Do not be afraid.

I am here now, in an altered, yet far more real state than your physical one. I am here with my mother and father, with Uncle Shepard and Aunt Marie, Adele, and Ben, and Samuel. We will all be here for a while until we are ready to return and learn new lessons, or to improve on those we left incomplete in our former lives.

Perhaps my message will not be believed. If people hear my words and scoff, it does not matter; they are simply not ready yet to understand; they will continue to be given chances until they do know the truth, the wonder, the miracle of their existence. The universe is very patient, for its Love goes on Forever, and to a far greater and more magnificent degree than any of you on earth can possibly imagine. Be joyful, all of you. All is well. It always has been and forever shall be well.

I, Sarah Bramble Adams, verify that every word of this manuscript has been written down exactly as it was channeled through me by the spirit of my grandmother, Barbara Traugott Stonegate. I began this composition on November 2, 1942, and completed it this day, December 4, 1942.

Afterword

"Wow! Wow!" I kept saying it over and over to myself after I read the manuscript. I could see why my grandmother had been hesitant to let me read it. Despite actually experiencing the automatic writing of her grandmother's book through her own pen, my grandmother still feared that people, even I who had loved her so well, might think her insane. I imagine in the 1940s, many people would have thought her crazy. Even in the twenty-first century, many probably will. But I do not.

I am not without some hesitation myself in publishing this book, but I choose to carry out the wish of my great-great-grandmother to make it public. Even if a million people should laugh at it, I trust it will benefit one person, and who can estimate the influence that one person may have? I also believe this story was meant specifically to come into my possession, for it came at a time when I most needed it myself.

The finding of my grandmother's manuscript became for me nothing less than the key to unlock the entire purpose of my being, the blueprint to an understanding of all the "odd" experiences I have known. I now feel connected to my family in an entirely new way—for so many of my family members had been remarkable—my grandmother, Sarah Bramble Adams, who could produce automatic writing—and her grandmother, Barbara Traugott Stonegate, who could tell her story from another realm, and who could see spirits in this one—and my Great-Great-Great Aunt Adele, who also saw a spirit, and her cousin, Ben Shepard, who appeared as one, and of course, the Stonegate ancestors, Samuel Stonegate who saw his sister's spirit, and Annabella Stonegate herself, perhaps the most powerful spirit of all.

I come from a remarkable family—and that explains to me so much about my own past—about the odd experiences of my childhood—feelings of floating above my bed and looking down to see myself sleeping, experiences of being able to predict who is on the other end of the telephone before I answer it, and my sensing when my own parents would die. My reading of this story began my own personal journey of self-discovery and acceptance, a journey I have only just begun, but which I trust will be just as remarkable. Someday I hope likewise to present my own story to the world, but for now, I am still creating it.

This story of my ancestors has been only the beginning for me, and I hope by sharing it that it becomes a new beginning for many.

Sybil Shelley
July 9, 2004
Marquette, Michigan

Be Sure to Read All of
Tyler R. Tichelaar's Marquette Books

IRON PIONEERS:
THE MARQUETTE TRILOGY: BOOK ONE

When iron ore is discovered in Michigan's Upper Peninsula in the 1840s, newlyweds Gerald Henning and his beautiful socialite wife Clara travel from Boston to the little village of Marquette on the shores of Lake Superior. They and their companions, Irish and German immigrants, French Canadians, and fellow New Englanders face blizzards and near starvation, devastating fires and financial hardships. Yet these iron pioneers persevere until their wilderness village becomes integral to the Union cause in the Civil War and then a prosperous modern city. Meticulously researched, warmly written, and spanning half a century, *Iron Pioneers* is a testament to the spirit that forged America.

THE QUEEN CITY
THE MARQUETTE TRILOGY: BOOK TWO

During the first half of the twentieth century, Marquette grows into the Queen City of the North. Here is the tale of a small town undergoing change as its horses are replaced by streetcars and automobiles, and its pioneers are replaced by new generations who prosper despite two World Wars and the Great Depression. Margaret Dalrymple finds her Scottish prince, though he is neither Scottish nor a prince. Molly Bergmann becomes an inspiration to her grandchildren. Jacob Whitman's children engage in a family feud. The Queen City's residents marry, divorce, have children, die, break their hearts, go to war, gossip, blackmail, raise families, move away, and then return to Marquette. And always, always they are in love with the haunting land that is their home.

SUPERIOR HERITAGE
THE MARQUETTE TRILOGY: BOOK THREE

The Marquette Trilogy comes to a satisfying conclusion as it brings together characters and plots from the earlier novels and culminates with Marquette's sesquicentennial celebrations in 1999. What happened to Madeleine Henning is finally revealed as secrets from the past shed light upon the present. Marquette's residents struggle with a difficult local economy, yet remain optimistic for the future. The novel's main character, John Vandelaare, is descended from all the early Marquette families in *Iron Pioneers* and *The Queen City*. While he cherishes his family's past, he questions whether he should remain in his hometown. Then an event happens that will change his life forever.

NARROW LIVES

Narrow Lives is the story of those whose lives were affected by Lysander Blackmore, the sinister banker first introduced to readers in *The Queen City*. It is a novel that stands alone, yet readers of *The Marquette Trilogy* will be reacquainted with some familiar characters. Written as a collection of connected short stories, each told in first person by a different character, *Narrow Lives* depicts the influence one person has, even in death, upon others, and it explores the prisons of grief, loneliness, and fear self-created when people doubt their own worthiness.

THE ONLY THING THAT LASTS

The story of Robert O'Neill, the famous novelist introduced in *The Marquette Trilogy.* As a young boy during World War I, Robert is forced to leave his South Carolina home to live in Marquette with his grandmother and aunt. He finds there a cold climate, but many warmhearted friends. An old-fashioned story that follows Robert's growth from childhood to successful writer and husband, the novel is written as Robert O'Neill's autobiography, his final gift to Marquette by memorializing the town of his youth.

MY MARQUETTE:
EXPLORE THE QUEEN CITY OF THE NORTH
—ITS HISTORY, PEOPLE, AND PLACES

My Marquette is the result of its author's lifelong love affair with his hometown. Join Tyler R. Tichelaar, seventh generation Marquette resident and author of *The Marquette Trilogy*, as he takes you on a tour of the history, people, and places of Marquette. Stories of the past and present, both true and fictional, will leave you understanding why Marquette really is "The Queen City of the North." Along the way, Tyler will describe his own experiences growing up in Marquette, recall family and friends he knew, and give away secrets about the people behind the characters in his novels. *My Marquette* offers a rare insight into an author's creation of fiction and a refreshing view of a city's history and relevance to today. Reading *My Marquette* is equal to being given a personal tour by someone who knows Marquette intimately.

For more information on Tyler's Marquette Books, visit:
www.MarquetteFiction.com

Join Tyler as he embarks on a new series of books about the Arthurian Legend

KING ARTHUR'S CHILDREN:
A STUDY IN FICTION AND TRADITION

Did you know King Arthur had many other children besides Mordred? Depending on which version of the legend you read, he had both sons and daughters, some of whom even survived him. From the ancient tale of Gwydre, the son who was gored to death by a boar, to Scottish traditions of Mordred as a beloved king, Tyler R. Tichelaar has studied all the references to King Arthur's children to show how they shed light upon a legend that has intrigued us for fifteen centuries.

King Arthur's Children: A Study in Fiction and Tradition is the first full-length analysis of every known treatment of King Arthur's children, from Welsh legends and French romances, to Scottish genealogies and modern novels by such authors as Parke Godwin, Stephen Lawhead, Debra Kemp, and Elizabeth Wein. *King Arthur's Children* explores an often overlooked theme in Arthurian literature and reveals King Arthur's bloodline may still exist today. This non-fiction study is a precursor to Tyler R. Tichelaar's upcoming novel *King Arthur's Legacy.*

THE GOTHIC WANDERER:
FROM TRANSGRESSION TO REDEMPTION

From the horrors of sixteenth century Italian castles to twenty-first century plagues, from the French Revolution to the liberation of Libya, Tyler R. Tichelaar takes readers on far more than a journey through literary history. *The Gothic Wanderer* is an exploration of man's deepest fears, his efforts to rise above them for the last two centuries, and how he may be on the brink finally of succeeding. Whether it's seeking immortal life, the fabulous philosopher's stone that will change lead into gold, or human blood as a vampire, or coping with more common "transgressions" like being a woman in a patriarchal society, being a Jew in a Christian land, or simply being addicted to gambling, the Gothic wanderer's journey toward damnation or redemption is never dull and always enlightening.

Tichelaar examines the figure of the Gothic wanderer in such well-known Gothic novels as *The Mysteries of Udolpho*, *Frankenstein*, and *Dracula*, as well as lesser known works like Fanny Burney's *The Wanderer*, Mary Shelley's *The Last Man*, and Edward Bulwer-Lytton's *Zanoni*. He also finds surprising Gothic elements in classics like Dickens' *A Tale of Two Cities* and Edgar Rice Burroughs' *Tarzan of the Apes*. From Matthew Lewis' *The Monk* to Stephenie Meyer's *Twilight*, Tichelaar explores a literary tradition whose characters reflect our greatest fears and deepest hopes. Readers will find here the revelation that not only are we all Gothic wanderers—but we are so only by our own choosing.

COMING IN 2013!

KING ARTHUR'S LEGACY:
BOOK I IN THE CHILDREN OF ARTHUR SERIES

He felt suddenly as if a siren's song were calling to him from across the sea, from an enchanted land, an island kingdom named England. He had always pictured England as a magical fairy tale realm, ever since his childhood when he had first read the legends of King Arthur and the Knights of the Round Table.

Magic existed in the thought of England's green hills, in the names of Windsor Castle, Stonehenge, and the Tower of London. It was one of the few lands still ruled by a monarch, perhaps a land where fairy tales might still come true. Maybe even a place where he might at last find a father.

All his life, Adam Morgan has sought his true identity and the father he never knew. When multiple coincidences lead him to England, he will not only find his father, but mutual love with a woman he can never have, and a family legacy he never imagined possible. Among England's green hills and crumbling castles, Adam's intuition awakens, and when a mysterious stranger appears with a tale of Britain's past, Adam discovers forces are at work to bring about the return of a king.

For updates on Tyler R. Tichelaar's Arthurian novels, visit:
www.ChildrenofArthur.com

About the Author

Tyler R. Tichelaar is a seventh generation Marquette, Michigan resident. Since age eight he wanted to be a writer, and he began writing his first novel at age sixteen.

Tyler has a Ph.D. in Literature from Western Michigan University, and Bachelor and Master's Degrees from Northern Michigan University. Tyler is the regular guest host of Authors Access Internet Radio and the current President of the Upper Peninsula Publishers and Authors Association. He is the owner of Marquette Fiction and Superior Book Promotions, a professional book review, editing, and proofreading service.

He spent thousands of hours researching and writing *The Marquette Trilogy: Iron Pioneers, The Queen City,* and *Superior Heritage*. In 2009, he was awarded the Best Historical Fiction Award in the Reader Views Literary Awards for his novel *Narrow Lives*. He has since gone on to sponsor that award. In 2011, he received the Barb H. Kelly Historic Preservation Award from the Marquette Beautification and Restoration Committee for his book *My Marquette* and he received the Marquette County Arts Award for an "Outstanding Writer."

Tyler lives in Marquette, Michigan where the roar of Lake Superior, mountains of snow, and sandstone architecture inspire his writing. He has many future books in the planning.